# MONKEY LOVE AND MURDER

# Monkey Love and Murder

## Edith McClintock

**FIVE STAR**

*A part of Gale, Cengage Learning*

GALE
CENGAGE Learning®

Detroit • New York • San Francisco • New Haven, Conn • Waterville, Maine • London

Copyright © 2013 by Edith McClintock.
Reader questions for discussion are located at the back of the book.
Five Star™ Publishing, a part of Gale, Cengage Learning.

**LIBRARY OF CONGRESS CATALOGING-IN-PUBLICATION DATA**

McClintock, Edith.
    Monkey love and murder / Edith McClintock. -- 1st ed.
        p. cm.
    ISBN 978-1-4328-2638-3 (hardcover) — ISBN 1-4328-2638-7 (hardcover)
    1. Scientific expeditions—Fiction. 2. Rain forests—Amazon River Region—Fiction. 3. Monkeys—Fiction. 4. Murder—Fiction. 5. South America—Fiction. 6. Romantic suspense fiction. I. Title.
PS3613.C35827M66 2013
813'.6—dc23                                                    2012032738

First Edition. First Printing: January 2013
Find us on Facebook– https://www.facebook.com/FiveStarCengage
Visit our website– http://www.gale.cengage.com/fivestar/
Contact Five Star™ Publishing at FiveStar@cengage.com

Printed in Mexico
1 2 3 4 5 6 7 17 16 15 14 13

For Kamala Griffith, my patroness

# CHAPTER 1

*Suriname, South America*

Brakes squealed in the distance and a shriek shot through the early evening hum of the courtyard restaurant. I jumped, twisting toward the street, expecting a smashed moped, or worse, a dead or bloody body. Instead a bug-eyed woman in her early forties was jogging toward us, a taxi driver honking and cursing her from the street as she jostled aside tables and people, waving her long arms and yelling, "Pumpkin, my favorite person. Whee!"

The woman threw her arms around my friend Ramesh, trapping him in a prolonged, enthusiastic hug. The surrounding customers, a mix of Dutch tourists and Surinamese professionals, stared at our table under the flowering Royal Poinciana, its branches heavy with bromeliads and twinkling white lights. But they seemed more amused than embarrassed. Unlike me. To them, the woman was just a loud American, a perfect stereotype. To me, she was one of my own, and I knew this wasn't typical behavior—enthusiastic, slightly endearing maybe, but not normal. When she finally released Ramesh, he introduced her as Dr. Alice Buchanan, a biological anthropology professor from Michigan, and me as Emma Parks, currently his best friend in all of Suriname.

Alice collapsed into a plastic chair at our table, the evening air thick with buzzing mosquitoes, the light breeze off the river barely denting the humidity. She blew at her crown of graying

7

bangs, inspecting me. "What are you? A missionary?"

"Peace Corps," I answered, annoyed. I touched my thick brown hair pulled back in a tight ponytail and glanced down at the loose cotton dress that hid my curves. I did look a little plain. Actually, I'd been too depressed to put much effort into my appearance during the past month. It was way too hot to wear make-up, but I liked to think my natural *je ne sais quoi* bespoke something more interesting than a missionary. But to be truthful, Peace Corps volunteers are not generally known for their style either.

"Emma just finished and I think she should stay here in Suriname," Ramesh said in his fast, rhythmic Guyanese accent, which slipped randomly between Creole and the Queen's English. He was twenty-five, my age, Hindustani and gay. I'd worked with him at a local health agency, my Peace Corps assignment, where he took care of the computers, battled the rats in my office, and kept me sane. He had a couple of side jobs, including one as a tour guide, which was probably how he knew Alice. But that life was over. Tomorrow I was finally going home, although I was feeling surprisingly scared and confused about my looming future—fortunately not my normal condition.

Alice slammed her long bony fingers against the table, nearly knocking over the small lamp in the middle. "I'm having an atrocious day. I just had two researchers screw me over claiming they can't come because they're pregnant. Pregnant? Like it's a disease? I've had malaria twice and kept working. Jesus, remember the insect living in my leg wound for weeks? That's why I keep the rum stocked."

Ramesh made cooing noises and patted her hand. "Alice has a research project at Kasima National Park," he explained. "Spider monkeys."

The waiter arrived with our *dyogo,* the large size of the local Parbo beer, and Alice grabbed hold of it first, filling her glass to the brim. "I can't do anything with so little help, and I have fantastic new plans, and I absolutely must, *must* have at least one more research assistant. I bet Jack got to them," she added under her breath. "He wants to destroy me."

I rolled my eyes at Ramesh, silently demanding to know why we'd been trapped into sharing our beer with this odd woman on my last night in Suriname. Ramesh winked, clearly enjoying my annoyance.

Alice's dark brown eyes fixed on me again, her head bopping like a marionette with a loose wire. "You speak Sranan?" she demanded, referring to Sranan Tongo, the *lingua franca* in Suriname.

"Ah, yeah." I shifted as far back as I could in my chair. The woman didn't seem *stable*.

"Sweetie!" Alice grabbed my arm, again drawing stares from the surrounding tables. "You have to come to Kasima. You don't want to go back to the States, to rush-hour traffic and dank, windowless cubicles. What kind of life is that?"

She grew more agitated and leaned close, her eyes bursting with newly formed admiration. "You speak Sranan. You'll be able to tell me what the workers think about IWC taking over the park. They've been acting strange lately. I need to know what's wrong with them." She clapped her hands. "There, it's settled. We're going to have so much fun.

"You'll have to be at camp by the end of April. That's not debatable. I need inside gossip before Jack arrives, and I'm not sure I can trust . . ." She stopped, her eyes searching the tables nearby. "Do you know Melvijn?"

"Ah, I don't think so," I answered, still trying to process Alice's rapid-fire manipulations about my future. "Should I?"

"He's Surinamese so I thought maybe you'd met him in Paramaribo and it's just . . ."

"She knows him," Ramesh said.

"Do I?" I asked, confused and distracted by Alice who was again cursing someone named Jack under her breath.

"How could you forget?" Ramesh asked. "He's a huge, sexy man. You danced with him at the salsa club when you first came to Suriname, 'member?"

"Oh, yeah," I said. "He seemed nice. Fun anyway."

"Melvijn's a rich man now," Ramesh added. "Driving around town in a fancy new truck. How you pay so well, Alice?"

Alice harrumphed and Ramesh grabbed my hand. "You gon' love the hottie Aussie! If I could live without TV, I would' mind a few months in the bush with him. Maybe I'll come—"

Alice interrupted. "Sweetie, you're Ramesh's friend, so I know I can trust you. There's something big coming, *really big*, and Jack can't get credit for it."

"Ah, who's Jack?" I asked.

"He's the big bad director of International Wildlife Conservation and a more conceited, arrogant gigolo you'd be hard pressed to find. Maybe you can find out what the other researchers know or, ah . . ." She paused again, turning to scan the sidewalk where a short Javanese man had stopped his bicycle, a caged songbird perched on the handle. "Never mind, sweetie, we'll talk about it later. Everybody's going to love you at camp!"

Management of Kasima National Park I learned, while Alice sedated herself with several more glasses of beer, was about to be transferred to International Wildlife Conservation, an American conservation group. Apparently there was a lot of local controversy about the decision—something about the nationalistic opposition party accusing the current government of selling out the people of Suriname. I'd never visited the park, since the flight and lodges were too expensive on my Peace Corps salary, but I'd heard it was the most beautiful spot in Suriname.

Under the crush of Ramesh and Alice's persuasions, and my

still depressed and possibly certifiable mental state, I accepted Alice's job offer. By the end of the night I'd agreed to join Alice's camp for six months. I did negotiate the six months at least. She wanted me to sign up for a full year.

Other than my start date and a need for rubber boots, Alice was extremely vague when it came to details, dismissing most of my questions with, "Don't worry, sweetie. You survived two years in local government. Watching spider monkeys will be as easy, peasy as pie. Just promise to stay away from those sneaky thieves at IWC, especially Jack West, and you'll do fine."

Given my non-existent qualifications to research monkeys (I didn't even know what a spider monkey looked like), Alice seemed to have either an overblown view of Peace Corps volunteers or less than rigorous standards in picking her research assistants.

That should have been my first warning.

"The weather will clear up soon," the pilot, a young bald man of indeterminate ethnicity, yelled over the roar of the ancient prop plane. "I'll go higher so it won't be as bumpy."

Paramaribo looked pristine and beautiful from the air, despite the rainy haze. We were still below the clouds and I could see the wooden yellow cathedral, now toy size, to my left, the Atlantic Ocean in the distance. We passed over the WWII freighter half sunk in the middle of the Suriname River, which winds along the edge of the city, and banked to the right, climbing into storm clouds.

Except for a few visits to friends living in Maroon villages and one visit with the health agency I'd worked with to a gold mining camp, I'd never been deep in the interior, which is largely tropical rainforest stretching south to the Amazon. My heart fluttered when the clouds wrapped the plane in white, but

I smiled at the same time. I was excited, for the first time in months.

After a bumpy fifteen minutes, we emerged from the clouds into mid-morning sun shining over brilliant green jungle scattered with flowering orange, red, and purple trees.

"Too much green," the pilot yelled, "it gets boring."

"No, it's beautiful," I murmured back, mesmerized by the view. The brown river sparkled in the morning sun, slithering through a soft carpet of moss stretching to eternity.

"If the plane goes down, no one will ever find you. The trees swallow you up. At least following the river, we have a chance."

"A chance to what?"

"A chance to find the plane." He laughed.

I didn't laugh in return. My heart sank to the pit of my stomach. What kind of pilot talks about crashing while flying a customer—even *if* said customer has hitched a ride for free in the co-pilot seat? Behind me were the paying customers, a group of partying Dutch girls and two confused Mormon boys in brilliantly white starched shirts and crisp black ties.

"A plane went down around here last year," the pilot yelled several times before I could understand him. "Supposedly smuggling songbirds—*twatwas*—they never found it."

"I heard about the crash." It had been a huge story in Suriname the year before, although I'd heard a different version. Ramesh told me the plane flew too low over a sacred Maroon area, which was why it crashed—brought down by bad *juju.*

"Top singing birds are worth up to forty thousand dollars in Holland," he added. "They know I won't take animals from where you're going, but it doesn't stop them from—" The rest was lost in the roar of the engine.

I didn't mind talking; conversation distracted me from the difficult parts—take-off, landing, flying—but the subject matter was not to my taste. Plus I preferred his eyes on the instruments rather than me. The plane dropped when we hit a dark cloud, a Dutch girl in the back screamed, and the pilot finally turned back to focus on flying. Clutching my hands in my lap, I tried to breathe deep and slow and not think about the bouncing plane crashing into the now invisible jungle below, or my Mom's strong warning I was making a terrible mistake. I desperately wanted another glimpse of the endless green rainforest.

I wasn't sure why I'd decided to join Alice's camp. I've always had a nagging wanderlust, but I'd thought once I finished Peace Corps I could settle into a traditional life of marriage, kids, and some sort of meaningful but not too stressful job. At least until Sonia—

"Don't think about that," I whispered to myself.

I grabbed my handkerchief, discreetly wiping away a tear. I probably should have taken Peace Corps up on the psychological counseling they'd offered rather than go for the sedatives. The nightmares had only become more intense, not fading as I'd hoped. Perhaps they would never go away, at least not until I made peace with the fact that, rather than accomplishing any great deeds in Suriname, I'd destroyed a life, maybe several lives.

"There's the runway," the pilot shouted. We broke through the clouds and the skies opened. He was pointing to a microscopic clearing in the forest ending mere feet from a massive, churning river. *Runway* seemed a somewhat inflated description of the rapidly approaching patch of grass. I closed my eyes and prayed.

# CHAPTER 2

"Sweetie, I'm so relieved you made it in time for tonight's party!" Alice yelled, trotting down the sloping grassy hill, two younger men in her wake. She wrapped me in a welcoming hug.

"Nick, meet your new field assistant, Emma Parks." She turned to a lean man in his late twenties wearing a wicked grin and a dark green t-shirt stretched tightly across his chest that read *"staatsfeind,"* which I believe means "enemy of the state."

"G'day. Welcome to Kasima," Nick said in an Australian accent that made the day a little warmer.

"Thanks," I managed, his eyes deep brown and kind. Several seconds later I realized he was still holding my hand and I jerked it away, embarrassed. I'm a sucker for an accent, although physically he wasn't my idea of an Australian. I'd pictured a surfer type, tanned, blond hair, but Nick looked like he had a fair mix of Greek or Italian ancestors in his DNA. The combination made breathing difficult.

"And this is Brian, the best looking man in Suriname." Alice winked and pressed her hand to his dark muscled shoulder. Brian, who towered several inches over all of us, shook my hand too. He looked young, although I guessed he might be about my age.

We unloaded my luggage and climbed to the top of the hill. A rocky path snaked downward through the trees to the grassy bank of the river, a scattering of huts visible in the clearing. The world was now green, the breeze a languid breath through the trees and branches, bringing a deep sweet smell of rotting jungle.

"Cupcake," Alice said. "I hate to run off so quickly, but your plane was late, and Nick and I have a meeting with the evil empire's local henchmen. We have to go kiss their butts so they don't toss us out."

Nick rolled his eyes at Alice and glanced apologetically at us. "Sorry about leaving you with the bags."

Alice and Nick disappeared down the hill and we followed with my few bags and the groceries I'd brought, emerging in a grassy lawn at the bottom of the steep hill. We turned toward a ramshackle wooden building with a sign that read *Watradagu*. A young Maroon man and two women, one ancient, one young, were playing cards on the front porch. The old woman, her brown face deeply lined and sagging, wore a long, curling, purple-gray wig and a white bra above her round belly. Wrapped around her hips was an orange and purple sarong-like skirt called a *pangi*. The younger woman was beautiful, with smooth black skin and large round eyes. She stopped in the middle of dealing, and all three turned to watch us approach.

Brian introduced me in Sranan as Alice's newest volunteer, but they didn't seem as impressed by my language skills as I'd expected. They continued to stare, not speaking. Maroons, descendants of West Africans who fled the colonial Dutch slave plantation, are not shy toward strangers, and I was a little disappointed with my welcome. It took a fair amount of effort to learn Sranan and I expected awe and wonder over my ability. Admittedly, it's an English-based language, but still, I'd worked hard to learn it.

Brian introduced Hortense first, the old woman with the purple-gray wig, and then Cedric, who was lighter skinned, with three shiny gold teeth.

"We dance at the party tonight," Cedric said to me, with the swagger of a man who understood his nature without having ever given it a single thought. But he was more interested in the boat engine Brian had brought him from town. They soon disappeared back up the hill to pick up the engine and the two women went back to their card game.

"I'm going down to look at the river," I announced, a little surprised again by the women's disinterest. I'd become too used to being the only white person in the room and therefore always unique, if only by default. But not here, it seemed. Perhaps they were too used to a constant stream of foreign researchers and tourists and had become jaded.

I turned to leave, but the old woman's gnarled hand darted out, grabbing my arm. She motioned for me to move closer and wrapped both hands around my head.

*"Takuu Akaa . . . winti . . ."* she whispered, droplets of spittle wetting my inner ear. I jumped away, missing the rest of the sentence. Her harsh whispering was a little painful. And wet.

*"Ai,"* I said, indicating I understood—a lie. "I'll be back in a few minutes." I turned away, shivering under the sun, surprised at the strange and slightly creepy words. I pulled out my handkerchief, wiping my ear.

*"Winti,"* Hortense had said and something else I didn't understand. Winti is the Afro-Surinamese religion, a bit like voodoo or Santeria, at least for the uninitiated like me. She must have been referring to the restrictions surrounding menstruation at Kasima.

Some Surinamese believed menstruating women can put spells on a man during sex or through cooking, but Maroons added in the ability to offend forest and river spirits. Alice had told me not to cook or swim in the river during that time, but chose to ignore the "no going into the forest rule," which destroyed any positive benefit as far as I could tell. Lying around in a hammock for a week each month while the men worked seemed like a great idea.

I slid down a black boulder polished smooth and soft by the relentless ebb and flow of the river and sat in the shade of a massive mango tree. Rounded rocks covered in green moss swelled out from the riverbank, white water surging over them in churning rapids. I curled into the root of the tree wondering if I'd made the right decision in coming to Kasima. I could have been home, safe in a comfortable bed. Outside the fall leaves would be turning red and orange, the days crisp and clear and growing shorter. I woke to shouting.

Nick poked his head over the top of the rock. "Hey down there. We're heading off. Care to join us?"

"Sorry, I fell asleep. I didn't sleep well last night." I shivered, remembering the nightmare that had kept me awake and shoved it to the recesses of my mind, along with all thoughts of Sonia.

Nick gave me a hand over the rock and we strolled toward the Watradagu building.

"Meet everyone on the island?"

"A few. Cedric, I think was his name, and this strange—"

"Cedric," he interrupted, "Jack West's favorite and my arch nemesis. I've been kissing his ass since I arrived, but no respect. Whenever Brian goes into the city, Cedric disappears. I bring him fish, I kill at soccer, I get him drunk . . . does it matter? No!" He scratched his chin. "Hmm . . . maybe it's my abject failure with women in his eyes—I so rarely go home with any of the Dutch chicks after the drumming parties." He glanced in my direction. "Too much information, eh?"

"Ah . . . yeah." We neared the Watradagu porch, empty now except for Brian. "There was this funny old woman named Hortense, too. She said something strange . . ."

"Hortense? She's a rare bird. I'm utterly terrified she'll make me dirty dance with her at the party tonight, shove my head between her huge, sweaty breasts, then drag me—" He slapped his face. "Bad Nick! Sorry, I promised Brian I'd behave today. I tend to embarrass him in public. An American chick I worked with in Costa Rica told me I'm a lovely guy, it's just not obvious for six or seven months. Since you're only here a few months, I thought we'd best start with good impressions. How'm I doing?"

"Oh, don't worry about me. I'm somewhat immune to male stupidity."

"*Touché*. How so?"

"It's a family defect. I have four older brothers. Four wild older brothers. You may have a hard time shocking me."

He cocked his head to the side. "A challenge. Can't wait to give it a try. Well then, I won't have to warn you that Americans seem particularly offended by my humor. Since you have four older brothers . . . Four, right?"

I nodded.

"Your mum and dad are certainly doing their part to populate the planet. Suppose we can't have the stupid people doing all the breeding, though. But good, so you already know when I take the piss out of you, it's just a sign of affection. I'm really a lovely person. So lovely in fact I'm not going to say a word about your grammar school pack. You aren't planning on using that in the field, I hope?"

I glanced down at my tiny, cheap backpack, which I *had* been planning to use in the field. "Let me get this straight. If you insult me, I should take it as a compliment?"

"Precisely. You catch on quick. I knew we were going to get along. So what'd my fave gal, the lovely Hortense, have to say?"

"Something about . . . a spirit," I answered, flustered when Nick brushed his hand along my neck.

"What'd you do, roll down the hill?" he muttered, picking at a twig stuck in my hair.

"What's that about a spirit?" Brian asked from the porch,

and I jerked around, having forgotten he was there. Nick's hand fell away.

"Don't get him started on spirits," Nick said. "Okay, party people, let's go grab the cold beer and make a move. Alice's going to meet us back at camp later."

"I don't think we should start drinking before dinner," Brian called to Nick, who was already strolling toward the river.

Nick yelled back, "No worries, mate. Don't I keep telling you that?" He disappeared into the lodge with a wooden sign that read *Anyumara*—some sort of river fish.

Brian waited for me at the entrance to the lodge. "Why'd you mention a spirit before?"

"Hortense said something to me about spirits in Sranan or maybe it was Saramaccan. *Takuu Akaa,* or something like that. I don't know what it means."

Brian watched me for several seconds before answering in his soft, patient voice, "The *Akaa's* an important spirit. When it leaves your body you become sick or have difficulties sleeping. Eventually you die. Your *Takuu Akaa* helps you resist spirits who'll try to occupy your body when you sleep."

"Creepy." Goose bumps gathered along my arm. "I've had really strange dreams lately, too." Brian held the lodge door open and we followed Nick into the kitchen.

"Hortense gave you a warning. Spirits and dangerous animals live in the forest. You should protect yourself. I can give you medicine to—"

"Mate, that's complete crap," Nick cut Brian off. "Believing a potion will protect you from snakes or evil spirits is superstitious nonsense. There's no proof—"

"It's real," Brian said. "I've seen a man eat glass and not bleed. How do you explain that?"

"Your medicine didn't stop you from stepping on a snake last week," Nick said.

"It didn't bite me," Brian answered.

"You stepped on a snake?" I asked. "Where? Did it strike?"

They ignored me, and Nick opened the door to the refrigerator, letting out a small moan of pleasure. "Come here my little beaut," he sang, wrapping two *dyogos* in a frozen towel and stashing them in his backpack.

I was glad to drop the conversation. I didn't want to get caught up in a discussion of science versus superstition or religion. My views were too confused, too repressed. I wanted to believe the world was solid and logical, explainable through science, but the spiritual, the mystical, my own family, were tugging on me too, trying to pull me under.

We met Cedric on the north side of the rocks and piled the luggage and vegetables in the center of a long and narrow dugout canoe, balancing while climbing across the faded green plank seats. Cedric steered the boat's small outboard motor into the strong current and we turned downstream. The sparkling brown river narrowed, the arching trees, heavy with bromeliads, ferns, and vines, enveloping us in a warm embrace.

Nick, who was sitting behind me, leaned forward, whispering, "I should probably warn you about Rosie and Diane."

# CHAPTER 3

Nick leaned back, stretching his arms along the wooden plank forming his seat back, his too confident smile causing chaos in several areas of my anatomy. I glanced away, afraid he would recognize my attraction. Although he was no doubt used to it. Probably expected it.

I took a deep breath and let my eyes settle back on him. "What do you mean?"

"Rosie and Diane are in an epic battle, and will try to draw you into it. I suggest you don't take sides. Be friendly with both but keep your distance."

"What are they fighting about?"

"Nothing real. Just the usual hurt feelings and misplaced words. That sort of thing can build out here when you're stuck together twenty-four/seven in a small, isolated cabin with few diversions. You're our newest distraction, so expect to be popular this week."

"Speaking of that," I said. "What's this party everyone keeps mentioning?"

"Nobody told you? It's IWC's celebration of taking over management of Kasima. The big shindig was in town. Alice's been raging for the past week about not getting an invite to that one. Tonight is for the park staff. And us, of course."

He gave me another knowing grin, and I turned around to face Brian, who was perched on the front end of the long canoe watching for rocks. The river widened again and Cedric pulled alongside a long, gently rounded black boulder on the shore, which he used as a dock for the boat. I recognized Melvijn, Ramesh's friend, on the rock with a redheaded girl. They both waved, smiling. Melvijn, tall and muscular, had a square face that blended most of the Surinamese cultures—Indian, Chinese, African, Dutch, and Javanese. He'd seemed very attached to city amusements when I'd met him a year or so earlier, and I wondered why he was now working for Alice.

He greeted me with a kiss, twice on each cheek, and did an impish jig that made me feel welcome. The American girl, Rosie, wasn't particularly attractive, but she did have a nice body displayed in a tiny red bikini, although it didn't seem very appropriate for a research camp in the middle of the rainforest. She looked at most twenty, and sounded thirteen as she gushed her welcome.

Nick, Rosie, and I grabbed my bags while Brian and Melvijn stayed behind to speak with Cedric. We hiked up the steep hill along a path about ten feet wide, and I was slightly out of breath by the time we reached the small clearing. The two simple cabins weren't much to look at, as they hadn't been built for tourists or visual pleasure. In fact, they'd be perfectly at home in the backwoods of the Missouri Ozarks, guarded by an old man in overalls, a sawed off shotgun, and a six-pack of Bud.

Having spent my summers romping in the Ozarks with my brothers, the cabins felt exactly right, with the jungle, a kaleidoscope of green teeming with bird, frog, and insect calls, looming on the edges of the neatly raked dirt yard. The smaller cabin on the left, nestled precariously on the side of the hill, was visible through rows of field pants, socks, and t-shirts drying in the shade of an awning attached to the main cabin. It was the newer of the two and still had a visible green trim and shiny corrugated metal roof.

"That's the shower," Rosie said as we passed through the

screen door of the main cabin, pointing to a small, wooden outbuilding on our right. The screened porch was a dumping ground for muddy boots and miscellaneous flip-flops, and I sat on the wooden bench and pulled off my shoes.

The interior was boiling hot and no more impressive than the exterior. Three small bedrooms lined the right side, and on the left were low shelves overflowing with equipment and supplies. The upper half of the wall was screened in, as was the kitchen along the back end of the cabin. I ran my hand along the rough surface of the kitchen table that dominated the room, noticing with pleasure the hammock and open-thatched hut, called a *kampu* in Suriname, out back, again remembering those idyllic summers in our Ozark cabin along the river.

It had been a rare day when I could claim and hold ownership of the single hammock. I could already feel my body gearing up for the race, ready to shove aside anyone who got in my way. But of course I didn't do that; I'm civilized now. I turned away, back to the tidy kitchen. Except for the *kampu*, everything was built for maximum utility with no thought given to decoration, beauty, or even much in the way of organization. But it was clean, which impressed me.

Nick was storing the beer in a plastic bucket under the sink when Rosie pulled me out of the kitchen and into my dark and dreary bedroom. Not sure what else to do, I started to unpack, uneasy about the sparse room with its plain bunk bed on one side, a twin bed on the other. The single bed, which I decided I would use, sat against the unscreened open window and I had visions of rats, bats, and snakes swarming through it at night.

"I can help you put up your mosquito net if you want," Rosie offered from her perch on the lower bunk bed—still wearing only her bikini. "You should set it up before it gets dark. We only use the light in the kitchen at night—so we don't drain the batteries. They store electricity from the solar panels."

Nick popped his head through the door. "Rosie, take care of Em. Show her 'round. And pack up something for tonight and tomorrow morning, eh. We're spending the night on the island."

Since it seemed like Rosie planned to hang around, I asked her how she'd ended up working for Alice while I continued piling my clothes on the rough, wooden shelves.

"My favorite anthropology professor knows Alice. He set it up for me. I thought I'd do a master's with Alice, but she's crazy and hates me, and I miss my boyfriend back home. When I first left, he told me he couldn't visit because of his wife, but I just received a letter and he said he's coming down. I don't know when. The satellite phone hasn't been working, so I'm a little afraid he might, like, you know, just show up someday, which would be bad with Alice still here, and he doesn't know about Melvijn . . ." She kept going.

It was a lot to take in and I stared at her as she jabbered on, barely taking a breath. I definitely should have met some of the researchers before committing to six months.

When I'd finished my mosquito net with Rosie's help, she took me on a longer tour, ending on the second cabin's back porch. A wall of green trees drooped over the edge of a tributary to the main river, the water flowing serenely past a tiny beach barely visible through an opening in the trees.

"Diane thinks this is her porch," Rosie announced, imitating someone smoking a cigarette and drinking tea or coffee with her pinkie extended. "But Nick says we all have equal access to both cabins, so don't listen to her. She's snooty just because she's working on her Ph.D. and gets to live in this cabin with Nick and Alice. I hate—"

"So what exactly does Nick do?" I interrupted, not wanting to get caught up in her fight with Diane.

"He fishes and drinks. Just kidding. He's cool. He has his Ph.D. from Cambridge, which Alice *loves* to tell everyone. She's a snob. He manages the project and trains us and makes sure the data is collected correctly and takes care of logistics, food, money. Sometimes he's a little *too* laid back though."

"Have you finished unpacking?" Nick asked, strolling on to the balcony, freshly showered and probably having heard our entire conversation. He was wearing jeans and a t-shirt, his wet hair curling just below his ears. "We're about to break open the *biiiriii.* Alice's treat, amazingly enough."

We followed Nick across the dirt yard, the lizards scattering for cover when we circled around the back of the main cabin. A woman, whom I assumed must be the "snooty" Diane, was draped across the picnic table, her halo of perfect blond ringlet curls in perplexing defiance of my previous understanding of hair, humidity, and the necessity of electricity to power a curling iron. She waved a dangling cigarette from her long thin fingers, and I walked over to introduce myself. Nick followed me, but Rosie left us, continuing to the kitchen.

Diane appeared to be in her mid-thirties, with light wrinkles around her glossy red lips and dark blue eyes. Even in her simple slacks and t-shirt she looked stylish, willowy, at ease. Until she moved, taking a long drag of her cigarette, her hands trembling ever so slightly, betraying her underlying tension. She finished her cigarette, rubbed the tip along the wooden picnic table, and tossed it into the jungle. It landed on an intricate shrine nestled in the roots of a shade tree just beyond the *kampu.*

"Join us for a beer before Alice gets back?" Nick asked after we'd finished introductions. I was barely paying attention to the conversation, my gaze still watching the cigarette butt glow and burn out on the batik print cloth covered in figurines and beads, a bottle of Mariënburg rum at the center. It bothered me—that shrine by the tree, but I couldn't look away.

Diane held up a cup of what looked like coffee to decline joining, and we turned to the cabin kitchen. She called after us:

"Did you finish the Kasima trail analysis yet? I need it before—"

Nick took a deep breath and turned back to Diane. "You'll get your report soon enough. One day's not going to make a difference."

Her face tightened in anger, her voice rising, "You said it would be finished last week. I promised. He'll think I'm—" She stopped, jerked her head, and pulled out another cigarette, lighting it immediately. "I don't know how you managed to do a Ph.D. You're lazy and a complete idiot—"

"Calm the fuck down, Diane. I don't give a rat's arse about what he wants. If Alice finds out you're handing over data or God knows what, I won't even contemplate that scene. And don't think I don't know you've been going behind my back bitching to her."

She blew the smoke directly in Nick's face. "You're delirious. I've barely talked to Alice in the last two weeks."

"Bullshit. I'm not stupid. I know exactly what's going on, which is the only reason I've been so tolerant of your *issues.* But watch yourself. My patience is wearing thin and you have way more to lose than I do, darlin'."

"Don't threaten me! I know—" She wiped away a tear. "I know who you met with last month in the city, and we both know what Alice will do if she finds out."

"Whinging to me won't help, but feel free to talk to Alice. I know you always do."

Diane's pale, freckled face turned bright red and Nick touched my shoulder, turning me toward the cabin kitchen.

"No loss. She never drinks anyway," Nick said, holding open the screened door into the kitchen, his warm hand resting on the curve of my lower back. "Given life is best served tall over twelve bottles of cheap beer, I can only assume she's a recovered alkie."

So much for making friends and staying neutral, I thought.

# CHAPTER 4

We followed Alice up narrow, wooden steps to reach Tigrikati's crowded balcony. The lodge was built on a rocky hill on the northern end of Loiri Island, the main tourist area where the plane had landed earlier. Alice sped off to flirt with Kevin Schipper, whom I'd met in passing at the two embassy events Peace Corps volunteers were invited to attend each year. He was American, probably in his late thirties, and worked for IWC, which was the extent of my knowledge. I'd usually been too busy gossiping and downing as much food and liquor as possible with Peace Corps friends to learn anything more—possibly the reason we weren't invited to more events.

A bigger group was gathered around a tall man who turned—I caught my breath. He was ruggedly handsome, with broad shoulders, rumpled salt and pepper hair, and a strong face that had seen, perhaps, too much sun. I involuntarily touched my own face, burnt to a crisp several hundred times during the past two years as I crossed the city under the blazing sun, realizing I was looking at my future.

"Is that Jack West?" Rosie asked, pushing in front of me. "How come no one mentioned he's gorgeous? Wow, I'd do—"

Diane pushed Rosie aside. "Grow up."

Nick poked his head between us. "Come on, no need to stare. Get a move on. We're stuck down here on the stairs. Besides, he's an old man—fifty at least. Have you no shame? At least Rosie has the excuse of being stuck in the woods for the last month, but Em, I thought better of you. If you want a true male Adonis, you need look no further than Melvijn. Look at this stomach. It's a magnificent work of art."

We glanced back and Nick tried to pull up Melvijn's shirt. Melvijn pushed him away. "Hands off, man. How many times do I have to tell you, this is only for the ladies." Melvijn lifted his shirt, slapping away Nick's attempt to rub his rippling stomach.

Kevin Schipper, who was wearing a traditional Maroon plaid cape tied at one shoulder, left Alice and joined us. "Help yourself to Parbos in the kitchen," he said, rubbing his shaved head. "We plan to start in about five minutes."

"Thanks, mate," Nick answered. "Exactly what we needed to hear. You should have told us it was dress-up required. I could have thrown a white sheet over my shoulder and come as a Greek god, that being half my heritage after all."

"Precisely why it wasn't mentioned." Kevin smiled, the expression transforming him from serious and slightly intimidating into a kind and attractive man. His steady blue eyes turned to me, and he gave me a quick welcome before turning away.

Nick pushed us apart. "Ladies, if you will please step aside and let the boys pass, we'll go fetch some drinks." Brian and Melvijn squeezed past us to follow Nick into the lodge.

There were a half dozen white men on the balcony, presumably all from IWC, and only one woman, who was busy snapping photos with her very expensive camera. The island workers, mostly men and easily identifiable by their casual dress and flip-flops, seemed to be staying together on one side of the balcony. I didn't know most of them, although I recognized Hortense, who'd put on a red tank top over her purple and yellow *pangi* for the special occasion.

"Who's that?" Rosie asked, indicating the woman with the camera. She was tiny, with almond skin and thick black hair pulled back in a silver clip.

"Laura Taylor," Nick said, returning with my beer and a rum and coke for Rosie. "She does communications for IWC out of D.C."

Melvijn emerged at the end of the balcony and approached the woman.

"Rosie," a voice said from the stairs. We turned in unison to find a dark, hawk-like man standing on the top step to the balcony.

Nick stepped toward him, shoulders tensed. "You weren't invited," he said. "You'd better leave before we have you thrown out."

Kevin's voice rang out across the balcony. "Everybody please move back against the wall. We'd like to begin."

The man laughed and turned back down the balcony steps.

"What the hell is he doing here?" Nick asked Rosie.

Rosie was silent, looking toward the opposite end of the balcony, seemingly more interested in Melvijn speaking to the woman with the camera.

"Rosie," Nick said, "don't talk to Arnaud. Walk away if he approaches you. I'll talk to Kevin about the situation, 'kay?"

Rosie nodded absently.

"Who's Arnaud?" I whispered as we crowded back against the wall of the lodge, leaving Jack West standing alone in front of the balcony railing. Behind him, across the river, Mount Kasima, a massive granite tabletop mountain, rose like an alien moon above a carpet of cloud and trees.

"The guy who threatened to kill me," Rosie whispered right before Jack West launched into his speech. He spoke each line first in English and then repeated it in Sranan: "I was twenty-three when I first came to Kasima, and I recognized the magic here. There are many great and beautiful places in the world, but Kasima National Park remains for me particularly special.

I'm proud International Wildlife Conservation will be playing such a critical role in protecting the most biologically diverse area in Suriname, as well as one of the largest tracts of undisturbed rainforest in the tropics."

At Jack's command, an ancient Maroon man wearing a plaid cape tied at one shoulder moved toward him, chanting. He circled Jack and opened a small Parbo bottle, splashing the beer on the floor and over the rail to the ground as part of the ceremony—a gift to the earth. Much of it landed on Jack's boot, but he didn't seem to mind.

Nick moved just in front of me, his right arm brushing against me. I leaned in, standing on my tiptoes to whisper. "Who's that guy Arnaud? Rosie says he threatened to kill her."

Nick stepped close enough for me to feel his breath against my neck. "Works for Natuur Tours. Buggered if I know what really went down. It was a mess, but supposedly, Arnaud was banned from bringing tourists out here. That clearly didn't happen."

"Someone should talk to his . . . ah . . . company. Get him fired." I was having a hard time focusing on the conversation, what with his hand now on my back, the fresh scent of soap on the curve of his neck, the little mole just below his dark curls.

"His brother's the owner," Nick whispered. "Rosie just needs to stay away from him." He pushed a strand of hair out of my eyes. "Want to sneak off and watch the sunset?"

I looked around the porch, realizing the speech was over. "What, you don't want to stay and schmooze?"

"Not at the moment." He detangled himself gracefully from his position half wrapped around me. "I'll go grab a couple of cold *biris*. Meet me at the bottom of the stairs, and whatever you do, don't let Rosie tag along. I think she'll be looking for company." Nick nodded to Melvijn who was still talking to the woman with the camera.

Rosie was leaning against the railing with one of the younger IWC staff, a stocky man in his late twenties. She seemed capable of taking care of herself.

Nick steered me under the porch a few minutes later and down a path to the rocks. "What a bore. Have you ever seen such a gathering of wankers in the jungle?"

"Wankers?"

"Something like idiots—it's hard to define exactly."

"Ah . . . No, but thanks for rescuing me. I didn't come to the jungle to circulate at a cocktail party."

"Now you mention it, why *did* you come?" He grabbed my hand, helping me slide down the rock.

We sat on the edge of a boulder and I thought about his question for a few minutes, taking off my flip-flops to soak my feet in the cool river. Nick pulled out two beers from his shorts pockets. He opened both with his pocketknife, passing one to me. "Honestly, I don't know," I said, opting for a partial truth. "It all happened so quickly. I'd had a rough few months and was feeling restless about going home, and suddenly there was Alice." I paused to gather my thick brown hair off my sweaty neck and twist it into a knot. "Alice is a little intense. Is she always like that?"

Nick choked violently on his sip of beer. "That's the understatement of the century. But count yourself lucky. She makes rather rash judgments, not always accurately, and can be cruel if she doesn't like you."

"I don't really care what she thinks of me," I said quickly and not quite honestly. "I'm just here to figure out what to do next."

"Hmmm. Feel free to let me know when you sort that out."

Something nibbled on my toe and I jerked it out of the water. "So, what about you? How long are you out here for?"

"I don't know. It's certainly beautiful, but I'd rather be studying sea turtles or dolphins. I guess I'm not as excited by monkeys as I should be."

"Ah, you like the ocean," I said. "Do you want to be a professor like Alice and set up a research site?"

"Maybe. The truth is, I'd really like to have a go at producing wildlife docos."

"Docos?" I asked. "You mean documentaries?"

"Good onya. Nice to see you know some proper English."

"That was my major. Journalism and film."

"Really? Alice said you were an English major. Which led me to assume your ignorance would be appalling."

"Hey!"

"Sorry. But true. This isn't going to be as easy as Alice makes it seem, you know."

I glanced at him, hurt. One minute he was flirting, the next insulting me. It was a little dizzying to navigate. "I admit I have no idea how I ended up here, but that doesn't mean I can't do the work. I knew nothing about malaria or dengue when I started at the Bureau of Public Health two years ago. By the end, I was the head of their education department. Okay, admittedly everybody else quit, but nevertheless . . ."

He raised a mocking eyebrow.

I grabbed my flip-flops, standing up. "I spent weeks in a gold mining camp dealing with situations you can't even imagine. I'll survive just fine here." That was a slight exaggeration, but I didn't correct myself.

Nick touched my arm, encouraging me to sit back down. "Fair enough. No reason to get upset. Didn't I warn you this morning? Now you're supposed to insult me back. It's a form of friendship, remember? Besides, we've heard really great things about you from Melvijn. He says you have a friend in common."

I sat back down, realizing I was overreacting. "I think we're going to have to become better friends if you want me to readily accept insults."

"Why do you think we're down here instead of at the party?"

I'd been kind of wondering that myself. I couldn't tell if he was interested in me personally or just interested in the latest diversion to land on the island.

"I thought we were escaping the wankers," I said and he laughed, clinking his beer against mine just as Brian called his name from the top of the rocks.

"Damn, never a second of privacy around here," Nick muttered. "What do you want?" he yelled back. "I'm occupied."

Brian peeked over the rock. "Alice asked me to find you, Nick. Diane told her you met with Laura last week about *the* job. She's threatening to fire you."

Nick jumped up, muttering to himself while climbing up the side of the rock. "I should have killed Diane when I had the chance. Now Alice has gotten herself in another froth. She's a few sandwiches short of a picnic as it is. Bugger."

# CHAPTER 5

The overhanging jungle reflected in the surprisingly still river just above the swirling rapids, the air quiet and bathed in a halo of soft blue. I'd never seen anything so beautiful, and I stayed on the rocks through the long twilight, nearly forgetting where I was until my stomach began grumbling and I realized it was time for dinner. Plus, it was almost dark and I didn't have a flashlight. I collected the empty beer bottles and climbed with difficulty back up the hill, scraping my knee along the way.

Up ahead, I could hear Alice's voice rising in anger. I crept forward, stopping in the shadows of the Tigrikati porch, the voices above me.

"You can't stand that I beat you at your own game. That's why you tried to destroy my research twenty years—"

A familiar male voice cut her off. "Alice, you'd think you could move on after all these years. There's limited space for research at Kasima, and I expect it to be substantive and applied. You don't fit here."

It was Jack West.

"Bastard!" Thumping followed her shriek. "You can't do this. Not now! I have friends too. I have a contract with the government! I'll hire a lawyer! I'll talk to my friends at the National Science Foundation."

"Jacobs? I doubt he'll care, since you've failed to publish anything meaningful in the last five years. Your contract is now void. I have more important things to deal with. Cheer up, Alice. All you have to do is find another park. It's not the end of the world."

Footsteps pounded across the porch and down the wooden steps.

"You pretentious son of a bitch, I'll kill you before I'll let you take away my monkeys," Alice screeched. Jack West disappeared down the hill and a glass bottle shattered above. Seconds later Alice rushed past.

Just my luck. I'd only been there a few hours, had yet to see any wildlife, and now we were being kicked out. I followed Alice down the hill, stumbling cautiously along the rocky trail in the dusk, wishing again I'd brought my flashlight. I could see light and people ahead, but they were farther down the sloping hill, under a *kampu*. Hopefully, I hadn't missed dinner. I hadn't eaten since breakfast and was now officially starving—I stopped in the dark, catching my breath in fright.

Arnaud, the man Rosie had said threatened to kill her, stepped out of the shadows, blocking the rocky cliff path that dropped to the invisible yet noisy rapids below.

"You late for party," he said softly in English, his sharp face hidden in the shadow of the mango tree. "You miss the rum I brought."

"Ah, too bad," I said, not sure what he was referring to and still a little nervous. I was within yelling distance of the party, but who knew if they would hear me over their own noise.

"Tell Rosie I want my photo," he said.

"What photo?" I asked. "What are you talking about?"

He stepped closer. I stood my ground, although I already regretted my question. His voice increased in intensity and he grabbed hold of my shoulder. "Melvijn use black magic on Rosie. I help her. Melvijn bad man. He—"

I shrugged off his hand, cutting him off. "I don't know what you're talking about. Can you please let me pass?" I'd had enough of Winti and black magic for the day.

Arnaud didn't move, and I had to edge around him, my foot loosening a rock that plummeted over the cliff edge. He too seemed crazy. Perhaps there was something in the water.

"I want my photo," he called after me. I turned down the hill to the *kampu* on the grassy lawn near the river, but stood at the edge of the party, watching the scene before entering. I'd hoped this feeling of detachment would have magically disappeared in the jungle, but it was still with me, heavy and real. Alice was laughing with Nick and Brian as she poured them shots from a bottle of local rum. It was Mariënburg rum, which is deadly stuff at ninety proof and way too strong for general consumption. I wondered who at IWC had made the crazy decision to buy it for the party.

It didn't look like Alice had fired Nick just yet, and she seemed completely recovered from her fight with Jack West. Or possibly she was just good at pretending. Kevin Schipper found me hovering. He held up another bottle of rum, slurring slightly, which, from my few interactions with him, did not seem like his normal condition at parties. He was more often a little stiff.

He handed me a small water glass, and continued pouring until rum splashed over the edge. He laughed when he noticed—a beautiful, rich sound—and I relaxed, following him into the *kampu*.

He raised his own glass just as Jack West appeared from behind, wrapping his arm around Kevin's shoulder. "I assume you're cheering our success in acquiring Kasima."

Kevin rubbed his bald head. "I'm not sure you want to use 'acquiring.' How about our success in taking the protection and management of Kasima to the next level? But actually, I was just congratulating Emma on joining Alice's—"

Jack interrupted, slapping Kevin on the back. "You've been a bureaucrat way too long, Kevin. You don't always have to play it so safe." He turned to me, the corner of his mouth curling upward in surprise, or possibly mockery. "So you've joined Alice's team? What bad timing."

"Jack!" Kevin said before turning away to greet a sweaty, middle-aged man and direct him to a seat near the head of the table.

Jack leaned over and whispered, "Don't get too comfortable. Alice is certifiable." I was still tingling from his warm breath on my neck when he walked away to sit at the head of the worn mahogany table stretched the *kampu's* length. I found a seat at one of the few open spaces left, next to a short Dutchman in his late fifties with an unhealthy bulging belly under his short-sleeved leisure suit. Frank Van Landsberg, as the Dutchman introduced himself, seemed disappointed to be sitting next to someone as unimportant as me and kept glancing down the table to Jack at the head, flanked by the unknown sweaty middle-aged man and Kevin Schipper.

Jack, who was dominating the discussion at his end of the table, seemed a little egotistical, but Frank was worse. He spent the dinner downing rum drinks and regaling me with a self-important history of his twenty years' working in forestry, most recently as head of the IWC office in Suriname. By the end, I was desperate to escape.

After dinner, we moved the table and chairs aside and Cedric, his gold teeth sparkling under the single light, introduced the drummers, who were all workers on the island. A group of young Dutch students joined the party, along with Arnaud, their tour guide. Only the Mormon boys from the plane stayed away. Everybody danced once the drumming started, and the men passed around bottles of rum, drinking it straight or mixing it with a little *stroop*, which is basically flavored sugar water. I saw Jack West toss back several shots with the drummers. At some point, Melvijn came by and handed me a shot of rum while I danced with Brian. Next to us, a Dutch girl picked up one of the small Maroon boys and twirled him in a circle as he giggled in delight.

A vivid flash of a lazy Sunday afternoon in town blurred my vision—Sonia and me twirling her young boys while samba records played on the ancient record player, her husband off at a Church of God revival. Sonia laughing, happy. I stumbled in the dirt, whether from the memory or the shot of rum, I wasn't sure. Brian grabbed hold of my arm to steady me and the song ended. The drummers were taking a break.

Cedric put on a salsa CD and I stepped to the side of the *kampu* to cool off. I took a deep breath and watched the bright, round moon floating above the trees. A full moon—when the demons and werewolves come out to play. Or as Mom, who's a doctor of sorts, always swears, the night emergency rooms go mad with gunshot wounds and loonies. I remembered another full moon and guilt washed over me, as it always did when I thought of Sonia—or tried not to think of her.

"Would you like to dance?" said a deep voice from behind. I turned, wiping away a few tears, and came face to face with Jack West again. He smiled and I felt a little giddy as we walked back under the *kampu*. For the past year I'd taken salsa lessons with friends from work and I was looking forward to showing off in front of Nick.

We swung onto the dusty ground, my feet in flip-flops now covered in dirt. He pulled me against his chest and we molded together, gliding—to the extent that's possible—across the dirt floor. "Kevin told me you wrote some of those stories about gold mining that were picked up in Europe," Jack finally said, breaking the awkward silence, since I couldn't figure out if we should be talking or just dancing.

"Yeah, that was kind of an accident—" I stumbled, stepping on Jack's toe when one of my flip-flops slid off. "Sorry."

He squeezed my back in response and pulled me closer, the music blasting from the tiny radio. I started to relax and enjoy the moment. He *was* gorgeous, and a good dancer too.

"I think you're being too modest, from what Kevin said. Send me an e-mail when you finish here." He drew me closer. "I'd be glad to help out, put in a good word for you at IWC."

His hand slipped lower on my back and I had a quick flash of him knocking back those shots with the drummers. I looked up and he was watching me, his blue eyes half-closed. He rubbed the small of my back with his thumb, his fingers drifting lower. My eyes dropped to the gathering beads of sweat on his tanned chest and throat. His skin looked hard and leathery up close, and I could see a few white hairs peaking through his tan vest straight out of central casting for a rugged explorer or war cor-respondent.

"You're a good dancer," he said. "I enjoyed watching you earlier."

I glanced at Alice on the edge of the *kampu*. She scowled, and I felt a wave of guilt. I didn't want her to think I was taking sides, and wondered if I should leave him in the middle of the song. My eyes moved to Nick next to the drummers, also watch-ing, expressionless.

I pulled back, putting several inches between our bodies.

"How's Alice treating you?" he asked, stepping in closer again.

"Good. I like her. I just arrived today and . . ." I paused, then jumped in. "Are you really kicking Alice out?"

He shouted with laughter and swung me out for a turn. "Word travels fast. Don't worry, just because Alice leaves doesn't mean other research won't continue. Besides, it'll prob-ably take several months to get her formally removed with as few messy confrontations as possible. Alice loves her dramatic scenes."

I didn't respond, and he didn't pull me in close again. "I

need some air to cool off," I said when the song ended. Faces and bodies were blurring around me under the lights.

Jack followed me into the dark. "Why don't we take a walk," he slurred in my ear, wrapping his arm around my waist.

I was startled and annoyed—I *was* young enough to be his daughter, even if it had taken me a while to remember that fact. I pushed him firmly away. "No thanks."

He stared at me, a flash of anger lighting his eyes, before he turned leisurely toward the *kampu*. So much for the job offer.

# Chapter 6

I slipped farther into the dark, checking behind to make sure Jack didn't follow, but he was watching the drumming start again. I stumbled down the path to a wooden bench just above the rapids and lay down, watching the bright stars swim dizzily above, the full moon rising in the night sky. The breeze felt fantastic and I began to dry off. The drumming eventually stopped and someone approached, pausing at the turn in the path. Whoever it was didn't seem to notice me, lying on the bench in the shade of the mango tree.

"With the new government, you're no longer useful."

"I still have connections. The government will change back again in a few years."

"You fucked me and my organization. I want you gone. The only reason I've been this reasonable is I want this situation kept quiet."

"It's just a few animals. I had to let it continue to get you Kasima."

"That's debatable."

"You haven't told anyone, have you, Jack?"

"I'm not interested in discussing this further. Resign by Friday or . . ." Frank Van Landsberg and Jack West passed out of my hearing up the path toward the Tigrikati lodge, presumably where the IWC guests were staying. Apparently the island was a vortex of disharmony and ill will.

Laughter drifted down the hill a few minutes later, and I

recognized Melvijn's strong accent and a woman's laughing reply. I twisted around. They didn't have a flashlight, but the full moon shone brightly on the path. They passed under the giant mango tree, Melvijn towering over the tiny Laura Taylor, her camera dangling from her hand.

At least a few people believed in peace and love. That made me feel a little better. Although Rosie was going to be upset.

Sometime later I was still lying on the bench when Diane appeared in front of me, her curly blond hair glistening in the moonlight. She was alone and looking out over the water. Possibly I'd dozed for a few seconds. I don't feel it's appropriate to describe it as passing out. She was standing so still I didn't notice her at first, not until she cried—long, soft sobs. She collapsed onto the ground, her feet dangling over the side of the cliff, muttering something under her breath. It sounded somewhat like: "Bastard, bastard, bastard."

I tried ignoring the sobs, telling myself I didn't know her well enough to get involved, but eventually her misery was too much to take and I sat up.

"Diane, are you okay?" I called, even though the answer was obvious.

She jerked around, teetering drunkenly on the side of the hill.

I leapt off the bench and raced toward her, grabbing her arm just in time to prevent her tumbling over the cliff. She dropped her flashlight in surprise and it plummeted over the edge, flipping as it fell, the beam slashing across us, highlighting the rocks and river before the churning rapids sucked it to the river bottom and the dim light vanished.

"Are you okay?" I asked again, pulling her away from the cliff. IWC needed to put up a fence of some sort. Sooner rather than later.

"I'm fine." She wrenched back her arm, wiping at her tears.

"Good, good. If you want to talk about—"

"Where'd he go?"

"Where'd who go?"

She wasn't paying attention to me, but peering under the bench, around the mango tree. "I know you're here, you bastard!"

"Ah, Diane, there's no one here. I think you should go to bed. Want me to help you walk back to the lodge?"

"Where'd he go?" she demanded again, sniffling.

"Maybe if you told me who *he* is, I could help you find him."

"Ha! Where are you, Jack? I'll fucking kill you."

With that she turned unsteadily down the path toward Tigrikati, the opposite direction from our cabin, but the same direction as Melvijn, Laura, Frank, and Jack. Mom was right about full moons.

I stumbled back up the path toward the *kampu,* wondering why Diane was upset with Jack until I saw a light approaching and heard Nick call my name, inviting me for a swim. He was with Cedric, and Arnaud for some reason, and four Dutch girls. The girls were drunk and loud, their Dutch stridently distinctive to the singsong Surinamese accent.

We followed the party crowd at a discrete distance down the hill to where the rocks created a protective barrier and sandy beach on the edge of the rapids. Water roared past on the other side of the rocks, drowning out the vibrating chorus of frogs, birds, and insects.

"What are you doing with Arnaud?" I asked.

"I'm keeping him away from Rosie for now. Brian was taking care of it, but he's making sure Alice gets to bed. She's sloshed. He said he'd be down in a few minutes. I haven't seen Rosie in a while, so I'm hoping she's gone to bed and we can avoid a scene."

I told him about the fight I'd overheard between Alice and

Jack, and asked him why Alice was mad at him earlier.

"I didn't *directly* lie . . . not if you consider time to be a flexible concept—you know, within the space-time continuum. It came down to my word against Diane's, and I think Alice believed me."

"What did Diane tell her?" I asked, thinking I'd have to watch myself with Nick if he has such a flexible view of lying. I stumbled on a rock and Nick grabbed my arm, continuing to hold it while we climbed over the rocky beach.

"She told Alice I met with Kevin and Laura last week about a job. I don't know how Diane knew. Maybe she overheard me talking to Brian. I'd tell Alice the truth if she didn't take every action as a personal betrayal. Besides, I didn't feel like dealing with her conspiracy theories about IWC wanting to destroy her. She doesn't understand we all need to start looking at alternate—"

"Then you're leaving?" My gloom deepened, even though it didn't matter. We were all leaving if Alice was kicked out.

"The chances are slim the project will even get funded." His hand slid down my arm. "The night's too beautiful to waste talking about Diane and Alice. How about something more interesting—like your dancing with Jack. That was certainly hot."

"Shut up!" I said softly, pushing him on his shoulder. "It was just dancing. That's how you dance salsa."

"If you say so. I was a bit jealous."

My heart gave a little lurch and I blushed, grateful for the dark.

"Time for that swim," Nick said, dropping my hand and slipping off his shirt.

I followed him, stripping down to my underwear and tiptoeing into the cold water. Which was probably a good indication I'd had way too much to drink. But in the moment a night swim seemed perfectly reasonable. The Dutch girls were already there, laughing and splashing with Cedric and Arnaud. It was dark in the little pool, despite the full moon, and all I could see were shadows.

"Don't step in the sand, scoot your feet," Nick said. "Stingrays hide just underneath."

I stopped.

"It's okay. They're tiny stingrays. It feels like a pin prick."

"Yeah, right." I splashed some water in his direction. We swam to a long, low boulder and Nick took my hand again to pull me out of the water, not letting go as we stepped carefully though the pools of water. I followed him to a slight dip facing the river and we lay down against the still warm, smooth rock.

I could hear him breathing softly next to me, his thumb circling my palm. Brilliant stars shimmered above. The full moon was now small and distant, isolated from the cozy band of stars and galaxy dust sweeping through the inky black sky. The air soft and sweet and a little cold. I slid closer to Nick.

"I'm not quite sure this is a good idea," he whispered, rolling over me, his breath soft and warm and smelling of rum.

"It's a very bad idea," I said, letting my fingers curl playfully in his unruly hair. My palm drifted to his stubbly cheek and I rubbed my thumb against his lips. He was so beautiful, it almost hurt. "I don't know anything about you."

"I'm not a settling sort. Fair warning."

"Definitely not fair."

"But worth it . . ." was the last thing I heard before his lips covered mine.

A few minutes later, I thought I heard a shout from the river and jerked up, knocking my chin against Nick's forehead.

"Ouch, that hurt." He rubbed his head. "You can just tell me to stop you don't need to—"

"Shh!"

"What does that mean? What—"

"Shh," I said again.

"Why do you keep—"

"Can you please be quiet for ten seconds? I heard someone yelling for help."

"*Luv,* it's probably the blood rushing to your brain. I have that affect on heaps of women."

The "luv" came out condescending, not to mention the heaps of women, so I punched him on the arm. Hard.

"You're a very violent woman, you know. Do you get some sort of masochistic pleasure from punching me? I'm certainly into experimenting, but violence seems . . ."

"Nick, just listen for a moment. Please."

"Okay, okay. What am I listening for? Yelling? It was probably just Cedric and the Dutch girls. He has a reputation for—"

I put my hand over his mouth. He licked my palm with the tip of his tongue, taking his time as he moved to a finger. I turned warm and mushy and was having a hard time remembering why I was sitting up.

I leaned toward him, but he sat up, dropping my hand. "Afraid I don't hear anything, Em. But I am getting chilly, let's—"

I pushed Nick aside and scrambled to the edge of the rock, sure I saw a human head bubble up from the rapids.

"Emma! My God, are you crazy?" Nick yelled as I dove into the river.

# CHAPTER 7

The current yanked me under, tossing me against the sandy river bottom and spitting me up, coughing and gasping for air. I kept my legs up and my head above water, and the current dragged me downstream. The river swept me forward, away from Nick shouting in the distance, his voice growing faint. I blocked his voice and let the river take me.

I kicked hard and fast toward the head, faintly visible in the light of the full moon. I was inches away when it disappeared again. I dove below, sensing more than feeling the outline of a body. I grasped for it in the murky water as we tumbled and turned in the foam, sliding across the slippery rocks. I felt the soft sand of the bottom and kicked myself back to the surface.

I took a deep breath of the cool night air and dove again, grasping soft skin. Finally. I wrapped my right hand around the cold, hard wrist and yanked upward, kicking from the bottom and tugging the body toward air.

I screamed for Nick. "I've got him!".

I heard Nick from somewhere upriver, but I couldn't tell if he was in the water with me or running along the rocks. I kept a strong grip on the hand and grasped for the edge of a jutting rock, hurtling forward. I missed. We swept toward another rock. I dove underwater, grasping the edge and dragging the dead weight through the water.

I pulled my head back up, gulping for air. But he needed air too. It was impossible to keep us both above water. I slammed my body into a hook in another rock, wedging myself into the space with my feet propped against the opposite edge. Waves crashed against us, and I edged further out of the water, the weight of the body straining my arm muscles. It had been a long time now. With no air. Hopefully it wasn't too late.

I flipped, grabbing hold with both hands, and dragged him out of the current. I couldn't fit him fully into the crook of the rock with me. Not with the current continuing to tug at his body. But I could keep his head above water. For now.

I screamed for Nick again. "I'm in the middle of the river. Where are you? I can't hold him much longer."

A boat engine revved in response and I heard a noise that may have been, "Hang on."

I looked down at the face. It was Jack West. The water pounded over us, but I kept his head out of the river. He didn't move or respond. I felt for a pulse. His neck felt strange and slippery. I couldn't tell for sure, in the dim moonlight and long shadow of the rock crevice, but his neck skin felt wrong. Like it had been cut.

I shook him. "Jack, Jack, wake up." Water washed over us again but still he didn't move.

The boat engine grew louder, and I heard a shout from what I thought might be the island. Another wave swept over us, knocking me sideways. I tried to keep my footing but lost hold of Jack. I dove for him, catching one arm. The body was in the main current again, the weight pulling me forward. I slipped, nearly losing my footing on the rock, barely able to keep my own head above water.

"Emma, where are you?" I heard Nick scream over the roar of the rapids and boat engine. I waved my hand over the top of the rock and yelled back but the sound was lost in the surge of foaming river.

I tried again, "I'm here!"

It was too late. He didn't hear me. The dugout canoe roared past, slamming more water over my head. I fell off the rock this time, and Jack slipped from my fingers. The current grabbed me.

I dove for Jack.

But he was gone.

I dove again and again, my eyes open in the black river, but there was no sign of him. I came up again, still tumbling downstream. I flipped to my back, keeping my feet up and letting the current pull me while I watched, realizing there was little chance of finding him while I was still in the river. I noticed a dark spot and moved toward it. The water was slowing down now, the rapids tapering off, and I let the current carry me into the hard, black rock.

I grasped hold and pulled myself up. Without Jack it wasn't so difficult. I scrambled to the top, my eyes straining to see in the dark. Clouds had moved over the moon and the water was black. I couldn't see anything. I called Jack's name anyway, knowing the attempt was useless.

Nick had managed to turn his canoe around and came into view as a murky shadow on the river.

"I'm up here," I yelled, but he didn't hear me over the roar of his outboard motor.

I screamed again, jumping and waving my arms.

"I see you," he finally called. His boat engine strained against the current, which, although calmer here, was still making it difficult for him to move alongside my rock.

"Jesus fucking Christ, Emma!" he yelled across the dark water. "Are you out of your mind? You could have drowned! And how the hell am I supposed to get you off that rock? I barely know how to drive this fucking thing." A piercing scrape and hissing from the engine confirmed his skills, and I nearly toppled off the rock in surprise.

"Shit," Nick muttered. "Cedric's going to kill me if I wreck his boat. I hope you have a good explanation for him."

"I saw a body in the river," I yelled back, feeling defensive. "It was Jack West. I think he's dead."

"Fuck," Nick said, adjusting the tiller and inching the canoe forward. Water was crashing over the sides of his boat and he seemed to be drifting farther away rather than closer.

"Why don't I swim out to you and you can pull me into the boat?" I yelled.

I could feel rather than see his glare. The muttering I could hear just fine.

"Come along," he finally called. "You survived those rapids, so you can probably manage a half meter crossing this far down. Just stay above water and away from the engine. And don't tip me. Please."

I scrambled to the topside of the rock and jumped into the river, just upstream from the canoe, swimming fast and hard through the current. I landed against the boat's bow, grasping hold of the warm wood, careful not to pull too hard. I clung to the top and edged myself along until I reached the middle.

"What's your plan now?" He'd turned off the engine and was letting us drift downstream.

"Are you watching where we're going?" I asked. "There're a lot of rocks."

"That's the understatement of the century. Why don't you worry about climbing into this canoe and let me do the rest, eh aqua girl?"

"I'm not sure I can climb in without tipping the boat."

"Ah, yes, the eternal canoe dilemma. Now she remembers."

"Can you lean over to the other side?" I asked, beginning to recognize the depth of anger brimming under his casual attitude. "I'll try and roll in."

He shifted his weight and I lifted a leg and arm over the

edge. The canoe teetered precariously and I slipped back into the water, losing my hold. Nick lunged forward, grabbing my arm.

I clutched the edge of the boat again. "I don't think this is going to work after all. Why don't I swim for shore and you can pick me up somewhere along the mainland?"

He didn't say anything but I could hear him taking a deep breath.

"Nick?"

"You're not swimming for shore. In fact you're not leaving my sight. I hear a boat engine. Maybe Cedric has finally realized his canoe's in mortal danger."

He started the engine back up, keeping us floating in the same spot.

The roar of a second outboard motor announced Cedric's arrival on the opposite side of Nick's boat. I inched around the front end and between the two boats. Both men lifted me out of the water and I landed in Nick's canoe, a combination of curses in Sranan and English raining down on me. Cedric still didn't know why we were there, since Nick hadn't yet enlightened him.

"I went in after Jack West," I told him, once I'd pushed myself upright, still breathless. "I lost him, he's floating downstream. He's hurt. We need to look for him."

Cedric turned to Nick, as if asking for confirmation and I looked down, realizing I was wearing only my underwear, thankfully black. I shivered, cold now that I was out of the water.

"If she said she saw Jack, she saw Jack," Nick said. Under his breath I heard him add, "Even if she is a drunk whack job for nearly killing herself in the process."

"I didn't come anywhere near to killing myself," I said.

"How the hell was I supposed to know that?" Nick nearly yelled. "You disappeared under pitch-black water and I couldn't see you or hear you for what seemed an eternity. I don't think I've ever been so scared in my life."

"What was I supposed to do, let him drown? We need to kkkeep ll—" I recognized a growing hysteria in my shaking voice and stopped talking.

"I look for him," Cedric said in English. "Go back Loiri Island before you destroy my boat. Tell Boss Van Landsberg and he organize search. I look now."

"I last saw him up there," I said, goosebumps forming along my outstretched arm. I hugged myself, rubbing my skin. Nick noticed and leaned forward to wrap a dirty towel that smelled of fish around my shoulders.

Cedric turned his boat into the rapids, gazing over the water.

"We should help him search," I said to Nick.

"Fucking hell. We'll be lucky to make it back to the island alive. I haven't the foggiest idea how to maneuver this damn hunk of wood, and you're shaking so hard you can barely speak. Don't tell Cedric, but it's only adrenaline that got me this far. Thank your lucky stars I like you or I'd have left you for the piranhas."

"But—"

Nick revved the engine and edged around the rock, turning the canoe toward the island while continuing to mutter to himself in between throwing me questions. "What the hell do I care about a tosser like Jack West? Let him drown. If I'd known you had such a fancy for him, I wouldn't have—Jesus, you almost killed yourself. Are you suicidal or just crazy? Who does that sort of thing?"

I didn't respond. My mind was focused on that soft, clean line of flesh I'd felt on Jack's neck. It was probably too late anyway, even by the time I'd caught him. He'd been underwater a long time, and with a cut like that . . . The rocks seemed too smooth, too worn down by the surging river to slice a neck so smooth and deep. I recoiled in horror at the thought, shutting it out.

# CHAPTER 8

I woke to a clatter of pots crashing to the floor in the kitchen just outside my door, followed by a curse. I curled into a ball and pulled the flimsy sheet over my head, my head throbbing. Last night was a blur, a nightmare, and I dreaded getting out of bed.

"Are they going to search more this arvo? We should help," Nick said from the kitchen.

"Man, when are you going to learn English?" Brian said. "What does 'this arvo' mean?"

"Mate, that *is* English, it means this afternoon. You just haven't been learning your English from the right people."

Softly this time, Brian said, "If we can escape. She'll never let us—"

"Leave it to me," Nick replied. "I know how to take care of her."

Brian made the typical Surinamese noise of disapproval, a click of his tongue against the roof of his mouth. "Man, you've got that backwards. She's got you twisted around her little finger like—"

I heard thumping followed by more banging pots. I rolled onto my side and gazed through the filmy haze of my mosquito net, listening to a plane hum in the distance. Lush palms glistened in the early morning sun just outside my screenless window. I rubbed my forehead, trying to massage away the pain and pull together the muddled scenes from the previous night.

I had a vague memory of finding one of the guides sleeping in a hammock just above the beach. He'd agreed to wake up Frank Van Landsberg at the Tigrikati lodge. I remembered being cold, shivering uncontrollably, barely able to stand up. I had another fuzzy memory of fighting with Nick over going to bed rather than searching for Jack. I couldn't remember anything after that. But somehow I'd ended up in my bed, wearing nothing but two sheets and a couple of towels.

I'd been stupid to drink so much, especially on my first night. Not to mention jumping into rapids to save Jack and making out with my new boss, who if I remembered correctly, had made it fairly clear he wasn't the "settling type." And although a lot of it was blurry, I did have a clear memory Nick had called me a "drunk whack job."

My window was open, but the air was still hot and muggy and my mouth was dry. I needed water and would have to face Nick. I stretched and sat up, pushed my mosquito net aside, and stepped onto the cool concrete to pull on a tank top and pair of shorts. I opened my door and stepped into the kitchen, not sure what to expect.

Nick smiled at me over his shoulder while Brian flipped the omelet. "Morning, Em. How's the drunken mermaid feeling? Hungry? We're making omelets." If he'd stuck to the smile, we might have been okay, but he raised an eyebrow, a condescending movement that held mountains of meaning. At least to me, in my tired and hungover state. Possibly I was being too sensitive and over-interpreting the move.

"Man, who's making the omelets?" Brian said. "You were dropping egg shells in the pan."

"Just to trick you into taking over, mate. Any special requests, Em?"

"I'm not hungry," I said, wincing at the bright sunlight streaming through the kitchen window. "What happened with

Jack? Did they find him? Why did I wake up naked?"

Nick shook his head, as if indicating I should keep quiet, even though he added, "Darling, it was that or let you sleep in your wet underwear. It was a hard choice, but I think I handled the sacrifice with manly fortitude."

"Nick collected all our sheets and gave them to you," Brian added.

"Oh," I said softly, regretting my tone.

Rosie's door swung open with a bang and we all jumped. She stumbled through the doorway and shuffled into the bathroom across from the kitchen. "I'm going to throw up," she mumbled, closing the door, although the wall was thin enough to still hear her retching.

I turned back to Brian and Nick. "What happened to Jack?"

"Ah, she's obsessed with Jack," Nick muttered to Brian, turning away. "She nearly killed herself last night over the poor bugger and now still, she can't let go."

"We spent half of last night searching for him," Brian said. "But we haven't found him yet. Everyone is sleeping right now, but they're going to search more this afternoon."

"Couldn't we help? Do it in shifts?" I asked.

"We need boat drivers, and they're all asleep," Brian said.

"I may have done a teeny bit of damage to one of their engines last night," Nick added. "As I believe I mentioned would come to pass. Cedric was none too pleased."

"One of the propellers came off," Brian added. "They'll have to send it into *Foto.*" Foto was the Sranan word for Paramaribo, the only real city in the country.

Rosie emerged from the bathroom pale and shaky and wobbled back to her bedroom. I followed her down the hallway with a glass of water, wanting to escape Nick and my confused emotions. I sat on the edge of her bed and unhooked her still-rolled mosquito net, spreading it over her mattress. "Here, drink this. You probably need it." She reached for the glass and lifted it to her mouth while still lying with her head hanging half off the bed.

"Have you seen Melvijn?" Tears were streaming down her cheeks, although I couldn't tell if they were related to throwing up or to Melvijn. She wiped her blotchy face with the side of her sheet. "He's an asshole. I saw him walk off with Diane while we danced, and he never came back. I hate her. She's so condescending, and she's always flirting with Melvijn. She's trying to steal him." She scratched her ankle, drawing blood.

"Diane and Melvijn? Really?" I didn't mention seeing him with the woman with the camera after the dancing had stopped. I wondered whether Rosie even cared about Melvijn, especially given her long line of other men, including the one she'd been flirting with the night before. But then the last could just have been a way to protect her pride before Melvijn disappeared into the night with someone new.

She rolled into a ball. "Can you get me a bag? I still feel sick."

I found her a paper bag and left her to get dressed, by which time Alice had woken up and was in the kitchen chatting cheerfully about returning to work.

"Morning, dumpling," she called. "I was just telling the boys how much I miss my monkeys. We should head back to camp as soon as possible. I heard Rosie in her room, but where are Diane and Mel—Oh, there you are." She clapped her hands at Diane and Melvijn's joint arrival on the front porch. "Come eat breakfast. We have a million things we need to go over today."

"Did you hear about Jack West?" I asked her, and everyone in the kitchen froze, as if I'd set off a ticking time bomb.

"Sweetie, I never want to hear about Jack." Alice turned to Nick. "Today I think we should work on those—"

I continued anyway, hoping she would help, despite her dislike. "He fell into the river last night. I think he's—"

Alice held up her hand to stop me just as a voice boomed through the front door of the lodge. It was Frank Van Landsberg, followed by Cedric. Frank stepped through the doorway, puffing out his chest like an aspiring alpha male. "Who is Emma?"

I raised my hand. He'd spent forty-five minutes regaling me with tales of his importance the night before at dinner, but the conversation had been completely one-sided so I wasn't surprised he didn't know my name.

"Cedric says you were the one who went swimming with Jack in the river," Frank said, his accent thick and guttural.

"Ah, not quite," I answered. "I was on the . . . ah . . . rocks, and I thought I heard someone cry for help. Then I saw a head in the river and jumped in. I didn't realize it was Jack until I caught him. I had him for a few minutes. I—" I hesitated, glancing at Nick. His fists were shoved deep in his navy green shorts pockets, but he wasn't looking at me. He was watching Diane.

"I think he'd been hurt," I continued. "He might have been dead. I . . . I tried to hold on to him but the current was too strong and the waves from the canoe knocked against us . . ."

"Ha!" Alice muttered, followed by a strained silence since none of us understood what she meant or how to respond.

Frank studied Alice, his mouth tight, his stomach straining against the fabric of his polyester shirt, then jerked his gaze back to me. "Possibly Mr. West fell off the cliff and got caught in the current. This afternoon the men will search again." He cleared his throat, patted his belly, and continued, "He is strong. Maybe he is just lost downriver. We radioed the city, and they will send out more men to search, maybe today . . . or tomorrow. I am sure I will find him before then."

No one from our group offered to help with the search, at least not in front of Alice, who was watching the river, vibrating with annoyance at having to waste her time talking about Jack. I studied her, then Frank, my attention finally settling on Diane, remembering that each had been upset with Jack the night before. I shivered.

Frank cleared his throat again. "With Jack missing, I am now in charge. If you saw anything last night, you need to inform me."

Alice sighed and continued watching the river. I struggled with answering, wondering if I should say anything. Wondering how I could possibly say anything. I decided to keep quiet for once in my life.

Diane, who looked tired but had still managed to pull her hair up in a neat ponytail and apply make-up over her puffy red eyes, did the opposite, pointing at me. "You went down to the river with Jack. I saw you leaving together. What'd you do to him?"

My face flushed with anger, shocked that she would accuse me of hurting Jack, especially after I'd held my tongue to protect her.

"I . . . I didn't go anywhere with him. *You* know that, Diane. I saw you by the cliffs. I was lying on the bench just down the hill from the *kampu* when you came down. *Remember?*" I emphasized *remember*, hoping she'd recall my saving her from tumbling over the side of the cliff. That she was the one who'd threatened Jack.

She looked surprised and suddenly scared. Maybe she hadn't remembered the incident on the cliffs. She'd certainly been drunk enough. Melvijn was watching us intently, a look of speculation on his face. I saw Cedric catch his eye and jerk his head, apparently indicating Melvijn should follow him outside, since they both slipped out of the cabin a few seconds later.

"Jack *was* there," Diane continued, her voice shaking. "I . . . I saw—" She frowned, as if trying to remember what she'd seen.

My eyes hardened. "The last I saw Jack on land was right after I left the party. He was walking toward Tigrikati." I turned to Frank. "With you."

Frank stared at me for a long moment, as if he was still trying to remember who I was or how he knew me. I shifted uncomfortably under his intense gaze. "So," he finally said, breaking the silence. "I will inform you when I locate Mr. West." He eyed me significantly and walked out.

# CHAPTER 9

I escaped after breakfast, my hangover needing a break from Alice's shrieks. I followed the trail toward the bench where I'd encountered Diane the night before. The island was quiet and empty, storm clouds hanging low in the sky. I stopped. Diane was there again. She hadn't eaten breakfast with us. In fact, she'd followed Frank out of the lodge and I'd watched them talking, gesturing toward me. I wondered what she'd told him.

I was a little worried about talking to her, but I had to ask her about the night before. I continued forward, collapsing next to her on the bench and dropping my bag. She mumbled a hello and took a long sip of coffee from her silver canteen, followed by a slow drag on her cigarette. Vultures were circling above and probably scavenging Jack's poor body somewhere downstream. I shuddered, sick at the thought of his body caught in an overhanging tree. Maybe it was an accident, his falling in the river. But then I remembered the cut on his neck and straightened my back, taking a deep breath.

Diane held up her shiny silver canteen of coffee. "Want some?"

She seemed to be offering a truce, and I decided to follow her lead, saying "Sure. Thanks."

She poured the coffee into her canteen cup, her hand shaking when she handed it to me. "So, you're planning to do a Ph.D. with Alice?"

"Ah . . . no. Definitely not. I don't know anything about

monkeys. I'm a little worried about the work, actually. I just came out here—Honestly, I don't really know why I'm here." I shrugged.

Diane bit her lip while studying my face. "Alice's field work is fairly simple, not to mention poorly managed by Nick. It's strange she let you join the team for only six months though. She and Nick had a massive fight about it. He threatened to quit."

She twisted a loose curl around her finger, possibly letting her comment sink in. I wasn't sure how to respond. Luckily I didn't need to.

"But I'm glad you're here," she continued. "I could use some intelligent female company. Rosie's trashy. Let me know if you need anything. I have extra field pants and tons of—"

"Diane," I said. "I don't want to be rude or anything. I know you're trying to make up for what you said earlier, and I'm grateful. I'd like to be friends. But I need to ask you something. When I saw you on the cliff last night, you threatened to kill Jack and then you headed toward Tigrikati. Did you two fight? Did anything happen? Maybe it was just an accident. I'm sure everyone would understand if something like that—"

Diane's eyes turned dark and cold, but she wasn't looking at me, she was staring past me. I followed her gaze to Laura Taylor, the woman with the camera from the night before, who was jogging down the hill.

She arrived slightly out of breath. "What happened to Jack?" she demanded, not bothering with small talk. Her tone was a little aggressive, given this was our first official introduction. She took in my flip-flop-clad feet and tan legs propped on a nearby rock, drifting to my tousled brown hair and slightly swollen lips. She zeroed in on my neck and I instinctively raised my hand to cover the red blotch before realizing the guilt behind that slight movement. I shoved my hand under my thigh, glancing at Diane.

"Didn't Frank tell you?" I asked. "I just talked to him twenty minutes ago. I saw Jack floating past in the river last night and jumped—"

"You what?"

"I tried to drag him out of the rapids, but lost him. That was hours ago, probably around midnight or one. Honestly, I don't understand why you all aren't still searching. I would help. He could still be alive." I didn't believe that last part though.

She pushed up her sunglasses. "Tell me exactly what happened. Every detail."

I told her the story again, although I didn't mention the cut across Jack's neck or any of the threats I'd heard against him during the drunken night. I thought I'd save those for the next person who asked nicely. And besides, I wanted to give Diane a chance to explain.

"Why the hell didn't I hear about this last night instead of some garbled story that Jack went for a swim with you and hadn't come back?" Laura demanded.

I leaned forward. "Who told you that?"

"I don't know. Cedric or Frank. Or maybe Nick. It was the middle of the night. We were all a little drunk."

"I can assure you I did not go for a *swim* with him. But I did see him in the water and he did *not* look alive."

"Damn," she said. "This is bad. I've got to go radio Kevin. I knew he shouldn't have left this morning. Jack's always wandering off to explore on his own. I didn't think anything had really happened." With that she stomped back up the path.

I glanced at Diane, who'd turned her intense gaze back on me. She was silent, making me uncomfortable. Her eyes kept drifting to the same telltale blotchy mark while her right forefinger, freshly manicured and painted a pale pink, tapped the wooden bench in a sign of nervousness, impatience, or possibly too much coffee.

"Don't fuck with me, Emma," she finally said, her voice ice cold. "I don't know what game you're playing, but I never threatened Jack and I certainly didn't go anywhere near Tigrikati last night. Everyone at the party knows you were the last to see him. That you left with him. Remember that."

"The boat back to your camp leaves now," Cedric announced behind us, and I jumped. He was pointing down the beach to his dugout canoe. He wasn't too far behind us, and I wondered if he'd overheard Diane.

Diane eased herself off the bench, picked up her Gucci overnight bag resting on the grass near her feet, and flicked her cigarette over the side of the hill with a quick, thoughtless motion.

"Hey!" I said, for some reason caring more about her trashing a pristine river than whether she might have just threatened me. I peeped over the cliff anyway, to the churning water and black rocks fifteen feet below. The cigarette butt was gone, but I noticed something tan hanging off a root protruding from the side of the steep hillside.

"Looks like one of the tourists dropped something down there," I told Cedric. "Maybe a bag."

He didn't bother to look.

"It might be important," I said, thinking it looked a bit like Jack's vest.

"I will send someone down later to find it," he said.

"I'm sure it's nothing." Diane grabbed my arm, squeezing it painfully. "Let's go. I don't want to be left behind."

Back at camp, we scattered to our bedrooms to sleep off the aftermath of the party, ignoring Alice's protestations that we spend the day reading the scientific articles she'd brought down. I woke in the heat of the afternoon and, despite the horror of the previous night and my suspicions about Diane, I felt recovered and alive in a way I hadn't felt in months, like I'd moved from black and white to color again.

I checked my floor for creepy crawlies before slipping out of bed, and tiptoed barefoot to the front of the quiet cabin. I was a little disoriented about time and thought everyone else might still be sleeping. I stepped off the porch and splashed my face with water from the outside faucet, the sunlight blinding in its intensity. The shower was running and I wondered briefly if it was Nick, until I realized the pink flip-flops outside the shower door looked a little too feminine. Now that I was feeling so much better I wanted to talk to him. Preferably in private.

I crossed the yard to his cabin and pulled open the screen door, catching Melvijn slipping out of Diane's room. He jumped when he saw me, putting his finger over his lips and pointing to Alice in a hammock stretched across the room, blocking Nick's closed door. Her thunderous snores ricocheted across the cabin and I felt deep pity for Nick and Diane having to endure that noise.

I stepped out of the cabin, turning to watch Melvijn stroll down to the river while shoving what looked like white envelopes into his backpack. He was quite the gigolo, with Laura Taylor last night and today with Diane, not to mention Rosie. Had Diane been crying over Melvijn the night before? Maybe that's why she'd gone toward Tigrikati. I'd swear she'd said Jack. But maybe I was wrong. I'd been a little drunk myself. Certainly too drunk to definitively accuse anyone of anything. Besides, both Alice and Frank had also fought with Jack. Either way, poor Rosie. But at least with all their drama, no one was going to notice anything between Nick and me.

I was standing in the cool shade between the two cabins thinking about what to say to Nick when something hard and squishy landed with a splash of pulpy goo on my hair, rolling off to fall with a wet plop across my feet. I looked up in surprise and another yellowish-green fruit tumbled toward me. I darted sideways and it landed with a splash in the dusty yard. Bending my neck back, I spotted several golden red monkeys with huge round bellies lounging on the lower branches of the tree. They were gorgeous, like shiny red teddy bears.

I gasped, forgetting everything else. It was my first monkey sighting. They'd knocked me in the head before I noticed, but we all have to start somewhere. I ran inside the main cabin to grab Alice's monkey book, noticing Diane crossing the yard to her cabin in a pale pink sarong with a white towel wrapped around her head. I briefly wondered whether I should warn Rosie about Melvijn and Diane, but dropped the idea, telling myself it was none of my business, and ran back outside. I flipped through the book, opening to the howler page. They were definitely red howler monkeys, with their long shaggy jaws and red fur shimmering in the afternoon sun.

"What are you reading?" Alice asked.

Startled, I dropped the book in the dirt.

"Too cool, the *Bagassa guianensis* is fruiting." She picked up a splattered fruit and rubbed it on her stained muumuu before taking a bite. "Hmm, tasty."

She held out the half-eaten fruit and I stared at it in horror. Did she expect me to taste it? The same fruit that was covered in howler monkey drool, had splattered in the dusty insect-riddled yard, and been slobbered on by Alice?

"It won't poison you, sweetie. I would never do anything to hurt you."

I plucked it from her offering palm, searching for a safe spot to take a quick nibble. The skin was a little tough but the pulp wasn't horrible—it tasted milky and bland, a bit like talcum powder diluted with water. Relieved, I let it fall to the ground. Alice beamed with approval, apparently satisfied I hadn't been too squeamish to try the fruit, and ran off to the cabin saying something about grabbing her camera.

On the river, an outboard motor roared its approach. A few minutes later Nick came around the cabin. He glanced at me, but turned to Alice who was busy setting up her tripod. "Cedric came by. They found Jack's jacket on the side of the hill. It looks like he fell in just above the rapids there."

# CHAPTER 10

The rest of the afternoon moved at a glacial pace and Nick disappeared, which meant I wasn't able to talk to him about us or my suspicions about Diane, or even Frank or Alice. Only Rosie hung around, since it was her turn to cook dinner. I joined her in the kitchen, doing most of the work, given she was in abject misery. We made fried rice, which seemed like an easy task, until she told me I first had to remove the boll weevils. The trick was to shake the uncooked pot of rice as water rinsed over it while simultaneously pouring off the rising black bugs. I did my best, although I still had to add in a few extra vegetables and spices at the end—for camouflage.

Everybody returned once it grew dark, Brian and Nick arriving triumphant with several skeletal-looking river fish. Which, given their level of swagger, was, at least in their own minds, the equivalent of dragging home a lion kill (a feat not biologically possible in Suriname, unless one counted the poor creature at the Paramaribo Zoo). They set up a small kerosene stove just outside the back door, with a wok full of boiling oil balanced on a lopsided burner. Brian dropped several pieces of fish in at a time, jumping back when the wok wobbled, splashing sizzling oil through the screen door and across the kitchen floor. Fortunately no one was injured.

We collected our food from the stovetop and I eyed the fish for several seconds trying to decide whether to taste a piece. It eyed me back, which settled my choice. I turned away, but Nick, who was next to me scooping fried rice onto his plate, picked up a piece for me. "Try this one," he said, raising his voice. "It's the tucunaré—fewer bones than the piranha, and did I mention I caught it?" I took the fish from his hand, figuring it was a positive sign, and sat down at the wooden table to taste it.

We ate the rest of dinner in silence, the soothing sound of gangsta rap playing in the background, courtesy of Brian. Small bugs fluttered around the dim bulb hanging above the table, occasionally dropping onto my plate to join the weevils in the fried rice. Next to me, Melvijn hulked over the table, crunching happily on his small piranha bones. Diane spat hers out, the bones forming small burial mounds. She caught me watching and narrowed her expertly highlighted eyes. I gave her a pretend smile and turned back to my fried rice and tasty fish.

Rosie and Alice were reading the magazines I'd brought from the States. Every few minutes Alice sighed, flipped a page of the gossip magazine, and tried to hide her self-satisfied smile. She caught me watching and frowned, attempting a look more gruesome than sad. At least I assumed that was what her facial contortions meant. Once she thought no one was watching, her gloating smile returned. I wondered again if she'd had anything to do with Jack's death. The idea seemed absurd but it was also a convenient turn of events for her, and she'd been acting inappropriately happy all day, even before I'd told her the news of his falling in the river. But then she always acted inappropriate, I remembered, so this was nothing new. And I was much more suspicious of Frank anyway. It didn't seem like he was about to be fired. Not now that Jack was dead.

The mosquitoes were getting worse, and I watched in horror as Melvijn grabbed a can of Raid resting on a wooden beam and sprayed it under the table, the toxic fumes drifting up. I coughed in response.

"Catch a bone, Em?" Nick asked, finally breaking the silence.

"No," I said, hacking again, "I'm just not fond of Raid at dinner."

Nick raised an eyebrow, standing up to wash his plate. "Well, just say so. Don't be passive-aggressive about it. Melvijn, no more Raid during dinner."

"Sure, boss," Melvijn said, and Rosie giggled.

Nick finished washing his plate and set it next to the sink to dry and Alice stood up. "I suggest you all get to bed early tonight. We've already missed enough days in the field due to IWC, and I want everybody working tomorrow. No excuses. Clearly none of us know anything about . . . about Jack."

She poured rum into a large plastic cup and opened a small bottle of pills. "Go to bed," she called, passing through the back door.

Instead we stayed at the table, Melvijn humming under his breath and watching Diane, while Rosie pretended to read her magazine but was secretly watching Melvijn watching Diane.

Nick muttered under his breath, "I'd have to kill Alice if she wasn't leaving soon. She was finally bearable this evening, and she had to go and ruin it at the end."

"Don't you think Alice's acting a little odd?" I asked.

Nick laughed. "I'm not sure I've ever known Alice to not act odd."

I glanced at Diane, who had pushed open the screen door but stopped when she heard my question. "But shouldn't we talk about what happened last night, what we saw—?" I stopped, everyone was watching me intently. Too intently. Feeling a growing animosity from my audience and unsure how to discuss Jack, I stuttered, "It's just I overheard—"

The door bounced shut and Diane stepped back into the kitchen, her face ashen. I looked around at the other startled faces. Melvijn winked at me then glanced at Diane. I knew I'd just made a serious enemy of Diane, but I thought it was better to have it all out in the open—everything I'd seen and heard, not just Diane's threat to kill Jack.

Nick interrupted, "Let me guess, Emma. You think Alice killed Jack? Knocked him over the head, flipped him over her shoulder, and dropped him in the river so she can keep her research station?"

"Alice didn't kill Jack," Brian said quietly but forcefully, his hands clinched in fists.

"We don't even know if he's dead yet," Diane jumped in. "You're being very stupid, Emma. I—" A branch crashed to the ground, and her voice caught in a high-pitched squeak.

We turned in unison and I half-expected to find Jack in the doorway.

Although I hadn't meant just Alice, I was annoyed with Nick and also wanted to diffuse some of the evil Diane was shooting my way, so I said, "He's dead. I'm sure of that. But for the sake of argument, how do you *know* Alice didn't kill him?" Eight critical eyes focused back on me. "I heard her threatening him before the party. She said she'd kill him before she'd let him take away her monkeys."

I glanced at Diane, her eyes still narrowed, her hands gripped in tight fists, and quickly looked away. She knew what I was thinking, that Alice wasn't the only one who'd threatened Jack.

"Emma," Nick said, "be careful saying things like that. You don't actually *know* anything. All we know is he fell in the river at some point. He could have done that completely on his own. He was certainly drunk enough."

"Alice couldn't have killed Jack," Brian said softly.

"No one killed Jack," Diane said. "Emma's just desperate for attention."

I ignored Diane and turned to Brian. "Why not?"

"Because she was with me, at least until I put her to bed. She'd passed out. I was in the bunk bed right outside her room, and she didn't leave it all night."

"How do you know if you were sleeping?" I asked.

"I wasn't sleeping. I couldn't fall asleep, not with her snoring. She sounds like a horse. It's awful. I was still awake when Nick brought you in. And by then you'd already seen him in the river. Right?"

"Satisfied, Sherlock?" Nick asked. "Can Brian and I play a game of chess now? Is that allowed, or are you going to grill me next?"

"I heard her too," Rosie said. "I came in to bed right before Brian and Alice. I was in the bedroom next door and . . . and waiting up for—" Her throat caught and she glanced at Melvijn. "I heard everything. I even heard Nick bring you in, Emma."

Melvijn stood and stretched, winking at me again. He added in Sranan, which only Brian and I understood, "All is good. Alice is not a killer." He grabbed his pack of Morellos from the table, saying in English to Diane, "Cigarette?"

She watched him silently for a minute before responding with a hesitant, "Sure."

# CHAPTER 11

I followed Diane and Melvijn outside, but sat down alone on the opposite side of the cabin to watch the bright stars and rising silvery moon. I was jittery, tensing each time a branch cracked in the nearby jungle, but I wanted some time alone to think. I believed Brian that Alice couldn't have killed Jack, but not because Brian said it. He might have lied to protect Alice, but I didn't believe Rosie would join in. She didn't even like Alice.

A twig snapped behind me and I nearly fell out of my plastic lawn chair.

"You know Brian is right," Melvijn said in his rough voice. He stepped out of the dark, his cigarette butt glowing.

"Shit, you scared me," I said, pressing my hand to my thumping heart. "You mean about Jack?" I added.

He nodded, squeezing into the chair next to me.

"Yeah," I said, thinking about Diane. "I . . . I didn't . . . I didn't really mean Alice. I saw Jack fighting with Frank too. And Diane . . . oh, never mind. I guess everyone in there is right. It's none of my business. I just thought . . . It doesn't matter." I didn't want to talk about Jack anymore, not after the way Nick and everyone else had responded. As if I was prying into something that was none of my business.

"Did you like Mr. West too?"

"No! Of course not. It's not that. I guess hearing him call for help from the river and then almost saving him. And then losing him . . . I feel a responsibility." Sonia's face floated in front of me. "It's hard to explain."

"Why did you come to Kasima? I thought you would go back to America. Ramesh told me your friend died."

Tears welled in my eyes and I wiped them away. "I . . . I wasn't ready to go home, after all. I wanted to see more of Suriname, more than just the city. I wanted to live in the rainforest."

"Why would you want to live in the bush?" He waved his hand at the jungle. "I don't understand white people who want to live with the dangerous animals. Not when you can live in the USA."

"Then you don't really like it out here?"

"Nah, I like *Foto*—the clubs and women. I do this for a few years to make money."

"For the money? For only two hundred dollars a month?"

He shrugged. "Alice pays in dollars, and I don't spend money here."

"Yeah, I guess so," I said. It still didn't seem like enough to get rich off, even in Suriname. Although it was a job, and they were hard to come by.

He hesitated and cleared his throat, watching the soft yellow from Diane's flashlight flicker along the rocky path to the shower. She glanced in our direction.

"Who were you with on the bench?" he asked once she'd moved on.

"Nobody," I answered, surprised at the abrupt change in the conversation.

He stayed quiet for a long time. "Be careful," he eventually said. "I saw some things too, but I don't talk about them." He tossed his cigarette into the bushes and stood up. "I like you. Forget what you saw. I take care of everything." I watched his cigarette land in the shrubs and burn out. Luckily it was the wet season. A branch cracked in the dark bushes just behind the

74

cigarette butt, and I jumped up too, hurrying inside to grab my towel. I needed a shower.

The cold water washed away the day's sweat and grime, but I kept scrubbing. I felt . . . not dirty . . . maybe contaminated was the better word. Melvijn's words had left me shivering, remembering the feel of Jack's hand slipping from mine, his head floating up one last time before going under. I couldn't get the images out of my head and somehow . . . I kept scrubbing.

An unearthly howl drifted off the river and I peered through the hazy screen circling the top of the shower stall. Moonlight bathed both cabins a ghostly white. The warm glow from my candle seemed to be the only man-made light in the yard, and I was glad to be inside the protective casing of the shower stall. The howling continued, followed by growling, and I imagined a jaguar ripping Jack's lifeless body apart, blood spurting against the mossy trees. I shook myself, letting go of the ghastly and probably biologically impossible image.

I turned off the water and pulled on my clothes, sure I caught the faint glow of a cigarette butt from under the *kampu,* now deep in the shadows of the overhanging branches. I pushed open the screen door and slipped on my flip-flops, shining my light furtively along the edges of the yard. I ran to the cabin, yanking the door shut behind me.

I caught my breath on the dark porch, annoyed for having been so scared just seconds before, for having run the fifteen feet from the shower to the cabin. I shook myself, gathered my courage, and stepped farther into the dark cabin, dropping my clothes in fright when a soft thud landed in the pitch-black kitchen. I froze, holding my breath.

"Shit!" I heard, followed by more cursing. I collected my scattered clothes and hurried to the kitchen.

Alice was there on her hands and knees, searching the floor. I flipped on the kitchen light, but she screeched, "No, no, turn it off. I don't want to wake everybody, I dropped something."

I giggled, feeling better. Alice's eccentricities were strangely soothing.

"What'd you drop?" I flipped the light switch off, although it took a minute or two to warm up and was not yet even on. I flashed my light under the table and around the edges of the room, sure everyone in the cabin was now awake and listening intently.

"A sleeping pill," she whispered, her voice loud enough to carry throughout the cabin. "For Diane. Something startled me. I dropped it."

"Did you hear that growling a few minutes ago?" I asked her.

She jerked up, her eyes cold and piercing in the glow from my flashlight. "I thought you were taking a shower."

"I . . . I was. I heard it from there. It sounded like a jaguar ripping apart some poor animal."

She laughed, relaxing. "Oh, you mean the howler monkeys?"

"No, no it was more like growling and shrieking. Almost a roar. It sounded like it was coming from the river."

"Definitely howlers."

"Really? I've heard howlers at Brownsberg Nature Park. They sound like a strong wind. This was different. Did . . . did you hear it?"

"Ah, no, I don't think so. It's been a difficult evening. Which is why I need that pill."

"What's wrong?" I asked, but she didn't respond. Instead, she threw back her head and released an exact imitation of the growling and shrieking I'd heard from the shower stall.

"Was that it, sweetie?" She sat back on her knees, smiling up at me.

From one of the bedrooms I heard a cough.

"Yeah." I took a step away from her.

"Howlers. No doubt the same troop we saw earlier. They're

still nearby and extra loud."

"You've convinced me." I turned my flashlight to the plastic trays of onion and garlic. I didn't see any pills, but something scary was glowing underneath the bottom tray holding the onions. Switching my light to the counter, I noticed several empty bottles of syrup water called *stroop*. I pushed them aside, immediately seeing a small white pill.

"Is this it?"

Alice jumped off the floor and snatched it from my palm.

"Thank God. It's my last one." She put it in her pocket. "You're wonderful, sweetie. I'm so glad you came."

She grasped my arm and leaned in, whispering, "We need to talk tomorrow. It's *extremely* important. Diane said you heard me arguing with Jack before the party and think I killed him. I know what it might have sounded like, but I promise I didn't hurt him, although I'm glad he's dead."

With that she skipped through the screen door, letting it slam against its wooden frame, sending a tremor through the cabin and no doubt waking anyone who against all odds had managed to sleep through her "whispers."

I turned back to my room, not surprised Diane had gone running to Alice already. I'd made an enemy of her with my questions. I climbed into bed, carefully tucking in my mosquito net and checking it thrice. It took me a long time to fall asleep, listening to a bat fluttering in the dark above, wondering if I should even stay at Kasima.

A door scraped open, waking me. I reached for my bedside lamp. The small knob clicked but the darkness remained. I flipped to my back, my body tensed in fear. I could feel her in the dark. Watching. The baby was crying in the next room. I couldn't move. A passing car's headlights flickered over her body. Her twisted neck. Her feet hovering inches above the faded, green carpet.

I screamed and screamed but no sound came out. And then it wasn't Sonia, but Jack. A pain cut through my neck and I was cold and clammy, choking and gasping for air. The darkness and cold spread deeper and blurred into nothingness. I yanked myself awake, through a long dark tunnel, and woke gasping for air, clutching my mosquito net, my heart racing.

I tried to focus in the dark, remembering I was in the rainforest and didn't have a bedside lamp. "It's only another mefloquine dream, only a mefloquine dream," I whispered, shaking myself awake and sitting up. I'd had similar dreams all week, a side effect of the malaria pills, I told myself. But this time it was different. Now it was Sonia and Jack. Both watching. Waiting. Wanting something.

The night was cold and quiet, the slightest creak audible. Dripping water from the overhanging tree splashed against the tin roof above. In the cabin, someone was tiptoeing. A beam from a flashlight flicked across the roof through the open screened area at the top of my room. The footsteps stopped at my closed door. I waited in silence. Not breathing. The door handle squeaked and the bottom of my door scratched against the concrete floor as it opened.

# CHAPTER 12

"Are you awake?" came a whisper from the dark doorway, followed by a soft hiccup.

"Yeah, come in," I said, so grateful there was a living breathing human being in my doorway, I didn't care why she was creeping into my room in the middle of the night.

"Can I sleep in the bunk bed?" Rosie asked, her voice quivering with tears. "I had a huge fight with Melvijn. I hate him!"

"Help yourself. But it doesn't have a sheet, and there's some sort of creature living in the bed."

"I . . . I brought two sheets," she said. "I'm so tired, I don't care. We've been down on the beach fighting for hours."

She wrestled with the mattress and sheets before climbing onto the creaking bunk bed and was soon snoring lightly. I slept soundly the rest of the night and didn't wake until I heard light noises in the cabin. I dressed and stumbled into the kitchen, empty except for Nick, who was at the stove boiling water.

"Morning," he sang. "I hope you're looking forward to a muggy day dodging branches thrown by our cantankerous Captain Sparrow. We won't head out to the field for a few hours, but eat a good brekkie or you won't make it through the day. We usually take leftovers from dinner for lunch, but I don't see any, so feel free to cook whatever you like. Just don't touch the Pringles. Alice will kill you."

"Is everyone already gone?" I rubbed sleep out of my eyes. I'd been so tired I hadn't even heard Rosie wake up and leave the room earlier.

"You must be a heavy sleeper to have missed them all in the kitchen this morning," Nick said. "They left about an hour ago. I'm going to give you an overview of the paperwork, and then we'll head out."

I moved to the kitchen sink and splashed my face with water. The hot morning already felt sticky and uncomfortable, although it was barely light outside. I hadn't realized I was going to be left alone with Nick for the morning. I wasn't sure how I was supposed to react to him. Were we more than friends or just simple co-workers who'd shared a few drunken kisses? I had a feeling he was regretting the romantic pull of stars and moonlight and too much rum, but I wasn't so sure how I felt. The physical attraction was still there, but perhaps the time and place were wrong. But either way, given I was new, not to mention unqualified for my new job, the whole situation left me vulnerable to his whims, and I needed to take control of the situation. I turned back to face him, wishing I could do this after a cup of coffee.

He beat me to it, saying, "Listen, I want to apologize for what happened at the party. I was a little drunk, you're attractive, and God knows I've been out here forever." He ran his hand through his thick black curls, and I felt a tightening around my heart. "But it was a mistake. I'm your boss . . . I don't want to cause problems with the other researchers or with Alice. I know this is completely my fault though. I should've been smarter. I'm a complete asshole, truly. Sorry."

"If nothing else, maybe Cedric respects you now," I muttered under my breath, pouring myself a glass of water at the faucet.

"What's that?"

"Nothing. No problem. It was never a problem. It's forgotten. So how exactly does the water work?"

It wasn't the truth, of course, but it was best to pretend none of it mattered. It could never have been more than a fun overseas romance anyway. We lived on opposite sides of the world. And he wasn't a settling sort, or so he'd said. It was easier this way, to avoid the inevitable pain when the relationship ended. I smiled at Nick, letting him know everything was okay. I still had my dignity after all. Mostly.

He let out a long breath, looking relieved, although he studied me peering through the screen window to the water pump. "You sure? You seem kind of angry."

Obviously I wasn't doing quite as good a job covering up my feelings as I'd hoped. I turned back to face him. "If I'm angry, it's not because we shared a few meaningless drunk kisses under a full moon, it's—Forget it. We're fine. Everything's fine."

Nick turned back to the stove and his boiling water, pouring it over a bowl of dry oatmeal while I pretended to examine the kitchen shelves. The unappealing breakfast choices were cereal, oatmeal, or peanut butter.

"Em, I really am sorry. It's not easy living in such close quarters, but for the most part we all get along, at least since I've been here. I know this is all completely my fault, but we need to find a way to be friends. Can you do that?"

"Of course." I pulled out the oatmeal, thinking he had a rather broad interpretation of *getting along*.

"Great." He pointed to the tiny gas stove. "There's still some hot water in the pot if you want it for the oatmeal. Should be enough. And you'll need at least two liters for the field. We have to pump water from the river every few days. The pump is seriously annoying and breaks down regularly, so try to keep your showers reasonable. Don't follow Diane's example. She takes thirty-minute showers. I make her pump water as often as possible, which she hates, but the water's perfectly safe."

I looked at the brown specks floating in my glass. Hopefully, the nauseated feeling in the pit of my stomach had more to do with Nick than the water. I turned to my peanut butter and oat-meal breakfast and tried to remind myself about the importance of dignity.

After breakfast, Nick showed me the daily logs and handed me a pile of scientific articles to read, explaining that Alice's long-term study examined the habitat, diet, feeding, and social organization of black spider monkeys.

"Alice is interested in foraging patterns, so we record everything the monkeys eat in fifteen-minute scans, along with dispersal patterns and group dynamics. We're also doing ad lib data and five-minute focal follows of individual monkeys. As part of the bigger picture, once a week we do a biological survey of the Mount Kasima trail to study impacts on wildlife from tourism, and every month we conduct a phenological status of trees."

He pointed out books and opened sealed containers, and I tried my best not to look as dumb as I felt. I understood the part about writing down a series of things about the monkeys every fifteen minutes, but not much else.

"You should study these. You'll need to ID them in the field." Nick pointed to fruit photos and videos of individual monkeys.

I flipped through the photos, each barely distinguishable from the next, while Nick continued talking: "Two to four people search for our main spider monkey troop, the Rangers, each day. Diane works with us, but she's also collecting her own research at the same time. She's doing some vocalization playback experiments for her dissertation. You get at least one full day off a week, but the schedule changes depending on the number of people at camp."

"Only one day off a week? Alice forgot to mention the part about slave labor."

"Count yourself lucky. Before I came they worked seven days a week, twelve hour days, year round."

He gathered together a pile of supplies, handing me one at a time: a radio, an umbrella, a folding metal stool, a machete—which he showed me how to tie on to the back of my pack—five small plastic bottles filled with an unknown liquid (to collect feces), a map of the study area to carry in a black plastic folder, and, finally, a snake-bite kit.

I studied the snake-bite kit. "What's the communications structure between us, the island, and town?"

"What do you mean? Communications structure? That's very fancy."

"What happens if there's an emergency? Like a snake bite?"

"You die if it's poisonous."

"That's not the most helpful response I've ever heard."

"You're not scared of snakes, are you?"

"Isn't everyone scared of snakes? Just seems like common sense."

His mouth twisted into a grin, as if he was relishing this newly discovered vulnerability, but he didn't tease me. "I'm not going to lie to you. We have some of the most venomous snakes in the world around here; they're common and aggressive."

I took a deep breath, continuing to study the kit.

"Most of the snakes you'll see aren't poisonous, and poisonous snakes don't always inject their venom—it's precious and wasted on humans too big to eat. But pay attention where you step. Even in the cabin. Brian killed a fer-de-lance he found on our front door-step last week."

"Seriously?"

"Yeah, but do me a favor, don't ask him about it. He'll give you some bullshit story how they always live in pairs and there may be another one hanging around, angry it lost its mate. He's already got Rosie believing his mumbo-jumbo spiritualism. I had to let Cedric do a ceremony to protect the yard just to stop the insanity."

"Is that the shrine behind the picnic table?"

"Yeah, seems a waste of perfectly good rum to me, but to each his own. Cedric claims to be some sort of obiaman or shaman. Frankly he seems a little too young and arrogant to make the shaman cut. But again, it's not my religion."

"How do you call the island?"

"We have a satellite phone that works occasionally. Although, since no one on the island has a satellite phone, it's actually quite useless in an emergency. A radio to call the island a kilometer upstream would be a little more useful. Or a boat with a motor. In an emergency, we'd have to blow the foghorn and hope they hear it on Loiri Island and come to find out what's wrong. Alice isn't into modern conveniences. Plus, she's cheap. So the moral of this long story is: wear your boots, look where you walk, don't be stupid and touch things like caterpillars, and hope you're one of the lucky ones."

"Safety training is not one of your better skills I see."

"Nope, we're all on our own in this God-forsaken world. Use your brain and stay out of other people's business, and that's about all you need to know."

He held up a pair of massive, ancient binoculars. "Have any?"

I pulled out the new pair my brothers had given me.

"Nice. We have some extra harness straps if you want to try them." I had no idea what he meant and stared at him blankly. He didn't seem to notice as he was plugging a small black radio into a system of strange cords hooked to a car battery. He turned on the radio and clicked the button with his thumb.

"G'day, ladies. Anyone awake out there?"

Dead silence. Nick muttered to himself, "Turn on your fucking radios."

He clicked the button again. "Ladies, come in."

A faint crackle came through. Nick thumped the radio and

adjusted the dial again, muttering, "Fucking radio," under his breath.

A long sustained crackle came through. He clicked the button and yelled, "Mate, I can't hear you. Repeat that."

Brian's voice crackled over the radio, ". . . Trail."

"Fucking hell." He clicked the button again. "Repeat that."

Brian suddenly came through yelling, "Pompi Trail, Pompi Trail, Pompi Trail, Pompi Trail."

"Pompi Trail. Got it, mate. No need to get your knickers in a twist."

Before heading out, Nick doused himself in bug spray. I looked at the variety of sprays lining the ledge and picked up a bottle that said "deet free" and "kid safe." Maybe cancer was too remote a concept to worry about when faced with a horde of malarial mosquitoes, but my mom's a doctor on the alternative spectrum, and I could never quite get her voice out of my head.

Nick looked over at me. "That crap doesn't work, try the real stuff or you'll be sorry later. Nothing seems to work for the chiggers. You're lucky it's the rainy season when they're not so bad."

I ignored his advice, spraying on the "kid safe" bug spray— another addition in a long line of terrible mistakes.

# CHAPTER 13

"Know anything about spider monkeys?" Nick asked as we hiked down the hill to the beach, picking up a winding path along the river and turning into the forest.

"No," I admitted, panting behind and wiping my sweaty face with my handkerchief in a vain attempt to look elegant. "I know you're upset Alice invited me to come out here, but she assured me I could learn everything I needed to know once I arrived."

Nick jerked around. "What do you mean she *invited* you to come out here?"

"Just that. We met one day in the city, and she invited me to come out. She was relentless."

He swung around and trotted down the path, cursing under his breath.

I jogged after him, my poorly attached machete and folding chair clanking rhythmically on my back, my rubber boots squishing through the mud. I sounded like a one-man marching band composed largely of cymbals.

Ten minutes later Nick abruptly stopped and turned around. "Listen, Alice does her own thing. I don't always agree with her, but that doesn't mean we resent you. I admit I was annoyed when Alice told me she was bringing on a do-gooding Peace Corp volunteer rather than a zoologist or biological anthropologist. And she'd let you join for only six months, no less. It wasn't fair to the other researchers who agreed to spend a full year out here. But I don't have anything against you personally. I'm . . . I'm glad you're here now. So no worries."

I gasped a thanks, slapping at the fist-size mosquitoes circling my head. "What do you mean do-gooding? What's wrong with Peace Corps volunteers?"

Nick continued hiking, calling behind him, "I'm sure you have the best intentions, but in the end you're just above missionaries in my opinion. From what I've heard, half the time you end up doing more harm than good."

That hit a little too close to home, and when I didn't respond Nick stopped and turned around again. "It's just my opinion. But look at you. You barely knew Jack, yet you feel the need to be involved in saving him or finding out who killed him. Why? How is it your business?"

"Why would I sit idly by and watch something bad happen? Especially when I could do something to stop it?"

"Even if you just make it worse?"

I studied the rocky path, thinking about Sonia and whispered, "I prefer to try."

"Like I said, trouble. Come on, let's speed up. You're practically a sloth."

*Don't get annoyed; take it as a compliment,* I told myself, but it didn't work, even when imagining it was coming from one of my brothers. I couldn't understand how Australians managed to have relationships if they were constantly insulting each other.

He crossed a side creek using a log, calling over his shoulder. "Back to the spider monkeys: they play an important role in the rainforest ecosystem by dispersing the larger canopy tree seeds— they swallow fruits whole and then defecate the intact seeds hours later. They're also unique in the way they split into small groups for foraging and come back together when food is available. Some days we work together in the field, but more often we split up to follow subgroups." Continuing to lecture, he pulled out his machete from the leather holster strapped to his backpack and chopped through an overhanging branch.

We crested a hill and Nick stopped. The forest, previously hilly and dense, opened up. Tree trunks adorned with bromeliads, ferns, and clinging liana vines stretched into the vaulted canopy above. Massive buttress roots spread gracefully like descending waves along the ground, holding up the towering kapok trees and strangler figs. In between the buttress roots, lush palms and tall ferns grew on the leaf-littered ground. It was magnificent.

"This is the beginning of our study area, which is about five square kilometers. Spider monkeys like primary tropical forests and swamp forests, the higher and wetter the better, which is mostly what you'll find in our study area." Nick pulled out his map, showing me our location. "We have three troops using this area. The Rangers are our primary troop, and they stay over here." Nick indicated the western half of the map. "But their range overlaps slightly with the other two smaller troops. We study them if we have enough researchers, but the Rangers are our main habituated troop."

"What's a habituated troop?" I regretted the question as soon as it was out of my mouth.

For a change, Nick didn't acknowledge its stupidity. "It means the monkeys become used to our presence, so we can study them in their natural setting. 'Course we also reduce their fear of humans, their main predator. Here it isn't such a problem because there isn't any hunting or trapping, but in other areas researchers use a certain noise when they approach their study animal—maybe a clicking noise. The animals learn that particular noise is safe, and if a human approaches without making the noise they flee."

"You sure there's no hunting or trapping in the park?"

"Maybe a little hunting, but not much. Why would you ask?"

I adjusted my backpack, which already hurt. "Just something

my pilot mentioned when we were flying in. He was talking about how much money you can get in Holland for certain song birds, and he said something about everyone knowing he wouldn't carry animals on his plane. He didn't mention Kasima specifically, but . . . that's what he seemed to be referring to."

"He probably meant Kwamalasamutu further south. There's a big animal trade from there."

"Maybe. Hey, is this a poison arrow frog?" I pointed to a tiny black frog with a yellow line down its back, but Nick didn't respond. I continued watching the tiny frog, which looked like a wet, plastic toy. When I glanced up, Nick was gone. I jumped up and ran down the path, my clamor no doubt scaring away every living creature for a square mile.

Nick glanced back at me once I'd caught up. "The Rangers have twenty-five monkeys, which is a large spider monkey troop. Monkeys form troops for protection against predators, but with spider monkeys you'll rarely see the whole troop together, although they communicate with each other all day through their calls. You'll learn to distinguish the sounds. Although with the racket you're making, you're not likely to hear much."

He turned me around and adjusted my straps, his lingering hands shooting a thread of electricity down my back. "You need to keep your machete off to the side."

I released my breath when he let go. Being friends would be a lot easier if he'd stop touching me.

"This is a great place to swim," Nick said, pausing a few minutes later at a beautiful waterfall.

White water rushed over rounded, mossy rocks, with emerald green foliage reflecting in the pool at the bottom of the falls. It was heaven: a waterfall on the way to work. I took a deep breath of the muggy air and sighed.

"And we both know you like to swim," he added. "I don't know how you survived those rapids, especially in the dark."

"Competitive swimming and water polo in college," I said. "I was never great, not like my brother, who was on his university's national championship team. But you don't have to worry about me drowning."

"Don't be *nuff nuff*, Em. Even lifeguards die in riptide. Remember that the next time you decide to jump into unknown rapids in the middle of the night. Drunk, no less."

"What the hell does *nuff nuff* mean? Never mind. I think I can figure it out. And I wasn't that drunk."

"Really?" He lifted an eyebrow.

"Okay, a little drunk, but I spent my summers on a river. You just have to keep your feet up, float and let the current take you where it wants. As long as you don't panic, you'll—"

"That current had dragged you into the middle of an Amazon river, swarming with piranhas, electric eels, stingrays, not to mention caiman and anacondas—and you with no shoes or clothes. In the middle of the night! And today you're worried about a few measly snakes?"

"Oh . . . I forgot about the anacondas. I didn't do it on purpose. I didn't think. I just saw his head and I—"

Nick held up his hand, putting his finger to his lips and calling me silently forward. I tiptoed closer and he pointed to rat-like creatures scurrying along the branches above us. "Red-handed tamarins," he whispered, his breath tickling my neck.

"Monkeys?" I was shocked my clanging hadn't scared them off.

He nodded.

"Weird. They look more like rats with long tails." I stepped back and pulled out my binoculars.

Unfortunately, I wasn't clear on how to use them, and the trees moved farther away. I pulled them back from my face, studying the binoculars in mystification. How difficult could binoculars be? Little kids use them. I turned them around and tried again, but couldn't focus. I tried squeezing one eye shut, which seemed to work, but I couldn't locate the tamarins in the lens, especially not with the sweat dripping into my eyes. I looked up without the binoculars. The monkeys were long gone.

"They move quickly." Nick smirked.

We hiked for another ten minutes before Nick stopped again, pulled out his radio and yelled—or more accurately "Whooed"—into the forest. A double "Whoo" came back and Brian crackled over the radio, "Kasima . . . and Steven's Creek." We walked on. "Can you hear that?" Nick asked. "That horse-whinny sound? That's a spider monkey excitement call. Sounds like we have a big group ahead."

We walked another five minutes until Nick grabbed my arm. "Listen."

I didn't hear anything except a cacophony of birds screeching overhead, but I kept my mouth shut. Always better to seem more intelligent than you are; that's my motto.

"Look up there."

The most amazing creatures swung into view: black and long, with small, wrinkly old-man faces. They were using their long shaggy arms, legs, and tails to toss themselves from branch to branch in a single, graceful, sweeping motion. Ballet music swelled in the background.

# CHAPTER 14

"It's the cutest thing I've ever seen," I whispered to Melvijn, Brian, and Nick, our eyes watching the lowest branch of a sprawling tree.

"Thanks, I hear that a lot," Melvijn said, handing the camera to Nick who took up recording the baby spider monkey—a ball of black fur with wrinkly skin around its mouth and big round eyes. The mother, Julia, was lounging on a branch, her long gangly arms dangling over the side, her sharp black eyes watching us suspiciously while the baby crawled over her head.

"The infant's only a month old," Brian said once Melvijn left to spend the rest of the afternoon recording monkey calls with Alice. "This is the first time we've seen him move around much." He pointed to another monkey nearby. "Over there is another of Julia's offspring—a daughter. She's nearly sexually mature and will probably leave the troop soon."

Julia, the baby clinging tightly to her belly, swung gracefully away with Nick in pursuit.

"Where are the rest of the monkeys?" I looked around, but couldn't see anything except dark shadows and dense jungle broken by piercing bands of sunlight.

Brian pointed to a branch about twenty-five feet above our heads. It took me several minutes of gazing into the canopy before I could distinguish a spider monkey with a shaggy black belly and eerie red face. Its humanlike fingers were grasping for a branch, its long tail curled around the limb above. Debris rained through the layers of leaves, ferns, and vines, landing softly on the rotting vegetation covering the ground. Brian knocked aside a spider web and reached into a fern, emerging triumphant with several of the small red fruits. "See the teeth marks?" he asked. "They're eating these, so we put them in the scan." He opened his black plastic folder and showed me a line of data, each beginning with a time at fifteen-minute intervals.

"This represents how many monkeys I can see." He went down the line. "This is their location on the map and their location in relation to the rest of the troop—if we know it; their height in the canopy; their travel direction; and any other species traveling with them. We also do ad-lib data." He flipped to another page with more writing, each line also beginning with a time. "We add in anything important that happens, with as much detail as possible. Mating, fights, grooming, alarm calls, and so on. That's Brutus up there. He's one of the dominant males. Did Nick give you the code page for the focal follows?"

"Nick gave me all sorts of stuff, but it'll probably take me weeks to understand it all. He said you've been here four years, trained tons of researchers, and could explain it best."

"Man, that's because he's lazy," he yelled down the path to Nick. He turned back to me. "Actually, I like training the new researchers and Nick doesn't have the patience."

"Have you been here long?"

"Since the beginning. I talked Alice into hiring Melvijn last year, since he needed to get away from *Foto*. His parents died when he was young and he grew up at my house. He's like a little brother."

"So you plan on doing this forever?"

He shrugged. "I want to stay, but I also have to look out for myself."

Nick sauntered up behind us. "And Alice doesn't pay very well. Brian's only had one small raise in four years. I keep telling him to take the job Kevin offered to manage the park. Screw Alice."

"Nick!" Brian looked away, embarrassed.

"Sorry, mate, but it's true. If Alice really appreciated you, she'd pay you more or get you that position at her uni." Nick continued past, still following the mother and her baby with the video camera.

Brian kept me busy learning the fifteen-minute scans and focal follows, which involved watching a single monkey for ten uninterrupted minutes. I did my best to follow the monkeys Brian pointed to, even when I had to charge through the hilly, muddy jungle in pursuit, desperately trying to watch the ground for snakes at the same time I watched the canopy. But I always lost the monkey, and quite often myself. Brian wouldn't respond unless I "whooed"—a strange noise to scream into the jungle. As soon as I tracked down Brian again, he'd send me off in another direction to follow another monkey. Or possibly the same monkey. To me, they all looked alike. Nick was always near us, but kept to himself, leaving the training to Brian.

An hour or so later, having lost another monkey, I was once again wandering through the jungle alone. Something landed on my arm and I glanced down at a yellow-and-black plaid caterpillar crawling off my sleeve and onto my arm. I eyed its stingray antennas with skepticism, remembering Nick mentioned I shouldn't touch caterpillars. I was unconvinced such a tiny pretty creature could cause any harm, but I shook my arm anyway, trying to flick it away. The caterpillar preferred to stay. I poked it with a small stick and it rolled into a ball, falling off my arm onto a pile of soft leaves. But not before leaving behind a vibrating itchy pain that spread up my arm. I stumbled down the path in search of Brian, feeling dizzy and nauseated, convinced I was in the early stages of anaphylactic shock.

I finally found him with Alice and Rosie after what seemed a long, painfully slow death. By then my arm still hurt, but the ache was lessoning and I decided to keep my imminent collapse to myself. I hated to embarrass myself, just in case I survived.

Alice saw me first, crying out, "Have you ever had so much fun in your life? Whee! I'm so exited you're here and want to dedicate your life to primatology."

In spite of the deadly caterpillar bite, not to mention my aching back and numerous lost monkeys, I realized I *was* having a great day, which I told Alice.

She clapped her hands in delight, bobbling on the tips of her toes. "I'm sure you can have the pick of any school you want, but I know you'll make the right choice and come do a Ph.D. with me when you're done here."

Stuttering in surprise, I glanced at Rosie, who was just behind Alice. Rosie made a gesture with her finger, indicating Alice was crazy and returned to picking at her chin. She looked miserable, stuck with Alice all day. And Rosie was somewhat right: no one would be fighting over me for a Ph.D. program in biological anthropology.

I laughed it off. "I barely know what I'm doing yet."

"Oh, you won't have any problems, cupcake. You're brilliant."

Brian cleared his throat and motioned for me to follow him, striking haphazardly at palm fronds while we hiked, his steady stream of instruction disappearing completely.

It finally hit me, what might be wrong with him, and I asked, "Are you planning to get a degree with Alice?"

He stopped on the trail. "The school won't accept my bachelor's degree from the university here. Alice says she's working on it, but I've been waiting for two years. I don't think it will ever happen. Maybe I will take the job from Kevin."

He leaned over to pick up a chewed orange-shaped fruit. "This is *Bagassa guianensis*," he added, changing the subject. "In Suriname we call it *gele bagasse*. It's a hardwood. Good timber. They eat it a lot. The code is Bagu. First two letters of the genus and species. You don't have to learn the actual name, just the letters. It's easier."

I took the fruit from his fingers, realizing it was the same fruit I'd seen at camp. I made a note for myself of the description, imprinting it in my memory. I was on my way—one fruit memorized and only several hundred more to go.

"Do you think Alice will be able to stay on now?" I asked him.

"They'll have to drag Alice from the park if they want to get rid of her."

"Who would get rid of her now? Frank Van Landsberg?"

"I don't know." Brian clicked his tongue in disapproval. "Frank is driving everyone on the island crazy, ordering them around like servants. Cedric said he yelled at Hortense yesterday because his cabin wasn't cleaned properly. He's a stupid, pompous little Dutchman."

We were approaching Nick, who was watching an enormous tree packed with spider monkeys gorging on its round fruits. "What's she got you talking about now?" Nick asked when he arrived behind him. "No doubt something that's none of her business." He pulled off the metal chair tied to his backpack and sat down on the path, smiling up at me.

The comment, followed by a warm smile, did come across almost like a compliment, so I let it go. "I was just wondering what'll happen to us," I said. "Is Frank everyone's boss now Jack is gone? Or is it Kevin?"

"Jack was never going to be the boss down here, even if Kasima was his obsession," Nick said. "He lives quite grandly in D.C. and normally only visited once a year, although he's been out here fairly frequently the past few months." Nick glanced at Brian, "I think we know why."

Brian chuckled, but didn't say anything.

I pulled off my chair with only a minor struggle and sat down next to Nick. "Why was he obsessed with Kasima?"

"He did his Ph.D. research out here years ago. He studied howlers, poor bugger. I think his research tent was on our same hill. Jack pushed for Kasima's creation and supposedly he's been trying to get control ever—"

Blood-chilling shrieks exploded the quiet of the afternoon, and the spider monkeys fled in all directions. The jungle danced, branches snapping and crashing to the ground, liana vines bouncing wildly. Low, menacing growls encircled us, but remained just out of view, sending chills of terror down my spine. Nick and Brian jumped up, knocking over their stools. They disappeared into the jungle, leaving me to fend for myself. I jerked left and right, confused and disoriented, seeing nothing but swaying jungle. Until a huge spider monkey sailed through the air above, barking and growling and dropping branches on my head. Swinging from his long tail, he shoved at a dead trunk, pushing it until it snapped, tumbling toward me.

# CHAPTER 15

The trunk plummeted to the ground, landing at my feet with a spray of papery bark. I fled up the winding path of the small rocky hill, charging through the thick piles of dead leaves, thinking only of escape. I turned a corner and plowed into Alice, who was running in my direction. We fell, a snarl of arms and legs, and tumbled off the path, landing in a muddy creek.

Laughing, I detangled myself and rolled away, pushing onto my knees. I knocked at the gnats circling my muddy head and wiped the mud from my eyes, only managing to further spread the bug-infested mess across my face. Alice looked about how I felt—her hair loose and tangled, her face caked in mud. But she didn't notice the humor in the situation. She jumped up, grabbed her pack, which was hanging half-open, and swung it over her shoulders. "Where are they?"

I stood up. "I don't know. What's going on? Nick and Brian ran off and left me."

"Shh!" Alice scoured the still noisy jungle. "There!" She charged up the slight hill from the creek, leaving me once more alone in the jungle. I looked down at my rubber boots still ankle deep in the muddy creek, noticing a half-submerged mini-cassette tape. I picked it up, turning it over and cleaning off the mud, surprised they were still using such ancient technology. Alice must have dropped it when we crashed.

I looked up the hill and noticed Melvijn watching me, a big grin on his face. He was holding a long pole with what appeared to be a tape recorder of some sort tied to the end. "You okay?" he asked.

"I crashed into Alice on the path. She's run off already."

"Need help getting out of there?"

"No. I'm fine."

"Where'd Alice go? I have the recording equipment. She's probably going crazy if there's a fight going on and I'm not recording it."

I pointed up the path. "She went that way, toward all the growling. But, here take this. She dropped it." I climbed up the small hill and handed him the mini-cassette. He jogged off with a backward wave of his hand.

I poured water onto my handkerchief and attempted to clean the mud off my face before turning reluctantly in Alice and Melvijn's direction. I wasn't eager to find the homicidal monkeys, but I also had no idea how to return to camp and figured desertion of post was not the best idea my first day in the field. I caught a glimpse of white to my right and followed it off trail.

Nick was calmly filming the canopy while branches and leaves fell around him. I crept up behind him. He was speaking softly to the camera. "The cap troop's alpha male is close, patrolling along a branch, looking alert. Captain Jack's nearby also. He looks a wee bit stressed."

"What happened?" I asked when Nick finally turned off the camera.

He swung around grinning, almost dancing in his excitement. "Sweet. Heaps of fun, eh? Your first day in the field and you see an intergroup encounter. They're rare. I've never seen anything like it. Obviously our tree was pretty damn popular. Everybody wanted a piece."

"What's an intergroup encounter?" I asked. It sounded sci-fi and somewhat risqué, but I guessed, despite appearances to the contrary, it did not mean the troop wanted to kill me. At least not the whole troop.

"In this case a fight between two capuchin troops with a few of our spideys hanging around the mix. Alice's going to be mad as a cut snake she missed it."

"She didn't. She's around here somewhere, hopefully with Melvijn. I ran into her on the trail. Literally. Bam! She barely seemed to notice, even after we tumbled into a muddy creek. Just jumped up and charged into the jungle. Somewhere in this direction . . ."

"That's Alice." Nick swiped my cheek, laughing. "You might want a long bath in the river when we get back. You've got mud all over your face and your . . ." His hand slid down my arm, jerking it forward, twisting my wrist. "Of all the . . . are those mosquito bites? I told you to use the bloody bug spray. You're not going to be able to sleep tonight." He dropped my arm, looking around. "Shit, where'd the monkeys go? You're distracting me."

He flipped on his radio. Brian was already on it, talking with Frank, who was apparently at the cabin using our radio system.

Nick interrupted them. "What's going on, mates? Why are you on the radio, Frank?"

"The police are here," Frank said through the radio. "You all need to come back now."

After some "whooing" into the jungle and a long argument by radio between Alice and Nick over whether to return immediately or wait for the end of the day, we finally met up on the main Kasima trail.

Diane walked up last in her shiny, quick-dry, North Face shirt and tight, camouflage pants, her hair and make-up perfectly arranged. Either she had some very impressive waterproof make-up on, or the woman simply didn't perspire. She glanced at me. "Wow, you're really sweating, Emma. Want a handkerchief?"

"My ancestors came from Scotland," I muttered and heard a choking laugh from Nick just ahead on the trail.

A little sweat was no longer high on my list of worries, however. I could barely move my neck from gazing upward at the monkeys and my back, my poor throbbing back. The pain was so intense all I could think about was sinking into the river for a three-hour soak. I stumbled along the trail behind Rosie, gazing enviously at her shiny red pack. It wasn't one of my brighter moments, not buying a new backpack, but I'd been hoarding my small Peace Corps remittance. Facing six months of unrelenting back pain, I was now deeply regretting the decision.

Alice, who was busy gathering rocks every few feet, soon fell to the back of the line. Halfway back, she pulled me aside, stopping to pick up another rock while the rest of the group continued marching forward to camp and the waiting police. Tired and desperate to submerge myself in the river, I could barely conceal my annoyance at the delay. A soft dripping rain began to trickle through the palms—just enough to smear my coating of mud and sweat interspersed with miscellaneous mosquitoes and black gnats, but not enough to wash me clean. And still Alice wasn't getting to the point.

I tapped my rubber boot against the rocky path. "You wanted to speak to me about Jack?"

She sighed, finally looking up from her rock. "It's about the police. You must realize, sweetie, I didn't mean it when I said I'd kill that lecherous slug. But maybe it's best you don't mention what you overheard. Sometimes they have strange ideas, especially with the body missing and all. No need to get them worked up. You understand, right?"

I shrugged noncommittally, which Alice completely misinterpreted. She threw her arms around me. "I knew you'd understand, pumpkin."

"Why do you hate him so much?" I asked, pulling away.

"Who? You mean Don Juan? Our king of cruelty and lust?"

"Ah. Yeah. If by that you mean Jack West." I was so tired, it was hard to keep my eyes open, much less follow Alice's obscure references.

"You must know a little if you overheard our fight. He hasn't changed since I was working on my Ph.D. I was only twenty-three and he was an assistant professor. An arrogant, careless narcissist even then. Right before I left to do my dissertation research in French Guiana, I reported him to the Dean. He'd been sleeping with several of his students and I didn't approve. He had a reputation for . . . coercion. But anyway, when I returned he'd been quietly forced out, although he always claimed he chose to leave. He moved to a position at the University of Spoiled Children, but not before he tried to sabotage my research."

She coughed and smirked, her fingers covering her mouth. "Of course I didn't let him get away with it. I made sure everyone knew all about Jack. At least in our world. But that's no excuse for the way he's acted, toward me or . . . anyone else."

The wind strengthened, howling through the trees. I tried increasing the pace, but Alice couldn't be hurried. She stopped, picked up another rock, examined it, and slipped it in her pocket, still talking, forcing me to slow down and listen.

"IWC opened an office in Paramaribo shortly after I built my research station here, but I've tried to avoid Jack. I knew he'd want me out of the park if he ever gained control." She stopped, looking skyward. She grabbed my arm and pointed to the canopy. "Listen!"

We stood still, listening in silence, the rain finally pounding down around us, drowning out the few noises I could distinguish. I had no idea what we were listening for until she jumped in excitement. "Did you hear it? Did you hear it? It's our harpy."

"Our what?"

"Our momma harpy. It's the most powerful bird in the world, with a wingspan of seven feet. Their talons are so powerful they can swoop in and rip a monkey or sloth completely in half." Rainwater streamed down her face and she swung her arms, demonstrating a gliding bird swooping in to snatch a monkey. "We have video of our adult harpy with a spider monkey in its talons. You *have* to watch it!"

She whispered, "This is top secret. Don't tell anyone from IWC, but we have an adult female harpy, a juvenile, and a nest in the middle of our study area, which is way cool. We found spider monkey bones last week at the site. Jack would have killed to find the nest." A flicker of unease passed across her face and she added, her voice lower, "But now he's dead."

"What do you think happened to him?" I figured I might as well ask, since we didn't seem to be heading back to camp anytime soon. Besides, the pounding rain was waking me up.

"What? The spider monkey?" Alice asked.

"No. No. Jack."

She pushed her wet bangs off her forehead and waved her hand. "Oh. Someone probably killed him. It was only a matter of time. His drinking and womanizing have gotten worse over the years. He isn't the sort to die naturally. I hope he went to a nice warm climate, where he belongs, leaving Kasima to those who deserve to be here."

"So you think you can stay on now?"

"I don't know. That's why I need to go into town and get a contract finalized with IWC. Frank's going to be a problem, of course, but with Kevin on my side I think . . . I just hope Jack didn't tell anyone at IWC about what I've found. I'm sure he knew."

"Knew what? What did you find?"

"Nothing, sweetie. Either way, it's all much easier with Jack gone."

"Do you know who killed him?"

She smiled. "No, but I have my suspicions."

"Who do you think did it?" I didn't really believe she'd tell me anything, but with Alice . . . who knew?

"Now why would I want to pay them back that way, when they've gone and done me such a wonderful favor?"

I lowered my voice even though we were completely alone. "Do you think it could've been Frank?"

She blinked. "Why do you ask?"

I told her about the argument I'd overhead between Frank and Jack the night of the party. I didn't mention Diane. I wasn't sure how close they were yet, or if she would believe me.

She clapped her hands, "Jack was going to fire Frank? This is fantastic news. Frank's always been Jack's main goon, blindly following his every whim. I've been worried he would follow through on Jack's orders to kick me out." She gave me another hug. "I'm so glad you're here."

"Do you think I should tell the police?"

"About what, sweetie?"

"About the fight. Between Frank and Jack."

"No. It won't help to get them involved. Don't worry about Frank. I'll take care of him."

"But if he killed Jack?" I asked.

"Oh, I don't care about that. This is much bigger than Jack."

# CHAPTER 16

"The *skowtu* are talking to Nick now," Melvijn told us when we arrived in the front yard. The rain had stopped; the air now thick and warm again. "Nick said Alice goes next."

Alice frowned at him, but made no move to comply. Instead she pulled off her boots, unpacked her backpack, and drifted into the kitchen. I followed her, pulling a chipped tin mug off a nail above the sink and moving to the small gas stove to boil water. We were at the kitchen table, Alice with a peanut butter and jelly sandwich, sighing every few minutes, me with my cup of instant coffee, trying to keep my eyes open, when Nick came through the back door. A short Javanese man in a police uniform followed him. Frank Van Landsberg came in last, studying the room with an air of ownership.

Nick introduced Sergeant Lam from the Suriname Police Department but didn't mention why he wanted to talk to us. Alice stood to shake hands, becoming nervous and giggly. She offered them drinks and began a stuttering, intricately detailed explanation of her research to the policeman, who didn't appear to speak English.

"I do not have the time for that right now," Frank finally cut Alice off. "Sergeant Lam will speak to you outside about Mr. West's death."

Alice followed them outside to the picnic bench under the *kampu,* glancing back to the cabin as if hoping one of us would rescue her.

"Why are the police here?" Rosie asked, picking at her chin again. "Did they find his body?"

"No," Nick said. "But Cedric told Brian it has something to do with Jack's vest they found on the side of the cliff. Brian's going to get the details out of him after the police leave."

Brian glanced up from the logbook he was updating. "Cedric will spill. Don't worry."

They called me out after Alice. Still in my field clothes, I wiped at my wet, grimy face with the side of my arm and sat down at the picnic table, hoping I didn't look as bad as I feared.

I leaned back on the bench, watching the soggy cigarettes floating in the damp ashtray between us and wondered whether I should mention Frank's fight with Jack to the sergeant. Was it fair to mention that but not tell him about Alice's fight or Diane's threat? Nick's accusations from the night before had left me confused.

"Tell Sergeant Lam about the party," Frank told me in English. "I will translate for you."

"I speak Sranan," I said and repeated what I'd told Frank and Laura earlier. I didn't trust Frank to translate properly if I spoke in English. He look surprised and annoyed I wasn't using him as a translator, but it didn't matter. I didn't tell the sergeant about any of the fights. It was too difficult with Frank listening to every word, possibly ready to twist the situation to make Alice look like the guilty party, if only to deflect suspicion from himself.

When I'd finished, Frank spoke to the sergeant in rapid Dutch, which I barely understood, before switching to English. "That is all. Should you need to speak to *me*, I will be here until tomorrow afternoon organizing the search. Send Melvijn Hardveld out."

Approaching the cabin, I glanced back at the *kampu* where Sergeant Lam was lighting Frank's cigar. Both turned to watch me, as if they were talking about me. I looked away. I had a feeling no one other than Alice would believe my suspicions about Frank.

Diane was pacing near the cabin, smoking a local cigarette, her hands shaking when she took a drag.

"What'd they ask?" she demanded and I stopped just outside the kitchen door.

"Just what happened," I said, looking past Diane, through the cabin's screen. Kevin Schipper was there, near the kitchen sink with an unknown woman.

"You know what I mean," Diane said. "Do they think someone killed him?"

I dragged my eyes back to Diane. "They didn't say."

"Did you spread any of your lies?"

"I don't know what you're talking about, Diane."

"Yes you do. You're jealous and trying to start rumors that I did something to . . . that I fought with Jack."

"I'm not, Diane. I'm sorry if you think I'm out to get you, but I haven't mentioned anything to anyone. And I won't unless I think it's really necessary."

I turned away, wondering about Diane. She was genuinely afraid I was going to say something to the police. But if she really thought Jack was still alive, or had simply fallen in the river drunk, would she really care? I stepped into the kitchen, telling Melvijn it was now his turn to speak to the police, and Kevin crossed the room.

"I heard the story about you trying to rescue Jack," he said. "What an amazing risk. I can't tell you how thankful we all are at IWC for what you did. Even . . . even if you weren't able to save him. You're a heroine."

He called over the woman he introduced as with the American Embassy but didn't mention her position. The American population in Suriname was microscopic, with most easily categorized as either embassy, Peace Corps, missionary, or mining, but I'd never seen this woman before, which meant she'd probably only recently arrived in the country.

"Beth's here to keep an eye on the situation," Kevin said. "Since Jack was an American citizen. It's up to the Surinamese police to investigate what happened, but we want to make sure it stays on their radar. Actually, we have a few questions too. Can we talk to you outside?"

Under the collective gaze of the group, I followed Kevin and the embassy woman out of the kitchen and down to the main beach. Cedric was there, wearing a bright red, Bob Marley t-shirt and smoking a cigarette. Kevin asked him in Dutch to give us some privacy for a few minutes and he left, wandering up the river path.

"Why are the police here? Do they think Jack was killed?" I asked Kevin. We were on the edge of the river and the sun moved out of the clouds, sending a sharp burst of light reflecting off the water. I squeezed my eyes in pain, turning away from the river and shading my eyes.

"I don't think they know anything for sure," Kevin answered. "But apparently Jack's jacket, the one Frank said you noticed on the hill, was covered in blood and had a long tear through the middle. Cedric thought it looked like a machete cut. It didn't make sense his jacket would be covered in blood before he landed on the rocks. But we heard all of this from Frank, who . . ."

He studied me carefully, glancing at the woman from the embassy before turning back to me. "I hope you'll keep this to yourself Emma, but we're not sure Frank is the most reliable witness. He's got powerful friends in the government and local police, and we wanted to hear your version firsthand."

"I felt a deep cut on Jack's neck," I said. "I . . . I . . . the rocks seem so smooth, you'd think if it was natural, he would have had bumps, maybe a concussion, but not a cut like that."

"Do you think he was dead when you caught him?"

"I . . . heard a yell a few minutes before I saw him in the river, so if he was dead it hadn't been very long. But . . . yeah, he was probably dead by then. By the time I lost hold of him anyway. He was underwater when I grabbed him and it took me a long time to drag him to the rock and get his head above water. But the waves were really strong and . . . I couldn't hold on, I lost . . ."

Kevin grabbed my hand, his eyes kind. "It's amazing you were able to catch him at all in those rapids, especially at night. I'm glad you're okay."

Relieved to finally have some sympathy and kindness, I spilled out everything I'd heard that night, including Jack's two fights, first with Alice and then with Frank, as well as Diane's crying and threat against Jack. I added Brian and Rosie's claims Alice couldn't have done it since she'd been asleep in her room at the time, and that I'd had a few drinks and my memory could have been faulty.

Kevin was still holding my hand when I finished and he squeezed it. "If anything happens, if you hear anything new, call me, okay? And maybe you shouldn't mention any of this to anyone else."

"Oh, I kind of mentioned something to Alice earlier. Just about Frank though."

"Alice is fine, just not to anyone on the island or the other researchers. Okay? And maybe try to stay clear of Frank."

I nodded agreement, catching a glimpse of red on the trail behind Kevin's head. They must know something more about Frank, I felt sure, if they were warning me away from him.

Kevin and the woman from the embassy followed me back up the hill, leaving to look for Alice in her cabin. I returned to the kitchen, where I found Nick boiling water at the stove.

Rosie was being interviewed outside, her flirtatious laugher drifting across the yard. Otherwise the cabin sounded empty.

"Is everyone else finished being interviewed?" I asked Nick, gazing out the screen window at Rosie.

"All done," Nick said. "How'd the gossip go with your new admirer?"

I turned away from the screen. "What are you talking about?"

"Kevin. You're his *heroine.*"

"Better than being a drunk whack job," I said, crossing the kitchen. "I'll take it."

Nick followed, grabbing me from behind. "Wait, Em." He put his hands on my shoulders, turning me around, and I felt the butterflies again, followed by a pang of desire when I remembered where those hands had touched me just two nights before. "I didn't mean it," he added. "Not in that way. It was a joke. I warned you about my sense of humor, didn't I?"

"It doesn't matter," I said, reminding myself I'd been rejected that morning, that he didn't feel the same way about me as I did about him. I stepped out of his arms. "I just want to go clean off and sit in the river for a couple of hours."

He shoved his hands in his short pockets, frowning. "So, what'd Kevin want to talk to you about?"

"He wanted to know the truth."

"Did you tell him?"

"Of course. All of it."

"Damn it, Em. This isn't the U.S. You don't want to get messed up with a death. You're asking for serious trouble. What about the police? Did you tell them too?"

"No. What good would that do? With Frank sitting right there?"

"Thank God for that at least. But what's Frank got to do with it?"

I froze, realizing Kevin had just asked me not to say anything.

But surely he didn't mean Nick. I looked around the kitchen, checking to make sure no one was nearby. "Frank is the main suspect."

"Who's main suspect?"

"Mine."

He shook his head. "And how do you come to that nice little conclusion?"

"Because Jack had just fired Frank for doing something sketchy or illegal. Something related to the park." I waved my arm. "And now look at him. He's leading the investigation into Jack's death and he's still running IWC."

"That's crazy, Em."

"Back there again are we? Kevin doesn't seem to think so. I'm going to the river." With that, I flounced out of the kitchen.

"Watch out for the anacondas," Nick called.

# CHAPTER 17

I changed into my bathing suit, grabbed a bucket for my dirty field clothes, and jogged down to the river. I sank onto the smooth rock, letting the rushing current massage my aching shoulders and neck. Parrots, always in pairs, squawked a noisy greeting as they passed, heading into the sleepy sun tumbling toward the jungle canopy.

Frank and his entourage left and Rosie came down, wearing a USC baseball cap and carrying a bucket of dirty clothes. Mine were still sitting on the edge of the river, completely forgotten. Rosie noticed them and offered to wash my clothes with hers. That worked well for me, since I couldn't move.

The river was shaded now, the air warm and soft. A gentle breeze blew across the water, storm clouds darkening the sky. It was pure bliss, and I let the day drift away, the rock massaging my back, the tiny fish gathering to nibble on my legs . . . I jerked my leg, a little worried when I remembered Nick's parting comment about anacondas.

"Is it normal for fish to nibble on your legs?" I asked Rosie. "They aren't piranhas are they?"

"Nah," she said, leaving the clothes to soak in the bucket. "The little fish are harmless, and supposedly piranhas don't attack large mammals. Don't go in with an open wound though." I settled back against the rock, albeit feeling a little less blissful.

"Melvijn went to the island," she added. "Do you think that woman, Laura, is there? He tried to deny sleeping with her, but

I don't believe him."

I was confused about all of her interweaving relationships, but I decided it was best not to ask for clarification. "I thought you broke up," I said instead.

"Only because he wouldn't tell me the truth." She sniffed. "At least Todd likes me . . ."

"Who's Todd?" I asked, immediately regretting the question.

"The guy from the IWC party. He's going to be in town for another week. Hopefully Alice will let me go with her on Saturday. It's my turn to go—"

I shook my head in disapproval. "Rosie, maybe you need a break from men. Why jump straight into something with Todd? And what about that other guy, Arnaud, and the photo? Did Nick talk to you about it?"

She laughed. "Like, whatever. I'm just having fun. Lighten up, Emma."

Given Rosie already had three known boyfriends, one married and one threatening to kill her, I didn't think I was being particularly judgmental about her adding another one so quickly, but I let it go.

"So you're not worried about Arnaud threatening you?"

"Nah, he just wants his photo back." She picked at her chin, looking less certain then she sounded.

"Why does he want it so badly?"

"He's superstitious. He's afraid I'll use it to put a spell on him or, like, steal his soul. Melvijn told me to hold on to it to protect myself."

I let the ridiculousness of that statement stand. Even my mother, who believes in all sorts of new age mumbo jumbo, probably wouldn't think you could steal someone's soul through a photo. The sun sank lower in the sky, and I reluctantly pulled myself out of the river to help Rosie wring out the clothes.

"What's USC stand for?" I asked her as I squeezed water

from her t-shirt with the same logo as her baseball cap.

"University of Southern California. I went to school there."

"Ah. I was thinking South Carolina or something like that."

"That's where Alice is from."

"South Carolina? Must be where she gets all the sweetie endearments."

"She doesn't call me sweetie. Just you and Brian and Nick. Haven't you noticed?"

"Oh? No. Sorry."

"She's so mean. I can't wait for her to leave. It was much better before, even with Diane. God, I have ten months to go. I don't know if I'm going to make it. I mean, why should I bother if I can't do a master's with Alice? That's the only reason I came. It's all Diane's fault!"

"How so?"

"She's so condescending, and she's always trying to make me look bad." She stopped, looking ready to burst into tears.

Not being able to help myself, in the face of her trembling lip, I patted her arm. "What is it, Rosie? What did Diane do?"

"She's always making fun of me in front of Alice." Rosie wiped away a tear. "I got her back at the party though."

My interest perked at that. "What happened at the party?"

She looked away, not meeting my gaze. "Just Diane getting her just desserts, that's all, but I left happy."

"When did you leave? Did you see Jack West?"

"Nope. I went off with Todd, but he said he was drunk and had to get up early, and so I went to bed."

"Were you the first back in the cabin?" I asked.

"You make it sound so pathetic. Not all of us can run off to shag two men in one night."

"I . . . I didn't sleep with Jack. Or Nick."

"Oh?" she asked, turning in surprise. "Was it Nick, too? I wondered, since you were down on the rocks together. And there's Kevin. He's cute too. Even if he's bald."

I picked up my bucket of damp laundry. "Rosie, you don't really believe any of that do you? Why is everyone so sure I ran off with Jack? Just because we danced together?"

She shrugged, and we turned to hike the short path back to the cabin. "You practically shagged, as our beloved Nick would say, on the dance floor and then you both disappeared. It's what everyone thought. Everyone was talking about it."

"Who's everyone?"

"Diane and . . ." She trailed off.

"So basically you and Diane."

She didn't respond.

"I went down to the bench by myself. I told you all that."

"We all thought you were lying, you know, since, he disappeared and all."

"I wasn't lying, Rosie! And why do you keep saying we all? Who else thinks I—"

I stumbled on a rock, grabbed a tree trunk to steady myself, and froze in terror; a long, gray snake with irregular dark bands raised its head a foot off the ground—ready to strike.

"Rosie, Rosie, what's that?" I whispered, nodding my head to indicate the snake.

"Don't move," she hissed, tiptoeing backward up the path, although I'd figured the "don't move" part out on my own.

My legs quivered and blood rushed to my head. I was about to die.

I watched the snake for what seemed a lifetime, noticing its speckled eyes and deadly fangs that inject venom the way a hypodermic needle inserts heroin. Sweat trickled down my forehead and into my eye. The velvety, intricately patterned scales shimmered in the afternoon light. I had a fleeting remembrance of the odd man during Peace Corps training who told us no fer-de-lance anti-venom existed in Suriname. I held still, barely breathing. An eternity later, the snake lowered its head and slithered into the leaves.

I was still frozen on the path when Rosie returned with Nick and Brian . . . and a machete.

"I thought you deserted me, Rosie," I said.

"No, I just went to grab a machete."

I pulled myself together and wiped away my tears, my hands still visibly shaking. "Sorry," I said, referring to the tears.

"It's okay." Rosie put her arm around me. "I'd be freaking too if a fer-de-lance tried to strike at me. I can't believe I walked right past it."

Especially creepy because it was still my "moon time," as my friend, a goddess worshipper calls it, and I'd gone in the river, despite the warning from Alice . . . and possibly Hortense.

"Where'd it go?" Brian asked. I pointed to the woods and Nick and Brian, both in swim trunks and shirtless, poked around on the edges of the path.

"You think it's the mate of the snake you killed?" Rosie asked Brian who was using the machete to push aside ferns and rocks.

"For Christ's sake, Rosie," Nick burst out. "Do you or do you not have a biology degree? Is that what they taught you about snake behavior at that so called school of yours?"

He waved us up the path. "Come on, the lot of you, Brian's got some fish to cook. I caught a tucunaré and he caught a couple of small piranhas, so he's very jealous."

"Man, I caught the tucunaré," Brian called, following Nick up the path. "You never catch anything but piranhas."

"He lives in a fantasy world," Nick said, stopping at the overhang. "The water's getting higher though, so we finally put out the net. Expect heaps of fish in the future."

Given all the tiny bones, more river fish was not something I was particularly looking forward to, but I kept quiet, hating to crush their egos. Brian left to cook dinner and Rosie followed him inside when I offered to hang her laundry. I pulled my field pants from the bucket first, clipping them to the front line; a quick rain began pounding the yard, dampening the dirt.

"Sorry about the anaconda joke earlier," Nick said, ducking under several lines of clothes and pulling off a towel. He wrapped it around his waist and pulled off his swim shorts underneath, nearly losing his hold on the towel, which barely covered him. I tried to look away, but my eyes weren't listening to my brain.

"Actually, I feel guilty," I said, a little overheated, even in the cooling rain. "Alice told me not to go in the river. But I couldn't help it. My neck was killing me . . . and I was so hot and dirty."

"What are you talking about?" he asked, catching my eye. "I got a little distracted by that last part. I can't seem to remember the rest."

More heat flushed my face and I threw a sock at his head, missing completely. "You know what I mean," I said. "Women aren't supposed to go in the river . . . at certain times of the month."

He shook his head sadly. "Em, not you too? Is it in the water out here or something? I had such high hopes for you."

*If he only knew,* I thought to myself. To him, I said, "I'm just saying. Day one I go in the river, and wham, Jack dies. Day two I go in the water and I almost die via a venomous snake. It's quite a coincidence."

He pulled on a clean pair of shorts under his towel and a dark blue t-shirt. "That's a bloody good scientific investigation you've put together. Although perhaps we should do a bit more experimentation? Why don't you have a little swim about tomorrow in the river and we test what happens. If no one dies, I win. If someone dies, you win."

"Funny. Very funny. Especially in light of recent events."

"It was too good to pass up." He joined me while I finished

hanging the laundry. "By the way, normally we have assigned lines. Alice puts her clothes wherever she wants, but once she leaves, people get territorial. Particularly Brian. He's a stickler for rules and order. You can ask Diane and Rosie which line to use. I don't think the front one is taken, but the rain blows in there."

A massive mosquito landed on my arm and I squished it. I wiped off the blood, remembering I'd forgotten to take my malaria pills that morning. "Hey, are you taking malaria pills?" I asked Nick who was fingering a red bra.

"You wore this in the field—"

"That's Rosie's," I said, and his hand dropped away. I steered him into the yard, away from the laundry. "Malaria."

"Ah, yeah. It's a small risk here, but it's also not safe to stay on those pills long-term. I think Rosie and Diane are both taking them. Brian and Melvijn not. Alice claims she's taken them for years with no side effect, but I've done heaps of research and none of it's good. They make you crazy. I have a news article about soldiers in the U.S. who killed their wives, and it turned out the only common link was malaria prophylaxis."

"I know, but malaria also kills millions of people a year."

"It's your decision." Nick watched me in the dusky early evening light. "But for me, I'd only take them if I knew malaria was definitely in the area."

I swallowed, remembering last night's nightmare about Sonia. "I've heard that before. I've had really intense dreams for several weeks; I think it's the malaria pills . . ."

I desperately hoped it was the malaria pills. The alternative, I wasn't ready to face.

# CHAPTER 18

"Wake up little chickadees! Wake up! Lots of packing to do." A pot clanged against the concrete floor and Alice squealed, "Brian, I can't find the flour!"

I reached for my alarm clock—6:00 A.M. Couldn't we sleep in the one day we didn't have to be in the field? Especially as I'd woken up halfway through the night from another nightmare and been unable to get back to sleep for hours. I pulled my pillow over my head, but had no choice but to get up once the kitchen filled with loud voices arguing over who should go into town with Alice the following day. Nick said Rosie could go, but Alice also wanted Brian to be there since Rosie didn't speak Dutch. Finally, following a torturous hour of arguments, tears, and wailing—the latter mostly in my head—it was decided both could go.

After breakfast, Alice handed out our assignments for double-checking, organizing, and packing the data collected and stored in various logs since her previous visit to Kasima six months earlier. Nick explained Alice always took hard copies of the logs and left the raw data in Suriname under her agreement with the government. She was taking it all to town the next day but would leave the original copies to mildew in the main cabin's attic upon her return.

"Those bastards at IWC think they're going to get hold of my data. Ha! I had a brilliant idea last night." She bounced around the kitchen, pointing to Nick, Diane, and me. "I want you three to go through the data and take out any interesting information. I want everything going to IWC to be as useless as possible. Nothing about the harpy sightings or any of the habitat mapping we've done." Despite Jack's death, Alice seemed as paranoid as ever, and I began to wonder about that pill she'd been looking for the night before and whether it had really been for Diane.

"Why don't you white out and renumber the pages after we pull out the important data," Diane suggested to me. "We don't have the decades it would take to train you on what is and isn't important." Nick didn't contradict her assessment of my abilities, probably because she was right, but it was still annoying.

Most everything Diane said or did in reference to me was an attempt to annoy. Apparently she wasn't ever going to forgive me for questioning her about Jack's death. And her tactics were petty. I'd found several of her field pants stacked in my room when I returned from the field the day before, even though I'd told her I didn't need them. Admittedly my field clothes *were* unstylish, and a bit holey, given I'd found most of them on the Peace Corps giveaway shelf in town. But I suspected she'd only made the offer because she knew they wouldn't fit and wanted to point out her smaller size. I didn't plan on giving her the satisfaction of returning them though. They would stay where they were, stacked on my shelf, never to be worn.

"Don't you think this is strange?" I asked Nick once Alice left to pack up the videos, photos, and fecal samples with Rosie, Melvijn, and Brian. "It seems like a lot of useless work, and personally I'd think IWC had better things to do than to steal Alice's data. Little things like save the rainforests." We were at the kitchen table with logbooks scattered around us, a grating electronica mix playing in the background—Nick's musical pick.

"Theft is all too common," Diane said, giving me an evil

look. "The first professor I worked with stole part of my thesis research and published it without crediting me."

"But IWC's a conservation organization," I said. "They don't need to 'publish or perish' the way professors do."

"Competition is competition," Nick said. "Alice's smart to protect herself, even with Jack dead. Melvijn told me he found Jack over here snooping through the Kasima trail data logs the morning of the party."

Diane gasped, although Nick didn't seem to notice, and the paper she was holding floated to the cement floor.

I handed it back. Her hands were shaking when she put it in the notebook, her breathing short and jerky.

Staring at the bulging blue notebook, an idea came to me, but I bided my time until Diane got up to leave the cabin. Assuming she'd gone to the outhouse, I turned to Nick, "Remember when I asked you about animal collecting in the park?"

"Vaguely," Nick answered, not looking up from his pile of field notes. "Why?"

"It just seems like Kasima would be a great place to collect wildlife," I said. "I mean, isn't it supposed to be one of the most biologically important areas in the region? Isn't that what Jack said? What if my pilot out here was right? I wouldn't put it past any of the workers to be involved. Pay's got to be next to nothing out here. And capturing animals, they could make some extra money on the side. And it's illegal, but it's probably not *that* illegal, right? It could explain what I heard Frank and Jack fighting over the night of the party. Maybe Frank was involved or let it happen."

"Let me get this straight, Em. You think Cedric and all the workers on the island have been capturing wildlife in the park and shipping it up river to Paramaribo?"

"Maybe, or sometimes by plane. My pilot said you could get forty thousand dollars for a little singing bird. There must be big money in it."

"That seems like a bit of an exaggeration. Maybe he was talking about a trained singing bird with a particularly beautiful voice. I'm not saying there isn't lots of money in the trade, but not usually for the people on the ground collecting the birds. It's the traders on the other end that make the money."

"Okay, that part's not important. I mean, who gets how much is just a matter of your perspective, isn't it? But it might explain why Jack was over here looking through the files, right? Let's say they've been catching a lot of birds. Wouldn't it be noticeable in Alice's data?"

Nick shrugged. "Sure. If it was on a massive scale over a long period of time. Once you'd analyzed all the numbers. But I find it hard to believe everyone on the island is in this massive conspiracy and none of us over here know anything about it. And frankly, I can think of plenty of other reasons Jack might have been over here picking through our files."

I frowned, remembering his conversation that first day at camp with Diane. He made some sort of accusation to her about turning over data. Had Diane been giving information to Jack? Could her anger at him the night of the party have had something to do with that?

I continued with my idea, expressing whatever thought came into my head without thinking about the repercussions. "But the trade is legal, right? Just not from a park."

"There are plenty of animals that can't be traded," Nick said. "But you're right. Wildlife trade is big here, and smuggling charges are nothing."

"See! And wouldn't IWC's taking over the park throw the smuggling into chaos? If they're going to have new management? It's a good reason to kill Jack, don't you think?"

"Now you're contradicting yourself, Emma. I thought you said Frank killed Jack?"

"I'm not completely clear on the details," I said, "but maybe if Frank was going to be fired, he couldn't control the island, ergo the trading would have to stop, especially if Kevin or someone else was going to take over day-to-day management."

"What do you mean Frank killed Jack?" Diane demanded from the doorway. She'd been so quiet I hadn't heard her return.

"Nothing, nothing," I said, turning pleading eyes on Nick, hoping he'd shut down the conversation now that Diane was back.

But he didn't notice. "Look, the wildlife smuggling is not out of the realm of possibility, I'll give you that. But I still think it's a crazy theory for what happened to Jack. You've got no proof, so why are you even speculating about it?"

"Maybe we should talk about it another time," I said.

Diane leaned against the table, her eyes cold and angry. "Emma, you need to stop making wild accusations about people and things you don't understand. You knew nothing about Jack. If he was over here, it was to see—"

She stopped, turned red, and I realized she'd been listening to the whole conversation. She must not have even left the cabin. Nick was watching her, his eyes soft. I frowned. Diane looked way too attractive in her tight red t-shirt, her legs too long and lean for him not to notice.

"That's none of your business," Diane continued, sitting back down in front of her blue notebook and flipping a page. "I know Cedric wouldn't have anything to do with wildlife smuggling in the park. And it couldn't happen without his knowledge. Are you accusing him too, Emma?"

"It's not a completely crazy idea," Nick said, staring into space, half talking to himself. "Most of the workers have been pretty upset about IWC taking over the park."

"That doesn't have anything to do with wildlife smuggling," Diane said. "It's Alice who's been stirring up the workers. She's been telling them IWC would fire them once they took over. Cedric told me all about it. She's not helping anyone spreading talk like that."

"Yeah," Nick agreed. "I've heard that too. But Alice isn't completely wrong either. IWC's management plan does call for turning Kasima into a high-end, luxury, rainforest destination with tennis courts and spas. I can't see Hortense with her purple wigs and bras fitting into that scenario. And Cedric, our favorite boat driver, who thinks he's going to be the new park manager, fishes in his underwear on the rock right in front of Tigrikati. A rich, elderly couple watching birds from their balcony won't find that appealing. It's sad. Hortense has been here over thirty years."

"I disagree completely," Diane said. "What's wrong with tennis courts, if it means IWC has the money to protect Kasima?"

"What good is saving the place if you turn the people living here into low-wage drones?" Nick asked.

"Isn't Hortense a maid?" I said, relieved the conversation had taken a new turn. "It's not exactly a management position."

Nick laughed. "She might be a maid, but I promise you it's Hortense who runs the island. And Cedric, through her."

Diane pulled off her designer sunglasses and shook out her blond curls, glancing in Nick's direction. I followed her gaze to Nick, but he was thumbing through a pile of paper and didn't seem to notice. "Alice needs to be more careful about what she says. I mean, I can stay on and finish my research whether she's here or not, but she's careless too. She needs to come up with better protocols and pick better research assistants. That last paper she published on linear dominance was a complete mess."

I squirmed in my seat, knowing she was referring partly to me. Nick glanced up. "No way. She's right that . . ."

Nick and Diane spent the next twenty minutes in a friendly argument about God knows what. Not understanding anything they were talking about, I was forced out of the conversation and returned to globbing on the whiteout and worrying. I'd made a critical mistake in not making sure Diane was out of earshot before I told Nick about my suspicions of Frank. I had a sinking feeling she was going to tell him what I'd said, just like she had with Alice.

# CHAPTER 19

We finished the packing by late afternoon, and Alice gave us the rest of the day off to, in her words, "Catch up on the breakthrough articles" she'd brought with her, most of them written by none other than Dr. Alice Buchanan. Instead, ignoring my conversation with Nick the night before, I headed for the river, first grabbing one of the black inner tubes from under the tin awning. It was too hot, and I needed to be alone to think. Hopefully the spirits, not that I believed in them—completely—would forgive me.

The river ran slower in front of our beach and I floated into the middle, paddling lazily across to the first rock, stepping through a small pool of water to reach the next. I walked to the end of the rock and sat down in the sun just above the small rapids. I lounged idly on the rocks for a long time, watching the water churn in foamy mounds, wondering whether I should contact Kevin about my wildlife smuggling idea. I wasn't sure if he was even still on the island.

Fifteen minutes later I was still on the rock when Nick and Brian emerged on the beach. They dragged the boat into the water and turned upstream, paddling along the edge of the river. They stopped directly across from me, near a pool of deep water. They were arguing back and forth and feeling around in the water.

"What exactly are you boys doing?" I called across. "Digging for treasure?"

"How the hell did you get out there?" Nick called back, startled. He lost his grip on the tree branch and almost toppled forward, saved only by Brian's tight grip.

"Isn't it dangerous to grab branches like that?" I yelled. "Snakes sun on branches overhanging rivers." Snake defense techniques I knew all about, despite my lack of qualifications in all other aspects of animal behavior.

"Don't you know sun tanning causes cancer?" Nick called back.

I ignored that. "What are you two doing?"

"We're looking for our net. The one Cedric gave us." Nick plunged his hands over the side of the swaying boat. "We set it out yesterday evening, but the river's gone up since then and we can't find it."

"Got it," Brian yelled.

"Catch anything?" Nick turned to Brian who was pulling on the net.

"It's stuck on something."

"Mate, don't pull it too hard. Cedric'll kill us if we ruin it."

"It won't budge. It's probably stuck on a branch. Climb down in the water and see if you can unhook it."

Nick slipped into the water just as Brian yelled, "*Kiri*. I think there's a . . . a hand in the net. Nick, get back in the boat!"

Nick scrambled into the canoe, flopping over the side.

"What is it?" I yelled. The net was on the far side of the boat and I couldn't see much.

They both ignored me, reaching to pull in the net together. They yanked it and an arm and half a shoulder came into view.

"Leave it in the water," I heard Nick say.

They crouched over the side of the boat and I couldn't tell if they were talking or not.

"What is it?" I yelled, although I already knew. No one answered. "Nick! What is it?" I shouted again.

"Jack." He leaned over the side of the boat, possibly to throw up.

Nick and Brian towed the body to shore, leaving me on my rock, now scared to go back in the water.

"How am I supposed to get back?" I called after them once I realized they weren't coming back in the canoe to pick me up.

"Don't you have an inner tube?" Nick shouted across the water.

"Under no conceivable scenario do I plan to climb into that water with hungry piranhas and dead body parts floating about . . ." The rest is best left unsaid. They were either transfixed by my heretofore unknown cursing ability or genuinely scared of me. Either way, Brian did return to transport me back to shore by rowboat while Nick disappeared up the hill.

As soon as we landed on the rock, I turned to the bloated body lying partially hidden under the tree line. I took a tentative step forward, building up my nerve to move closer. Jack's face was barely recognizable, no doubt due to the piranhas. I took another step, mesmerized and horrified at the same time. I'd only ever seen one dead body before. Not so long ago. *Don't think about that,* I told myself. But this one was different. The body was so bloated, it barely looked like a human anymore and the neck—

"Emma, what are you doing?" Brian called from his perch on the rock.

I whipped around as if released from a trance. "I . . . don't know. I just wanted to see his neck. It felt like it was cut, when I caught him in the river."

He cleared his throat. "It's better to leave that to the police."

"I . . . I guess so." I joined him on the rock, no longer particularly anxious to examine the body anyway. We watched the river rather than the body until Nick returned with a foghorn, Alice, Rosie, Melvijn, and Diane trailing behind him.

Only Melvijn wanted a closer look.

"Don't touch him," Alice yelled at Melvijn who was leaning over the body.

"Alice's right," Nick called. "Come back here and wait, Melvijn. Don't touch anything."

Melvijn stepped back and pulled out a cigarette, lighting it while he continued to study the body. He finally turned around and came to sit next to me on the far side of the rock.

"It's dangerous to cross a woman," he whispered in Sranan, the words barely audible.

"What do you mean?" I whispered back.

He smiled, nodding toward Diane, Rosie, and Alice huddled on the opposite side of the rock facing the river. Diane had her arms wrapped around her knees and was rocking softly, her hands gripped tightly. She loosened her hands, and I caught a glimpse of her thumb shoved deep into her palm, as if she were purposely trying to cause herself pain.

"What are you two talking about?" Rosie asked, turning to watch us.

"Nothing," I said, wondering if Diane was trying to keep herself from crying.

The sun blinded us before finally descending behind the wall of forest across the river, the tension palpable while we waited for the police to arrive. I was still thinking about the circling piranhas, hungry for another dead body. I shivered, not sure I'd be going back in the river any time soon. Nick continued blowing the foghorn every few minutes until we finally heard a motor on the river.

Cedric arrived with Frank and the policeman, and they sent us up the hill while they examined the body. Even though no one was hungry, Rosie finished cooking dinner while we waited. Eventually Frank called Alice and Nick outside and Diane paced, peering out the screen every few minutes.

"What did the sergeant say?" she burst out as soon as Nick returned, followed by Alice, who poured herself and Nick rum drinks.

"They're pretty sure it was murder," Nick answered. "They're taking his body to town tomorrow for an autopsy. None of us are allowed to leave the country until this is sorted out."

"Holy shit," said Rosie, "they really think it could be one of us?"

"Of course not," said Alice. "It's just a formality."

"I don't know about that," Nick said.

Rosie turned to Diane, a look of malice on her face. "Looks like you're going to miss your friend's wedding in Texas, Diane."

"No . . . no, I'm not," Diane stuttered. "I . . . I'm not leaving for another two weeks." She proceeded to burst into tears and run from the cabin.

"What's wrong with her?" Rosie asked.

"She's just a sensitive soul," Alice said, making a poor attempt at frowning. "I'm starving, what's for dinner, Rosie?"

"I'm going to go talk to her," Brian said, leaving us in the kitchen.

We were silent through Rosie's potato goulash dinner—until Nick pulled out a bottle of rum, pouring drinks for all, including Diane, who'd returned with Brian halfway through dinner.

"I think we need something to take our mind off Jack," Nick said, passing out drinks before he sat back down to shuffle a deck of cards. He turned to me. "Ever played poker, Em?"

"I may have once or twice," I said, smiling innocently at Nick who was next to me. "But I don't remember the rules." He was looking particularly attractive, his lean jaw covered in soft stubble, his black hair still wet and messy. I was fighting an urge to run my fingers through the thick curls, to smooth them into place.

Everyone joined in except Alice, who was banging and clanking and making an excessive amount of noise in the next room. Presumably she was packing, but why it involved her tearing apart the front of the cabin I wasn't sure.

We played a practice round and then started the official game, with lots of laughter, boasting, and trash talk—some of it a bit ghoulish in light of finding Jack's body only a few hours before, but it was probably a natural reaction and helped us to deal with the horror. Diane seemed recovered and continued to target me with her barbed comments. But I took them in stride, along with all of her poker chips. I claimed beginner's luck, although no one seemed to believe me.

Nick dealt a round, his arm brushing and then lingering against mine when he passed the cards, his voice teasing in a falsetto, "Oh, boys, I don't know how to play. Show me what to do next. Is the ace high or low? Silly me can't remember." He flipped his imaginary long hair. He gave me a pointed look. "I think we've been taken by a shark. Don't think we'll be fooled again, though. Should have suspected as much when she wanted to play for money."

I laughed, tipsy from the rum, and left my arm resting against Nick. Alice stumbled into the room and Nick jerked his arm away, leaning back in his chair. She stopped in the doorway, watching the game with a frown of disapproval on her pale face. She glanced around the table at our rum drinks, her eyes stopping on my pile of chips.

"What's up, Alice?" Nick asked, propping his hands on his head, his muscles nicely displayed.

She didn't say anything. In fact she barely seemed to notice Nick. She was staring at Melvijn slumped over on the table, his head on his arm. She watched him pull himself up and gather in his cards for the round. He waved his arm at us, swaying in his seat. "I'm taking you all down this time. All the way down!"

"Please!" Rosie said. "You're losing. I wonder why."

Alice jerked to Rosie, staring at the USC baseball cap she was wearing again.

Melvijn waved his hand in Rosie's direction, as if she were a mosquito he was shooing away.

"Don't do that," Rosie yelled, slapping his arm. "Who do you think you are? You think you're so special just because you're—" Melvijn's hand snaked out, grabbing Rosie's shoulder. She stopped, her mouth gaping open at him.

"Did any of you take anything from my bag today?" Alice demanded from the doorway, her voice sharp. We swiveled in unison to Alice, surprised at her tone. Her eyes were darting between Melvijn and Rosie.

I glanced at the others, who were shrugging or shaking their heads.

"What'd you lose?" Nick asked.

"I bet Emma took it," Diane said. "She stole stuff from me too."

"I did not, Diane! What are you talking about?"

"You're a liar and a thief," Diane yelled at me and ran out of the cabin again with a slam of the door.

"What the hell was that about?" Nick asked.

Alice was studying me and didn't answer Nick's question.

"I have no idea," I said. "She's crazy. Personally I think it's a combination of too much coffee and cigarettes mixed with malaria pills. That's enough to make anyone batty. And she certainly qualifies."

Alice stiffened her shoulders, sighed, and followed Diane out the kitchen door. It slammed shut, rattling the cabin, and Melvijn stood up to follow Alice out, winking at me as he went.

Nick whispered in my ear, "I'm going to check in with Diane. Don't let her get to you." He brushed a strand of hair behind my ear and pulled away. He stared at me for a heartbeat or two, and I saw an unexpected hunger there. The world turned still and I couldn't look away. Or breathe. Until he shook his head and straightened, as if surprised by his own need. I released my breath, catching a swift, accusing look from Rosie.

# Chapter 20

"Cupcakes, I am going to miss you all so much," Alice kept repeating, followed by last minute instructions on how to collect the monkey data. She was acting as if she were leaving for a month rather than a week.

"Now don't push the IDs. If you don't know which monkey you have, don't do a focal follow." We were sprawled on benches in the shade of a *kampu*, waiting for the sound of a plane engine while Alice continued talking. "Don't forget to call me on Tuesday and let me know what's happening. I'll get stressed if I don't hear from you at least once this week." Her eyes darted to the policeman who was nearby with Kevin, Frank, and the woman from the American Embassy.

They were all leaving on the same plane, presumably with Jack. I didn't see the body anywhere and assumed it must be inside the small cement building on the edge of the airstrip. I wanted to speak to Kevin privately about my wildlife smuggling theory, but Frank was too close. He'd been hovering nearby ever since we arrived at the airstrip.

When the plane bounced to a landing on the grassy strip, I was watching the cockpit window, hoping it was the same pilot I'd flown out with only three days before. I completely missed Ramesh waving from a back window as the plane rolled to a stop—until Alice pointed him out, screaming, "Whee, Ramesh!" and charged across the grassy runway to the plane, leaving us to carry her luggage. Ramesh bounded out behind the unknown pilot, greeting Alice with a jumping hug. He gave Melvijn a fist bump and a long complicated hand greeting and then turned to me, bouncing in excitement. He hugged me, whispering he'd heard all my naughty gossip. I, of course, had no idea what he was talking about.

But I couldn't ask him for clarification as he had to pull off food and help his tour group, an elderly American couple, but I promised to come find him as soon as we finished with Alice. We loaded the boxes of data on the plane and Alice hugged us all, whispering to me, "Watch Melvijn and Diane for me. They're treacherous." Brian and Rosie followed her on the plane and I skipped down the hill in search of Ramesh, not even waiting for take-off. I found him at the Anyumara lodge, with his elderly American tourists.

"Are you one of the monkey researchers?" the tiny wrinkled woman called as I approached.

"Yeah." I stepped onto the porch, nodding to Ramesh, who was lounging on a worn bench.

"Ramesh said he'd bring us by to see the monkeys you're studying."

Her husband, a tall heavy-set man, creaked up the steps behind me.

The little old woman grabbed my arm. "We're so excited, even though we have a hard time understanding his accent. It's awfully fast, isn't it? Are you *saved?*"

I froze, smiling at the woman, her face eager. She tried again, saying, "Are you a Christian?"

Missionaries, I realized, belatedly recognizing the "born-again look" in the woman's wide smile and glassy eyed gaze. The wooden cross hanging around her neck and her husband's "New Hallow First Disciple Church" t-shirt should have been obvious clues.

"Ah . . . I, ah . . ." I looked to Ramesh for help and backed up. The woman's husband stepped behind me, blocking my escape.

"Where are you from?" he asked firmly.

"Missouri." My brain flickered back to life, and I pulled out the bag of black licorice from my backpack, which Ramesh had told me to bring to make friends on the island. "Want some candy?"

It worked, more or less. The woman seemed to forget about the status of my soul and explained enthusiastically, while chomping on a licorice stick, that their original calling was to do missionary work in Florida, converting Jewish retirees. They chose Suriname only after reading Florida would soon be over-run by snakes and bears. I gave her the benefit of the doubt about the snakes, but the bears comment seemed a little fruity. "Can you excuse us for a minute?" I asked when they began circling back to my eternal salvation. "I have to talk to Ramesh about something." I nodded at Ramesh, who seemed to be enjoying the show a little too much.

He pushed himself lazily off the bench and slipped his arm through mine as we strolled down the hill. Loud enough for half the island to overhear he said, "Story is you bagged yourself the hottie Aussie."

"Shh!" I nodded toward the elderly couple. "Who'd you hear that from anyway? You've only been here a few minutes."

He grinned. "From Arnaud. He works for Natuur Tours. My tour's through 'em. Arnaud's been banned again. He thinks Melvijn's behind it."

"Ah, Arnaud. We've had the pleasure of meeting. Dear God, word travels fast. This is worse than Peace Corps. But unfortunately, nothing's going on there. Arnaud is behind the times."

"What wrong with him?" His eyes brightened. "He gay?"

"No, he's not gay. Just not interested."

"He gay then."

I leaned my head on his shoulder. "I've missed you. And you're very kind, but unfortunately not every man has such impeccable taste."

"You should throw yourself at him." He glanced back at the lodge. "I've got only a few minutes. They're excited to convert a Hindu. I'm the first of my kind they've met. Little do they know. But tell me what happened with Jack West. Arnaud says you found him in the river?"

The higher rocks, which were rarely submerged by the river, were rough and reddish brown, and I laid out my sarong before sitting down next to Ramesh. I was catching him up on everything when Nick appeared behind us.

"We haven't met yet," Nick said, offering Ramesh his hand and studying our cozy position together on the rocks: our shoulders pressed together, Ramesh's hand leaning on my knee while he twisted a small branch.

"Nick, Ramesh. Ramesh, Nick," I said, making the introductions with a wave of my hand. I didn't stand up.

Ramesh jumped up to shake Nick's hand, putting on his best British English. "I've certainly heard all about *you*. And seen you around *Foto*. I picked up a Kasima tour with Natuur Tours so I could catch up with Emma. I work occasionally as a tour guide, but my main job is at the BOG. Computers."

Nick nodded. "So you two know each other well then?"

Ramesh caught the questioning note in Nick's voice, and to my delight decided not to set him straight. He sat back down, throwing his arm about my shoulders. "Sure. We know each other really well." He winked at me—a wide, obvious wink that Nick couldn't possibly miss. "In fact, I convinced her to stay in Suriname. For good, hopefully. I couldn't wait to get out here and see her again." He ruffled my hair and copied one of Alice's endearments. "I missed you, sweetie." It was a bit too much, which I was sure Nick would notice.

But all he said was, "Ah," and rubbed his forehead, nodding slightly before he turned away. He stopped and looked back. "It's going to be a couple of hours until we head back to camp. You'll have plenty of time to catch up." He nodded at Ramesh. "Nice meeting you."

We watched him stroll down to the little pool of water near the rapids where Diane was sunning on the warm rocks.

I poked Ramesh. "Nice job. Thanks."

He grinned. "You're very welcome. Although maybe he's not worth the trouble."

"Hmm." I watched Nick pull off his shirt and slide into the pool of water. "I think he may be worth it."

"Enough about your hottie Aussie and my jealousy. Tell me about Jack West. The paper says he was murdered."

"It seems so. This might sound a little crazy, but I think it's possible his murder may have something to do with wildlife smuggling in the park." I told him about the pilot's comments my first day flying into Kasima and my theory about wildlife smuggling. I started to tell him about the conversation I'd overheard between Jack and Frank, but Ramesh stopped me, glancing around.

"Emma, no, no, you're wrong." He grabbed my hand on the rock, squeezing it tightly, a little too tightly. "Have you told anyone?"

I tried loosening his hold and he jerked his hand away. I looked at him warily, wondering how well I really knew him. "No. I mean, just to Nick and accidentally to Diane, but they didn't believe it. I . . . I don't even know if I believe it. It's just a theory. I have a few other theories too . . ."

"It's not possible. Why anyone gon murder Jack West over that? It's nothing. Just a little fine." He gazed at Nick and Diane, who were laughing on the rocks below us. Diane, her willowy body clothed in a sleek blue suit, pointed to a shiny-green hummingbird hovering in the air in front of her, its very long beak in front of her nose. It zoomed backward and returned, again hovering nose to beak. I always kept my suspicions of Diane in the back of my mind, but I didn't want to mention them to Ramesh, not when I was so unsure.

"Those hummingbirds scare me," Ramesh said. He nodded at Nick and Diane. "Those two?"

"No!" I turned away from Nick and Diane.

"You told me after Sonia's funeral you gon stop interfering in other people's lives," Ramesh said.

"You had to bring that up, huh?" I stood up, knocking the leaves and dirt from my shorts and shoving my sarong back in my backpack. "Actually, I've been having nightmares about Sonia ever since I came back to Suriname. Every single freaking night. Since Jack's death, they've been mixed up together. Sometimes I see Sonia. Other nights it's Jack. Last night it was both. I don't feel like I'm interfering. I feel like I'm involved. Like they want me involved. That they won't let me go until I figure out what happened."

Ramesh took a step away from me. He too believed in Winti and spirit possession, and I could tell I was scaring him.

"What do you think?" I asked when he didn't respond.

"You're not scared?"

"Sometimes." I shook myself. "No. I probably just have too much time out here. To think and worry. That's my problem. But then . . . You know Hortense, right?"

He nodded.

"My first day out here, she whispered something about *winti* and my *Takuu Akaa*, which Brian said is supposed to help me resist spirits trying to occupy my body when I sleep. How could she know that? About the nightmares, I mean? And there's something there, because I can't seem to resist them. I see them every night in my dreams. Nightmares." I ran a shaky hand through my hair. "I think I'm going a little crazy. Maybe a lot crazy. I stopped taking my malaria pills this morning. Maybe that will help."

He studied me. "Go talk to Hortense."

The noon sun was beating down on us but I shivered. "Why? You think she can give me something to stop the nightmares? To exorcise the spirits?"

"Maybe," he said. "And about Jack too. The rumor is he was Cedric's father."

# CHAPTER 21

Lightning forked across the sky, crackling in a boom of thunder; I turned toward a scattering of small, thatched roof houses and towering coconut palms just behind the Anyumara lodge. Stormy winds whipped the palm fronds and scattered the grassy path with pink frangipani petals, cooling the thick heat of the afternoon and stirring up a sweet, bitter smell of rotting mangoes.

Instead of rain, a gray fog swept up from the river, wafting over the moss-covered rocks and thick piles of rotting leaves and settling comfortably around my waist, as if it planned to visit for a while. I plunged forward, ducking under a dried palm frond hanging across the path to protect the village from evil spirits, which refuse to bow down to pass under the fronds. I don't know why the spirits can't simply walk around the fronds, but spirits have their own rules. Or so my grandmother always said.

I rounded a tree and stopped. Melvijn and Cedric were arguing ahead on the foggy path. Melvijn was gripping Cedric's t-shirt, jerking him roughly. They were face-to-face, and I couldn't make out the words, but Melvijn seemed to be doing the talking in a low, furious whisper. Cedric grabbed at Melvijn's hands, pushing them away and sauntered back to the village.

Melvijn stomped up the path in my direction, stopping when he noticed me. "Are you looking for me?" he asked in Sranan, immediately hiding his anger with an impish grin.

"I was going to stop in to say hello to Hortense. Is everything okay?"

He clicked his tongue in disapproval. "It's nothing. Cedric owes me some money and he doesn't want to pay. But he will." He swung me around in a quick dance. "We need another drumming party." With that he turned and walked away, as if he didn't have a care in the world, singing, *I got money in my pocket, baby, money on the way.*"

·I continued in the opposite direction, following the dusty path toward the village, wondering what scheme Melvijn was up to.

Cedric was next to the first hut, holding a small bottle of clear Mariënburg rum. I waved as I passed, keeping my head down, not wanting to speak to him so soon after his fight with Melvijn. Maybe later he'd be a little calmer. But he called in English, "Where you go?"

I took a deep breath and paused. "To find Hortense. Do you know which is her house?"

He came closer. "Why you look for Hortense? What you need? I help you."

"Oh, thanks, but I just wanted to bring her a present."

"You bring Hortense present and not me?"

"It's just candy. You want some?" I dug through my backpack, passing over my second to last bag of candy. I wasn't sure if Diane had told him about the smuggling yet, but he didn't seem angry with me, so I guessed not.

"Why Boss Alice go to *Foto* so soon? With police?" he asked, opening the bag, offering me a red M&M.

"Oh, she didn't go with the police. It was just a coincidence they were on the same plane. She went in for some meetings with IWC. To finalize her contract with them so she can stay at Kasima."

"Boss Alice say IWC bad and should not have this land. That

IWC fire us. Now she change mind."

"I don't think it has anything to do with that. She doesn't have a choice. She has to be friendly to IWC if she wants to stay here and watch her monkeys."

"Not her monkeys," Cedric said. "This is our land. Maybe IWC not keep Kasima for long."

"You want the government to manage the park again?"

Cedric smiled, his gold teeth glistening. "No, Saramakans! Not the government. This is Saramakan land. We do what we want here."

I vaguely remembered Maroons had just won some sort of international ruling giving them new rights to their ancestral land and wondered if the area included Kasima. "Ah, yeah, of course. You're Saramakan, right? What village does your father come from?"

He glanced at me, startled by the question then shrugged. "My mother, she come from Abenaston."

Maroon villages were matrilineal, so it wasn't a particularly strange answer. "And your father?" I tried again.

He pulled out a cigarette and mumbled something it was probably best I didn't understand, adding, "You have man in *Foto?*"

I'd been expecting that at some point. "No, I have a boyfriend in America," I lied, knowing after two years in Suriname where this was headed. "We plan to marry next year when I go home."

"He not love you if he stay in America," Cedric said. "You take Surinamese man."

"No, no. I only like one man at a time." I turned to leave and he pointed me to the last hut at the end of the village.

I continued along the path, feeling my back tingling. I let out my breath. Diane was right about Alice stirring up the workers against IWC. I wondered if Kevin and Frank knew what she'd been doing.

I found Hortense in front of a small wooden house with a thatch roof at the end of the village. She was with the same younger woman who'd been with her my first day on Loiri Island. Her door was painted in a colorful pattern, the dirt yard neatly raked with Zenlike lines that eliminated any hiding areas for snakes. They were sitting under a plastic overhang, protected from the rain, which still hadn't arrived.

*"Fawaka,"* I called in greeting. Hortense didn't seem to have heard the news about my wildlife smuggling suspicions. She smiled and waved me over. I wasn't sure how I was going to ask her about Cedric's father, especially without making it seem like I thought Cedric had any connection to Jack's death. But I was more scared to ask her about spirits and wasn't sure if I would even do it.

Although I'd half-joked about it with Nick and Ramesh, and despite certain family history, I didn't believe in an afterlife where spirits would hang around to haunt my dreams. It was just my guilty subconscious dealing with Sonia's death, plus Jack's murder combined with the malaria pills. That's what I kept telling myself. Although it was hard to remember those facts in the middle of the night with howling monkeys in the dark jungle, anacondas circling in the murky river, and the memory of Jack's bloated face, unrecognizable after three days swimming with the piranhas.

I jerked back to the present, centering my vision on the two little boys playing in the dirt with nothing but strings tied around their waists. The strings were supposed to protect them from evil spirits, I remembered, kind of like a Kabbalah bracelet.

"Are the boys your sons?" I asked the younger woman in Sranan. I sat on the carved wooden bench across from Hortense, and pulled out the last of my candy, offering some to the kids.

"*Ai,*" the younger woman said, leaning over to help herself to the candy.

"My grandchildren," Hortense said proudly.

"Oh, Cedric's your brother?" I asked the younger woman.

Hortense smiled, her wrinkles crinkling. "*Ai.* You like Cedric? You take him with you to America."

"No, no. I have a boyfriend," I lied again. They both giggled in response. "Where is Cedric's father? Does he live here on the island too?"

"No, no," Hortense said, shaking her head and sweeping her hand as if Cedric's father were very far away.

"You have a brother?" the younger woman asked.

"*Ai,* four older brothers," I answered.

"*Soo,*" Hortense said.

"They come visit you here?"

"No, they've never visited," I answered. "They live in Missouri and Washington, D.C."

"*Konimai* lived in Washington," Hortense said, staring over my shoulder, her jaw churning.

I wasn't sure what *Konimai* meant. It was a Saramakan word, but I thought she must be referring to Jack. This was going to be easier than I thought.

"Is *Konimai* Jack West?" I asked.

"*Ai.*" She nodded.

"Did you know him very well?"

"I came from Abenaston thirty years ago, with my man. He died long ago. *Konimai* came later. He was good to me. But he changed. That's why he died."

"You, you . . . ?" I stuttered in English, surprised at how quickly she'd admitted the connection. I switched back to Sranan. "Jack West—*Konimai*—was your man?" I just couldn't picture this wrinkled old woman who looked well over seventy with Jack. "How old are you?"

145

She took a long time to answer. When she did she simply said, "Fifty-eight." Only fifty-eight; two years older than Mom and probably around Jack's age. It was a hard life here. I made a mental note to remember to use more sunscreen.

"Why did *Konimai* die?" I asked.

The two little boys returned to grab more candy and run off again. Hortense yelled at them in Saramakan but they continued weaving through the scattering of huts until they disappeared into the fog.

"I told *Konimai* he wakes the ancient spirits," Hortense said. "He wanted to bring in more tourists to walk sacred grounds and put up new buildings. The spirits took him away."

"You mean it was the spirits that killed him, not a man or woman?"

Hortense didn't answer my question.

"Was Jack, *Konimai*, murdered?" I tried again.

"*Ai*," she answered.

"Do you know who killed him?"

Hortense waved her hand and said something to her daughter in Saramakan. They both laughed. I smiled, not understanding, but still hoping Hortense would answer my question.

"Nick. He's your man?" the younger woman asked, giggling.

"Ah . . . no." I watched Hortense, sure she knew more about what had happened to Jack, although it didn't look like she was going to tell me.

"You go back to England with him?" She bit into a piece of candy.

I sighed. Was there anyone who wasn't talking about my non-existent relationship with Nick? Cedric and Arnaud must have mentioned our night on the rocks to half the country. And now they all thought I had a boyfriend back in the U.S. too. "Ah . . . no, but he's from Australia, not England. It's *langa fara*." Very far away. The younger woman said something in Saramakan and they giggled again, pointing at me.

"How old are you?" she asked.

"Twenty-five."

"*Soo.* So old. Why you not married?"

There were few things that could have pushed me to ask Hortense about Winti, but apparently, and surprisingly, my unmarried state was one of them. I turned to Hortense. "What did you mean when you told me about the *Takuu Akaa* my first day on Loiri Island?"

Another crash of lightning heralded the rain and I moved my bench under their protective plastic overhang. Hortense twisted a lock from her purple wig and motioned for me to come closer. When I hesitated, scared she was going to whisper in my ear again, she came toward me, her gnarled hands grabbing my head. We performed a tug of war until I finally offered her my ear, my hand firmly cupped over it. She patted my chest, whispering harshly, "Your *dyodyo,* she is with you. Here." I jerked back, knocking over my small wooden bench and falling onto the wet ground.

# CHAPTER 22

I had two more nightmares the following week, but I wasn't willing to believe Hortense's version of my problem, that my *dyodyo* was attached to me. I'd had to ask Melvijn about the *dyodyo* while we were out in the field since I didn't want Nick to overhear our conversation. He explained it was a guardian angel in the Winti religion and wanted to know why I was asking. I didn't tell him the truth for a variety of reasons, but primarily because I was still telling myself I didn't believe in spirits and ghosts. Well, not completely and not during the day. Besides, I had fiends more diabolical than nightmares to deal with in the lonely hours before daylight, namely chiggers. My skin grew red and raw from itching and my stomach was bumpy with welts. I longed for meds that actually worked, and spent hours fantasizing about ripping my skin to shreds. Rum seemed the only cure.

I finally had time to study the plant and monkey ID photos, and I began to feel more confident in the field. I was on my own now. Each morning we left camp by six-thirty, the day barely lit. I searched along damp paths covered in leaves a foot deep, machete out, keeping a careful eye on the ground and nose to the air so as not to step on a poisonous fer-de-lance or stumble into a herd of charging pingos. Pingos, or peccaries, as they're known outside Suriname, are similar to wild boars in appearance and roam in herds of up to 200 individuals.

"You'll smell them long before you see them," Nick assured

me one morning while we hiked to the study area with Melvijn. "They have massive scent glands on their backs that secrete a hellacious smell—like a dead body or decaying meat, but not quite as bad as our dunny. The smell marks territories and keeps herd cohesion, but they're also aggressive and dangerous. If you smell one, climb up a strong tree or on top of a big rock and stay there until you're sure they're gone."

"What if I don't have anything to climb?"

"Then run like hell," Nick said. "Run through brush if you can so they have to scatter. A herd chased Melvijn clear across the study area a few months ago. Brian and I found scattered pieces of his equipment for weeks along—"

"I had my revenge at dinner," Melvijn interrupted from behind. "Cedric brought us a pingo he'd killed that morning and we ate it for dinner—*switi!*"

I wasn't particularly successful in the field, at least not those first few days. Each morning I circled my designated paths, stopping every few feet to listen carefully for monkeys moving or calling in the distance, but the raucous screeching of macaws, parrots, and screaming pihas drowned out any other noise. The birds not only sounded like the monkeys, but they also dropped fruits and pods from high in the canopy—just like their primate friends.

One morning I triumphantly announced to Nick and Diane I'd found the Rangers. I couldn't see them—they were too high in a tree—but I was sure they were up there taunting me. Within seconds of arriving at my towering kapok tree, Nick informed me I'd in fact found four toucans. He and Diane gave each other a look I did not appreciate, and Diane thoughtfully suggested I try using my binoculars. I stomped off to continue searching.

Even with all the frustrations, I fell completely and irretrievably in love with the rainforest that week—the deep rich smells of dirt and decay and teeming, thriving life; the warm soft light of the rocky moss-covered paths hidden beneath layers of climbing and tumbling lianas and roots; soaring tree trunks wrapped in colorful bromeliads, orchids, moss, and lichens; and the canopy of leaves of every conceivable size and shape. Each day was a new adventure, new wildlife (some good, some terrifying) and ever changing forest, from the sunlit traveling palm groves to the dense, swampy marshes near the river; to the rocky, open forests with the towering trees the spider monkeys loved. I enjoyed watching the spider monkeys too, but I could have been just as happy watching any number of wildlife. It was simply being in the rainforest I loved most.

Relationships at camp were not great, although generally uneventful, and at least Diane didn't accuse me of stealing any of her stuff again. We didn't talk about Jack, which seemed strange since we talked about everything else. But no one else seemed interested the few times I tried. Nick complained about Melvijn being messy and not washing his dishes; and Diane, who was perpetually moody and jumpy, argued occasionally with Nick, although most of their arguments were over research issues and rather boring. Melvijn seemed excited and happy most of the time, spending his few hours off smoking with Diane or playing card games with me. Cedric didn't come around much, so I wasn't sure if they'd made up or not.

Diane and I acted friendly, but it was a show. We'd mostly decided to ignore each other, although she could be picky when it came to collecting data, and would often make me redo or clarify my notes at the end of the day, pointing out my mistakes in front of Nick and Melvijn.

Most nights were uneventful and routine. We arrived back from the field exhausted, washed and hung up our field clothes, showered, then ate and entered data before falling into an exhausted sleep. Even though I'd quit my malaria pills, the nightmares didn't go away. The rainy season had arrived and the rainstorms, violent and sudden, came each day. Water fell in a solid mass that beat down everything in its path. I was relieved our camp was located high on a hill, especially at night when I heard trees cracking and falling deep in the jungle.

The monkeys were not so lucky, and we had one suspected tragedy midweek. Julia and her baby disappeared. No one knew what happened. They both simply vanished the day after Alice left, and we weren't sure if they'd migrated to another troop, which Nick said was strange behavior for a mother with a baby, or if a harpy eagle or some other animal had made an attempt for the baby and harmed Julia in the process. We went to the harpy nest but didn't find any spider monkey bones, which gave Nick hope they would both reappear.

I woke on the morning Alice, Brian, and Rosie were arriving back from the city to an elephantine size rat scurrying across the attic. I climbed reluctantly out from under my mosquito net to investigate, opening my door to find feet and legs emerging from the hole in the roof and stepping down the ladder. Melvijn jumped the last couple of feet to the floor.

"What's in the attic?" I asked.

"I was looking for a soccer ball," he said. His answer didn't fit his defensive body language, but I dropped the subject since Diane and Nick had arrived from the other cabin to make breakfast. Melvijn disappeared into his room and after breakfast, Cedric, who'd stopped by the night before for the first time all week, came by to pick up Melvijn and Diane, who had volunteered to meet Alice's plane and carry supplies. According to Cedric, Kevin Schipper, Frank Van Landsberg, and Laura Taylor were also coming in on the same flight, although we weren't sure why. Nick didn't think it was worth his time to go to the island and was taking the day off to fish.

Bored, I decided it was time to clean out my now smelly

backpack. I started with the front flap. I reached into the main portion to grab my water bottle and felt an odd sensation. I yanked out my arm, staring at it in horror. It was a writhing black mass from elbow to fingers.

I raced for the shower, jumping in fully clothed, scratching, pulling, and slapping at my arm. My vision blurred and I turned cold and clammy. I grabbed hold of the shower shelf, watching the black clumps of tiny ants swirl into the drain. Stripping naked, I kicked my clothes away and continued to hold my arm under the water, rubbing it with soap. Still dizzy, I stumbled into the yard and grabbed my sarong off the line, just as Nick appeared, heading for the river and a day of fishing.

"Wow, what do I—what's wrong?" He looked at my arm. "Shit, what happened?"

"Ants. In my bag. I left some chips . . . I don't feel so good."

He grabbed my arm, walking me to a plastic lawn chair in front of the cabin. Eventually I stood up and tied the sarong above my chest. My arm was slightly red, but otherwise fine, but I was still shaking. I grabbed a can of bug spray off the shelf and pulled open my bag, spraying until a thick cloud fogged the cabin. I kept spraying until I'd killed every last ant. And quite a few brain cells.

Nick took me back to his room and applied lotion to my still shaking arm. He made me lie down on his bed and climbed in next to me, massaging my back. The massage worked, and I calmed down, finally drifting off to sleep. A plane passed overhead midday and I woke curled next to Nick. He was awake.

"Em," he whispered, his finger drifting down my cheek and neck, stopping at the top of the sarong. "I've been trying to resist. It's this sarong you're wearing. I'm only human." He slipped his hand into my hair, wrapping chunks around his fist, pulling me closer. "I keep telling myself to stay away, but I only have so much self-control." His other hand drifted over my shoulder and down my arm, teasing lightly, leaving goosebumps in its wake. "If only you'd stop your constant caresses, your incessant touching. It's really quiet unseemly, the way you've been throwing yourself at me."

"Bastard," I whispered, trying and failing to untie my sarong, "I'm not the slightest bit interested. I'm just humoring you, hoping for a sexual harassment lawsuit against you and Alice."

"You need to wear this more often." Nick pushed away my fingers to work on the sarong knot. "Although perhaps not so tightly. Damn, what kind of knot is this? I think I should use my teeth." He gave up on the knot, slipping the sarong open.

I held out my palm, stopping him mid-nuzzle. "Just as long as we're clear it's you who've lured me to your bed while I was incapacitated. I only surrendered because you promised drugs for my pain. And I want a codicil stipulating you're the one who's been doing all the caressing and fondling all week."

His slid my hand away. "Yes, yes, fine, I admit it." He trailed light kisses in the crook of my neck. "In fact, I baited your pack as the opening to an hour of depravity." His mouth closed over mine and I sank my hands into his hair.

We spent the next hour tangled together, forgetting about time and the other researchers. Until a motor roared on the river. By then I'd almost forgotten about the ants or pretty much anything that wasn't happiness and joy. I didn't want to go down to the beach to greet the boat, and I reluctantly followed Nick.

"We have to keep this a secret, Em," Nick announced as the canoe approached, releasing my hand.

"I've never been much good at following rules," I said.

"Em, I'm serious. Alice would fire me if she knew, and I don't want anyone feeling uncomfortable or claiming I favor you. It's not going to be easy. You'll probably get upset with me."

"No I won't," I promised. But it was already a lie, and I was already annoyed. It wasn't enough, those few hours alone together, and I resented all of them—Alice, Rosie, Brian, Melvijn, and Diane, and even Cedric—for intruding on my little piece of happiness. Cedric cut the engine on the canoe and hopped out to steady the boat. I watched them climb off the boat and unload the boxes of food, no one speaking. They seemed tense.

Alice grilled Nick about the monkeys as we hiked up the hill. Halfway up, Rosie, who must have gone shopping in the city, as she was now wearing a skintight hot-pink tube dress, leaned over to whisper, "Frank offered Melvijn the park manager job. Brian's, like, totally upset because Kevin promised him the job months ago."

# CHAPTER 23

"Once a month we visit each numbered tree and write down whether it's flowering or fruiting and whether there are any signs the fruits are being eaten by monkeys," Nick said, explaining the "phenology transect," or seasonal tree survey, we were conducting the next morning. We stopped and Nick pointed out our first tree, about five feet off the path and marked with a round metal tag and bright orange flagging tape. The tree did not appear to have any fruit or flowers. Even I was competent enough to recognize flowers and fruit. Or so I thought.

"What do you think?" Nick asked, letting me study the next tree while he nibbled the back of my neck. Luckily for him I'd skipped the bug spray that morning.

"You expect me to think while you're doing that?"

"Losing your multitasking skills are you?"

"I don't think I ever had any."

"I'll step away then. Do continue your perusal."

Disappointed, as I vastly preferred the kisses, I studied the tree's branches and circled the massive trunk, poking through the piles of dead leaves with my rubber boot. "No fruits or flowers."

"Sure about that?"

I pulled out my binoculars, studying the leaves and tree branches up close, noticing small dark nuts. They were the same color as the bark and barely distinguishable. I settled my binoculars back against my chest. "There's some sort of nut. I think. Does that count?"

"Yeah, that would count. I take it you've never had a botany class? Where did you say you went to school?"

"I had a perfectly decent education, thank you very much. Although maybe a little light on the sciences. I don't think I ever saw a botany class listed as an option. Not all of us can be blessed with a Cambridge education. It's certainly done you well with Alice if nothing else . . . Ouch! That hurt!" I added when he pinched me.

"My mother paid heaps of money for my degree. Show it some respect."

"Wait till we're in a city. I've got plenty of useful skills."

He didn't respond and I glanced up, realizing we would probably never visit a city together. That in six months, maybe less if IWC still kicked Alice out, we'd both go our separate ways. Nothing had really changed.

Despite that realization, it was still a wonderful morning, just the two of us. We were free to play and show affection without worrying about Alice, who had a morning meeting on Loiri Island and wasn't expected in the field. And the transects were far enough apart, spanning the entire study area, so there was no chance we would run into any of the other researchers who were all working alone. We took full advantage of that.

Although Nick did the rest of the tree surveys, he did assign me the leaf litter plots, not because there was much to learn, but because I suspected he didn't feel like crawling through the piles of rotting, decaying leaves looking for the tiny marker flags. My job was to measure the leaf litter at each marker by sticking a ruler into the ground and noting how high the dead leaves came up on the ruler. Then I held a hanger bent into a box shape to the sky and randomly decided the percentage of tree cover I saw through the square.

I can't say I enjoyed crawling around on my hands and knees

in the wet leaves and mud, knocking off ants and scorpions, but I did it in the name of science. What kind of science, I wasn't sure. I did ask, and Nick gave me a detailed explanation about the first incidence of yearly biological events and its importance for studying climate change on the monkeys. I didn't understand much, but then I was a little distracted digging spiders out of my cleavage.

At eleven, we finally remembered to turn on our radios and spoke to Brian and Diane, although we didn't hear anything from Rosie or Melvijn at the opposite end of the study site. Brian said they'd heard from Rosie at ten, but hadn't heard anything from Melvijn all morning, which wasn't strange since he was the farthest out. Nick had assigned Melvijn and Rosie the more difficult transects, which were farther away and muddy, as some sort of punishment—because Melvijn was leaving abruptly and taking what Nick felt was Brian's job, and because Rosie had annoyed him that morning with her nonstop chatter about her week in *Foto*.

We finished just before one in the afternoon and arrived back to an empty kitchen. We went down to the river after a lunch of ramen noodles and black tea, and I propped an inner tube on top of our submerged rock and floated in the cool brown river. The wispy clouds passed overhead, the afternoon light draping the jungle in soft green. My eyes drifted lazily over Nick while he shaved. He was propped on a chair in the river, holding a small mirror, his lean back muscles rippling with each soft drag of the razor. Life was wonderful; nothing to worry about; nothing important to accomplish. I wanted to stay forever in this exact moment. I was in love with Nick, I realized, and I didn't care what that meant for the future.

Rosie yelled from halfway up the hill, interrupting my daydreaming, "Have you seen Melvijn? His boots and backpack aren't on the porch. I don't think he came back from the field!"

She was still wearing her dirty clothes and looked like she'd just returned from the field herself.

"I'm sure he's back," I yelled, annoyed at the interruption. "He probably went fishing with Brian. Have you checked with him?"

Nick finished his shaving, wiping the razor and mirror in the river. "I'll check with Brian," he called. "I saw him a few minutes ago. He's upriver around the corner."

Rosie yelled back, "I went down the path to the other beach, but I didn't see anybody." She looked worried and serious too, a new and unexpected side of Rosie.

I followed Nick reluctantly out of the water, still sure everything was right with the world. We found Brian just upriver, but he was alone. He came back to the cabin with us, where we found Alice, Diane, and Rosie gathered around the kitchen table. No one had seen Melvijn come back or heard from him all day, including Rosie, who was last to see him when she left him on the Kasima trail that morning.

"He always forgets to turn on his radio, so I didn't worry about him not checking in," Diane said, even though Melvijn checking in wasn't her responsibility. She took a long sip of her ever-present canteen of coffee, her hands shaking.

I blushed, remembering Nick and I had forgotten to check in a few times ourselves, having been busy with other activities.

"I thought I heard him in his room when we first came back," I said. "He was moving boxes, but he didn't come out for lunch. Maybe he got back earlier and left with Cedric."

"Alice," Nick said, "what time did you get back from the island? Did you notice if Melvijn was around?"

"Cedric dropped me off around noon," Alice said. "I was on the beach when he left and then went up and took a nap. I didn't see Melvijn anywhere."

"What about a tourist boat?" Diane asked.

Alice shook her head. "There weren't any tourists on the island. Just the IWC goons."

"We have to search for him," Rosie said, on the verge of hysteria. "Something has happened to him. I can feel it!"

"Calm down, Rosie," Nick said. "He may have decided to finish his whole area. Although he should have told us, and it's already five o'clock. You'd think he'd be back by now."

"He's not exactly known for taking on extra work," Alice said. She turned to Brian, who'd been quiet through the exchange. "Sorry, Brian, but you know it's true." Brian looked at the kitchen floor and didn't respond.

Alice touched his arm. "Sweetie, I talked to Kevin about the park manager job today. He said Frank never even told him he was going to offer it to Melvijn. He was pretty upset about the whole situation. But really, it's for the best. We're going to get you to Michigan this year. I promise."

Nick turned on the radio, calling Melvijn, but there was no response. He rubbed his neck. "Damn. Okay. Put on your field clothes again and grab a flashlight and water. We'll meet on the beach in ten minutes."

Nick was blowing the foghorn when I arrived at the beach with Rosie and Diane just behind me. Alice and Brian were already there too, Alice digging in the dirt while Brian paced nearby.

"Nick, let Emma take care of that," Brian said as soon as Rosie and Diane arrived. "We need to search."

Nick handed me the foghorn. "Em, since you speak Sranan and don't know the trails very well, we think you should stay here and keep blowing the foghorn until someone comes from the damn island. We're going to search on the east side, the area Melvijn was covering. If Cedric comes, tell him what happened and send him back to get all the men on the island. Got it?" He swung his pack on his back then stopped when Alice turned back.

"Sweetie," Alice said. "When Cedric comes, go with him to the island and make sure he radios Gum Air. We need a plane on standby. Just in case."

I nodded, close to tears, thinking of all the things that could go wrong. The jungle didn't seem so beautiful anymore. I continued blowing the foghorn as the group disappeared into the dark forest, then turned to the river to wait.

# CHAPTER 24

Cedric arrived within ten minutes, and we sped back to Loiri Island, the rapids having transformed during the past week by the rising water into a wide, expansive river. Cedric hopped out to round up the men on the island and make sure Melvijn wasn't around somewhere. I raced up the hill to Tigrikati, the lodge's worn wooden steps barely visible under the shade of the trees. I nearly collided with Kevin, who was coming down the stairs.

"We heard the foghorn," he said. "I've been worried. What happened?"

"It's Melvijn. He's missing. He hasn't come back from the field. Everyone else is out looking for him right now. Alice said we should radio Gum Air too, and ask them to have a plane ready."

"I'll change quickly and go over to the radio room. I think they keep a plane ready for emergencies."

I followed him up the stairs to the wide porch. Laura and Frank were there, Frank sitting at a small wooden table with an ashtray and a half-empty bottle of rum. Kevin explained the situation and then disappeared into the lodge.

Frank looked drunk, but Laura was leaning against the porch railing and gazing across the river at the sun setting in the distance.

"Are you coming?" I asked her.

She jerked around. "Coming to what?"

"To search for Melvijn."

Her eyes flitted to her flip-flops and slacks, her flimsy tank top. "I . . . I'm not really dressed. Or qualified. I'm sure I wouldn't be any help." She frowned. "Are you sure about Melvijn? Couldn't he have . . ." She trailed off, looking confused and a little scared.

"We don't know anything yet. But he should have been back ages ago."

"Don't worry about Melvijn," Frank slurred. "He can take care of himself. He's good at that."

"When did he disappear?" Laura asked. "What happened?"

"We don't know. We haven't heard from him all day. Rosie noticed he hadn't come back this afternoon. Around four."

Laura drummed her red nails along the porch railing. "Rosie noticed, huh? She's the silly redhead?"

"I wouldn't say she was silly . . . exactly."

She didn't say anything else, but followed Kevin into the lodge, leaving me alone with Frank. He stood up and stumbled toward me, grabbing hold of my shoulder. Strong alcohol fumes hit me as he leaned in to whisper, "Diane told me about the lies you're spreading. But I know all about you. Sergeant Lam told me about your friend Sonia, that her husband went to the police claiming you killed her. But no one would believe him. But maybe they'll believe him now. With Jack dead. Who's next, Melvijn?"

I slapped him and he staggered back, just as Kevin and Laura returned to the porch.

"What's going on?" Kevin demanded, his accusing eyes turning to Frank.

Frank seemed to shake himself awake. "Nothing," he muttered in Dutch and stumbled into the lodge.

"Are you okay?" Kevin asked.

"Fine," I said. "I'd like to go. Are you ready?"

"Please forgive Frank," Laura said. "He's been under a lot of stress since Jack's death. We all are."

"Fuck Frank and his bottle of rum," Kevin said. "Emma, go wait on the rocks. I'll be down in a few minutes."

I raced down the lodge stairs and across the wide grassy lawn, not stopping until I reached the rocks and Cedric's dugout canoe. The sky rumbled and burst open, the rain pouring down as I shivered alone on the rocks. How dare Frank accuse me . . . who did he talk to? Sonia's husband? Was he back from Holland? I knew he blamed me; he'd said so, that one horrible day at the funeral, but to go to the police? For what? Did he actually think I'd killed her? Strung her from the roof . . . I clasped my hands around my knees and rocked. *Don't think about that. Don't think about that.* I looked over my shoulder. What was taking everyone so long?

It *had* been partly my fault. She'd come to me looking for help. How could I not have told her the truth? My truth anyway. I jumped up to pace across the rock. But how could I have known she would do that? It wasn't—*Don't think about it. Don't think about it.*

I heard the men approaching. Finally.

Kevin was the first one down. "Are you okay? What did Frank say to you? Did it have anything to do with overhearing Jack firing him?"

"I . . . I don't know. Maybe, probably. I don't want to talk about it. Are we ready to go back?"

"Yeah, we're taking two boats. Climb in." He sat next to me on the bench. "The invitation's always open. If you ever need to talk."

"Thanks," I mumbled, staring out at jungle as we sped downstream, a white mist drifting off the darkening river.

The sun was gone by the time we reached camp and set out along the Kasima trail in the dark, a terrifying task even with flashlights and eight men crowding the trail. But I was glad to be searching. It was better to have something to do, than to wait and wonder. To think.

We met Nick and Alice on the Jaguar trail and divided into groups of two to search in the falling rain. I was with Cedric, his voice booming, "Mellll . . . vijn," through the rainy forest followed by the thump of the flat edge of his machete against a buttress root, the sound echoing through the dark. I concentrated on staying close to Cedric, who was moving quickly and not concerned about whether I kept up. Our flashlights seemed insignificant against the pitch black of the canopy, and the forest roared with strange and unknown noises. It seemed impossible we could find Melvijn in the pounding black rain.

Something fluttered against my cheek and I jumped, remembering the venomous bushmaster snake, which hunts at night by leaping through the air. A tree fell in the distance, but Cedric kept going, crossing a barely passable creek, which was normally ankle deep but now reached my waist. I thought we should turn around, but he plowed ahead, wading into the thick black water, holding his machete and radio over his head. I had no choice but to follow, occasionally holding on to the back of his shirt for support.

Our boots were soon full of water, but still he didn't stop, not until Alice's voice crackled over the radio, ordering everyone back to camp. She said there was still no sign of Melvijn, but it was too dangerous to keep searching in the nonstop deluge.

Rosie was yelling at Alice and Nick for deserting Melvijn when we arrived back at the beach, a destination I hadn't been so sure I would ever see again. Nick, demonstrating more patience than Alice, who was simply ignoring Rosie, took her up to the cabin and put her to bed while the rest of the returning searchers gathered by the river. We huddled together, watching Cedric, who'd had the foresight to bring fireworks. He lit a bottle rocket under a traveling palm and jumped back when the streaks shot out of his hand, the explosions briefly lighting the night sky and dark river. We all hoped Melvijn would see the fireworks and find his way back to the camp, although if the rain continued, he wouldn't be able to follow the Kasima trail until the water went down. I watched the exploding stars fizzle and die, tears rolling down my cheeks. Brian was silent next to me, but I could tell he was upset.

"Are you okay?" I asked, touching his shoulder.

"What will I tell his grandmother? I saw her in *Foto* two days ago. She told me to take care of him, to protect him. She's afraid of the jungle and was worried about him out here." Brian's shoulders shook under my outstretched arm. I didn't tell him I thought Melvijn would be okay. I didn't want to lie.

Alice joined us, taking Brian's hand. "He'll be fine. He's a tough guy, and he knows how to survive out there. He's just lost. Why don't you try and get some sleep?" She pulled him up the hill and I followed them back to the cabin.

I don't think any of us slept well, except maybe Rosie, who was snoring in the bunk bed next to me. I tossed and turned as the storm grew more violent. Eventually I drifted somewhere between consciousness and dreaming, imagining Frank chasing Melvijn through a creek, a bright green tree viper wrapped tightly around his bloodstained neck.

We met again at daylight to continue the search, the rain taking a break. Kevin and the men from the island joined us, along with Frank this time. Everyone searched alone so we could cover more space and hear signs of movement off trail. I was supposed to follow the length of a rocky creek passing through Melvijn's pheno-transect at the very edge of the study site. The morning was dark and damp, and the rarely used paths were overgrown. I kept a slow pace, sticking close to the water so as not to get lost, jumping each time an animal fled through the bushes or a branch snapped in the distance.

I swung my machete half-heartedly at a branch and stopped. Monkeys were chattering up ahead. I crept closer. A troop of brown capuchins were gorging themselves on an arripa palm's long yellow fruit, too busy eating to feel threatened. A capuchin, barely more than a baby, jumped into the tree above to watch me, her round eyes and ears moving inquisitively under her sharp widow's peak. Her tree bounced and I caught my breath—a massive, horned capuchin had landed above the baby, baring his teeth in a threatening gesture. The baby swung away and the angry capuchin jumped to the ground, just as a train seemed to roar through the jungle. The troop shrieked in terror and scrambled away.

Confused, I crouched, tensed and terrified as the jungle shifted dizzily. I looked up, watching powerless as a hundred foot tree teetered drunkenly above, slowed only by the attached lianas and neighboring trees. Just when I thought I might be safe, it exploded in a shower of leaves and branches. I dove for the water, grabbing for the rocky bottom and letting the water out of my lungs. The creek shuddered and turned dark.

I came up gasping for air, the water cold and riddled with wreckage from the gigantic tree now straddling the creek bank above my head. I coughed up water and stumbled toward the rocky bank, catching my breath in horror.

Lifeless eyes stared up from under a tangle of roots dangling over the creek bank. A flash of green slithered over the body and disappeared beneath the water.

# CHAPTER 25

I scrambled for the creek bank and threw myself over the muddy edge, ignoring the branches ripping at my clothes and face. Back on land, I sank to my knees and turned on my radio. I yelled, between gasps of air, for Nick and Brian, who I thought were closest to me, but no one responded.

I studied the dark, wet jungle, wondering where to turn for help. A branch snapped nearby and my heart stopped. Soft footsteps in the wet muddy leaves crept nearer. I wrenched my machete from its holster and jumped up screaming. Whatever or whoever it was made a hurried retreat through the wet brush, but I kept my machete out, my back to the creek. The jungle held its breath, waiting.

The forgotten radio crackled to life at my feet and I jumped again.

"Emma, where are you?" Nick asked.

I grabbed the radio from the pile of dead leaves, flipping it on. "I found him," I answered, breathless and so relieved tears were running down my face. "He's dead. A tree fell on me, but I'm okay. I'm on the edge of Sneki Creek, near . . . damn . . . let me look at the map." I yanked out my map folder and the attached pen swung loose, dangling from its string. I grabbed for it and missed. I grabbed again, catching it and ripping it off in annoyance, cutting my hand on the string. I studied my wet map, ignoring the pain in my hand, the blood dripping onto the plastic cover. "I'm on the southeast corner of the map. Right before it ends. I'll keep screaming." And I did.

Nick arrived first, breathless but calm. He shook me. "Em, you can stop now. Please—stop!"

I laughed, somewhat hysterically.

"Where is he, Em?"

I pointed to the tree straddling the creek. "He's under there, but I'm not going back down, there's a tree viper in the water. I think the viper killed him. Frank's right. Everybody keeps dying around me." Tears rolled down my muddy cheeks.

Nick stared at me confused, then wiped the blood mixed with tears off my face with his handkerchief. I looked down at my muddy, bleeding hands, everything now in slow motion. I remembered the falling tree, the water, the climb up the creek bank. Nick kissed my forehead, holding me for a moment in his arms. He murmured something calming, his hand resting softly on my muddy hair. I thought about his poor white shirt, probably now covered in blood and mud from rubbing against me. "What were you doing in the creek?" he asked. "Jesus Christ, is that the tree that fell?"

I nodded. "I dove into the creek. That's what saved me."

"Fucking hell." He squeezed tighter. "You seem to attract dang—"

"Excuse me?" I said, my head still resting against his chest. "You're blaming me for the tree fall?"

He rubbed my neck. "Jesus, Emma, that's not what I meant. Trees fall all the time. I just want you to be careful, that's all. God, you're a difficult woman. You're torture—" He set me gently away. "Why don't you sit down?" He unfolded his metal stool, but I didn't sit.

I touched his chest. "Sorry about the stains. I like this shirt. You look like a pirate."

He grabbed my hand, rubbing it against his heart and lifting it to kiss my wrist.

A "whoo" echoed through the jungle and Nick dropped my hand. A minute later Brian came crashing through the trees.

"Where is he?" he asked, scanning the jungle.

Nick pointed to the tree trunk but held on to Brian to prevent him from jumping into the creek. "Let's try and reach Alice or Kevin before we go down. We're going to need to cut away some of the trunk and branches."

He clicked on his radio. "Anyone out there? Alice? Kevin?"

Kevin came on the radio.

"We've found him," Nick said. "He's dead. It's best you come with Cedric, since you're closer and send everyone else back to camp to wait." He gave Kevin instructions on finding the spot.

I collapsed on the stool, staring at the river while Nick and Brian began cutting away the branches and massive trunk so we could reach Melvijn, their muscles rippling with each swing of a machete. I was confused, moving in a fog. My mind jumped erratically, never settling on any one thought, but never far from the vision of Melvijn's dead eyes staring up from under the tangled roots.

I didn't notice the rustling until three tiny armadillos emerged from the covering shrub, wandering aimlessly, their long noses digging through the dirt at my feet, even sniffing my boots. They seemed unaware two men were nearby, machetes in hand. I watched them root in the pile of dead leaves and then disappear back into the brush. I didn't move. Time was still.

I jumped, startled by the snapping fingers waving in front of my face. "I know you're in shock and all," Nick announced, crouched in front of me, "and I do sympathize, but get a grip. No lazy chicks allowed. Got that?" He pulled on my arm. "Come on, get up and help."

"Kev—" Brian said.

Nick cut him off. "Melvijn was practically your brother. If you can handle it, so can she."

Anger woke me from my self-pity and I pushed myself up, shoving Nick away. I wobbled and Nick grabbed my arm. I looked around, realizing I'd lost a fragment of time while sitting there perched on the metal stool. Nick and Brian had already finished cutting through the tree and were pulling off branches. I pointed at Nick. "You told me to sit down."

"I know, darling, but I was getting a little worried about you. You weren't focusing. Here take this." Ever the romantic, he dumped a pile of branches in my arm and pushed me away from the river. I stumbled toward the trees, barely dodging his swinging machete when he went back to work on the trunk.

By the time Kevin arrived with Cedric, the creek bank was clear. Nick, Brian, and Kevin climbed into the creek and Cedric cut down several small trees. I stayed on the bank, keeping myself busy collecting palm fronds to fasten Cedric's tree trunks into a stretcher. Frank eventually arrived too, yelling orders into the creek bed, which everyone ignored.

Frank put a hand on my shoulder. "Sorry you had to find him. Why do you not sit down? Why are you carrying trees?" He yelled at Cedric in Dutch, but Cedric just shrugged his shoulders and kept working on the stretcher.

Kevin climbed out of the creek bank, noticing us talking. He walked over, turning to Frank. "Did you apologize?"

"I'm fine," I said, although I was anything but that. I just wanted to be left alone for a few minutes to sort myself out. To try and think clearly and figure out what was happening. I needed to do that somewhere far away from Frank, who both scared and repelled me, despite his feigned concern.

Kevin frowned. "I might not know exactly what happened last night, but I do know Frank owes you an apology for whatever he said to upset you. If for nothing else than for his drinking."

Frank puffed out his chest, turning bright red. He looked

livid, but his hate appeared to be aimed at Kevin.

"Frank," Kevin said.

"I am sorry for whatever I said last night," Frank said. "I do not recall exactly what it might have been. But if I offended you, I am deeply sorry."

He walked away and I let out my breath. I actually believed that he didn't remember what he'd said, but he still knew about Sonia. He knew her husband blamed me for her death. And more: what I hadn't known, that her husband had gone to the police with his accusations. I wobbled again. Kevin grabbed my arm, pulling me to the chair.

He was kneeling in front of me, his hand resting on my knee when Nick emerged from the creek bed, eyeing us with a questioning lift of his eyebrow.

"We're ready," Nick called to Kevin.

Kevin joined them in pulling Melvijn's body out of the creek. I kept my eyes focused in the opposite direction. They were quick and set him on the makeshift stretcher. They'd found Melvijn's backpack under his body, and Frank carried it as we hiked back to camp. I stayed at the back of the line during the hike, although Frank kept offering for me to move in front of him. He probably thought it was unchivalrous for me to walk in the back.

The jungle crept closer and I stumbled along the path, desperate not to fall behind. The trees now appeared menacing and practiced at concealing danger. It wasn't the jungle I was afraid of, though. I was wrong about Melvijn. The tree viper didn't kill him. It couldn't slice a gash from ear to ear. More likely a machete. A man with a machete.

# CHAPTER 26

"Nonsense," Alice said, gulping her rum and *stroop* mix on the porch overlooking the river. "We're not going to the island. How dare *you* insinuate we had anything to do with this." She glared at a defiant Cedric.

"It is safer together. To wait for police." Cedric's eyes darted between us. He looked angry, as if he thought one of us had killed Melvijn. I was more concerned about his own role in Melvijn's death, remembering the fight between him and Melvijn the week before. But then I remembered how relentless Cedric had been the night before while searching for Melvijn, and I couldn't believe he'd done it. Unless it had been guilt that kept him searching.

"We're staying here," Alice said again, dismissing Cedric. She returned to patting Brian's hand, chatting cheerfully about her new agreement with IWC, which she said they were close to signing. It seemed a strange topic of conversation, but given the circumstances I assumed she was trying to distract Brian, to keep him from thinking about Melvijn.

Rosie was not in much better shape than Brian. She was staring at the river, hiccupping softly and watching the afternoon sun shimmer on a brilliant blue morpho butterfly flitting between the railings.

Eventually, Nick joined us on the balcony. "Alice, they're insisting we return to the island tonight. Cedric says you're refusing."

Alice harrumphed.

"Cedric was just following Kevin's orders," Nick said.

"This is ridiculous. They're interrupting my work. They have no right. The police can come here. We'll cooperate fully. I don't see why we need—"

"Alice," Nick pleaded. "Don't you think it's best we don't make waves? Given the circumstances? Melvijn worked for us. It looks bad."

Alice finally gave in and we bunked again in the Anyumara lodge, the same place we'd stayed the night Jack West died. I dropped my bag and went to sit by the river. My head was beginning to clear, and I was thinking too much. My mind had moved on from Frank and was now circling around the thought that one of us had killed Melvijn. It wasn't possible, I kept telling myself.

Sure, Rosie was justifiably mad at him, but could she slice a machete through his neck? And Brian? Maybe he was upset about the job, but they'd been friends since childhood. And what reason did Diane have to kill Melvijn? They didn't act like they were involved, despite that day I'd caught him coming out of her room. And if they were, they'd always seemed friendly, although maybe she'd caught him flirting with Laura. But even with my dislike of Diane, that didn't seem like a very good motive for killing anyone.

Kevin, his head glistening in the afternoon sun, slid onto the bench next to me and we watched the river surge past in silence for a long time until I finally turned to face his steady blue eyes. "Do you think one of us killed Melvijn?"

"No. I don't. But be careful what you say to the police. They may have their own agenda."

"So who killed him then?"

He rubbed his forehead and looked over the river, seeming

tense. "I don't know, but there seem to be a lot of rumors flying around."

"Like what?"

He cleared his throat. "I . . . maybe I should warn you that some of the workers seem to think you're jinxed. Or something like that. There've been two deaths since you arrived—"

"They think I killed Jack and Melvijn?"

"No, no, I didn't say that. No one's saying you killed them. It's just . . ."

"What?" I asked. "Is it Frank?"

He frowned. "I don't think it's Frank. I hadn't thought about that. But it seems to be the workers. They think maybe you brought an evil spirit out here. I know it sounds crazy, and I don't quite understand it, but I thought you should be warned. It won't matter to the police of course. They need proof. But sometimes even a rumor can . . . you know. You've been here long enough."

"I'm scared," I said, realizing Hortense must have told everyone on the island about the spirit she thought I was dragging around. What if the police were superstitious too? Or worse, what if they were listening to Frank?

Kevin reached over and patted my hand. "I spoke to Alice. It took some convincing, but she's agreed you should all come into town until this is sorted out. I know you probably have friends there, but if you'd like, you can stay at my house with the rest of the group. It's big, and everybody else will be there, although Brian will probably want to stay at his own house. We'll figure this out. If we don't, you won't come back here. Okay?"

I thought about Nick, and somehow the idea of not coming back, of having to say goodbye, frightened me almost as much as thinking about who'd killed Melvijn.

Kevin and I were still watching the river when Nick came

down to tell me dinner was ready. Kevin rested his hand on my shoulder as we turned to follow Nick up the short hill, a touch that did not go unnoticed by Nick. We stopped at the break in the paths and Kevin said, "Will you be okay tonight?"

I nodded, trying hard not to tear up. "I'm feeling better."

"I'm at Tigrikati if you need me."

"Thanks."

Kevin turned down the path, leaving us.

"That was a touching scene."

"He's just being kind, Nick."

"I haven't noticed him being so concerned about Diane or Rosie."

"You're the one who wants to keep our relationship a secret. It's hardly fair to get mad when another man is being nice to me simply because a few short hours ago I discovered a friend's murdered body in a jungle creek. Right after a hundred-foot tree nearly squished me into subatomic particles."

"You're not the only one who's upset. He was like a brother to Brian."

"Yeah, I get that all your sympathy's with Brian. But I'm not asking for your compassion or approval, I'm just explaining Kevin's actions. And if you have a problem with his flirting, then step up and tell him we're together. Or whatever it is we happen to be. I certainly don't know."

"Emma, this isn't the time for—"

I took a deep breath. "I know, but I'm a little stressed at the moment."

"Sorry too," Nick said, still not touching me or comforting me the way Kevin had so easily.

I followed him back to the lodge, where we ate dinner in silence. A light breeze drifted off the river. No tourists passed. The island was empty. Even the workers avoided us. I finished my rice and brown beans first, impatient with the scraping silverware and Brian's sniffles. I'd become inappropriately wound up and tired of all of the secrets, of no one wanting to discuss openly what was happening. Especially if I was the one being blamed.

"We have to talk about this," I finally said. "We can't keep hiding from it, hoping it will magically go away." My voice echoed across the porch, hanging in the silence above the table. I glanced at the anxious faces, realizing I'd experienced a similar scene already, right after Jack's death.

"Emma," Nick said, shaking his head, but I ignored him.

"Are we all going to sit around and act like nothing happened? Somebody killed Melvijn. What if his death is connected to Jack's?"

Brian jumped up, knocking against the table. He stared at me, his mouth gaping, then walked out, disappearing across the dark lawn.

"Great job, Em," Nick said. "He just found his best friend, practically his brother, hacked open with a machete, and you want to breezily discuss it over dinner like it's a joke or something?"

"I . . . I . . . didn't—"

"You need to shut your big fat mouth," Diane interrupted. "You never think of anyone but yourself. Alice's stupid little dilettante. You think you can waltz in here and tell us what we should think? None of us wanted you here in the first place. You're a useless thief. You can't even tell a capuchin from a squirrel monkey, much less—"

"Enough, Diane!" Alice said. "You should all go to bed. Everyone's exhausted."

"I'm going to find Brian," Nick said, leaving the rest of us at the table.

I wasn't surprised at the venom from Diane, but I was hurt by Nick's indifference.

"You're a jealous bitch," Rosie told Diane.

"Rosie, stay out of it," Alice said.

But Rosie grabbed the bottle of rum from the table and pulled my arm. "Let's go, Em."

"I can't believe Diane," I said, after we climbed down to the rocks. "What did I ever do to her?"

"Don't you know? You're clueless." She laughed. "Diane's been after Nick since she arrived. I don't know. They might have gotten together before I came. But I guess after, like, whatever happened between them, she decided she hated him. Maybe because of his girlfriend in Australia. She's been reporting bad things about him to Alice ever since, but Alice makes up her own mind. And you and Nick haven't fooled anybody. Diane's just jealous."

"I don't believe it," I said, referring to her thinking Nick and Diane had hooked up.

"It's true! She acts all snotty and prissy, but she's after every guy out here."

"Maybe you're right, but I still don't understand why everyone is so afraid to talk about Melvijn. Doesn't anyone want to know the truth?"

"It's easier for you. You didn't know Melvijn very well. For you it's more of, like, an academic puzzle than something real."

"That's not true. I mean, I know I didn't really know him, not like you did, but it's not just academic to me. I liked Melvijn, even if he was pretty creepy about women."

Suddenly it hit me, what Rosie had said, and I collapsed onto the hard rock. "What did you mean, about Nick's girlfriend in Australia?"

She laughed. "You mean he never told you about her? Men!" She paused, letting that sink in. "She's on TV and does lots of wildlife documentaries back in Australia."

I felt sick to my stomach. It was too much, finding Melvijn

and now this. Rosie noticed my distress and squatted next to me on the rock. "Hey, maybe they broke up." She patted my shoulder. "Who knows? But when I first got out here, Nick talked about her all the time. He even said she might come out to visit. I've noticed he hasn't mentioned her lately, not since you arrived. I can't believe he didn't say anything to you. I just thought maybe you two had an understanding . . ."

# Chapter 27

The whitewashed clapboard house rose amidst a thick grove of palm, papaya, and shade trees, forming a fortress against the heat and noise of Paramaribo. A cozy porch with ferns and hanging flowers enclosed the front of the house, white curtains billowing from the open windows with dark green shutters. We followed Kevin up the faded green staircase, the wooden boards creaking under our weight when we settled on the balcony's couch and chairs.

Alice, who'd been in the taxi with us, had asked to be dropped at the American Embassy, but the rest of us were there: Nick leaning forward in his chair, his chin propped on clasped hands; Rosie, next to me on the couch, hunched over, her arms wrapped around her stomach; Diane, on my other side, straight, her feet flat on the balcony floor.

Kevin faced us, his back against the balcony railing, "I know each of you already spoke to the police on Loiri Island this morning." He paused and cleared his throat. "I imagine it's hard to speak to the police when you're in a foreign country, scared your friend's been murdered, and worried about what justice might be like here. What your rights are. I've already spoken to Alice about this, but I want you to know you should feel free to come to me if there's something you're holding back, something you might know, something you saw . . . Whatever it is, maybe even something you haven't thought of yet. It can be completely confidential. Even if it means you . . .

ah . . . um, you need help from the embassy. Come and talk to me."

I shifted restlessly, trapped between Rosie and Diane. Hadn't Kevin said he didn't suspect us? What had changed? I peeked a glance at Nick, his knuckles clenched in tight balls under his chin as he stared toward the river. I followed his gaze across the busy street to where a Maroon family was squatting in an abandoned, half-built adobe structure. Past the adobe, on the brown river, a decrepit fishing boat chugged along, black smoke billowing from its engine. Could Kevin have invited us to stay with him just to watch us? To keep all the suspects in one place? Or was it just me he wanted to watch?

A massive white cat jumped into my lap and I nearly screamed in fright.

"That's Kiwi," Kevin said. "She moved in a few weeks ago. I hope none of you are allergic."

"Mate, seriously?" Nick said. "Kiwi? Who picked out that name?"

I didn't wait for an answer. I passed the cat to Nick and jumped off the couch, needing to get away from everyone. I couldn't think clearly. "I'm going out to do e-mail and buy a cell phone card," I said. I grabbed my khaki satchel from the wooden floor and swung the strap over my chest.

"It's late," Kevin called. "How are you going to get into town?"

"I'll grab a bus on Anton Drachtenweg."

"I think you should stay here . . ." But I was already out the open gate and turning toward the river.

It didn't take long to catch a mini-bus to downtown, but it was after four on a Saturday, and the shops had closed for the day. I stopped at the Internet café, the only business open, to read e-mails. I didn't answer any. I wasn't sure what I could possibly say at that point and left the café after only an hour, wandering on to the hostel Peace Corps volunteers stayed at while in town. I was hoping to find someone unrelated to Kasima to talk to, but the gates were locked, and the building empty except for the manager. I turned back toward the central bus stop, ignoring the men across the street yelling propositions first in Dutch, then in English, then switching to French as they tried to pin down my nationality.

The mini-bus chugged out of the plaza on the edge of the Suriname River and swerved through downtown's tight streets lined with whitewashed colonial buildings. We turned north, passing the presidential palace and palm garden, a relentless mix of reggae, hip-hop, dancehall, and Hindi music blasting from the small radio. I still wasn't feeling great, but a couple more hours away from Kasima had helped me put at least a small part of my situation into perspective. Nick hadn't lied to me, and he certainly never promised me anything. In fact, quite the opposite. I'd have to talk to him and then decide what to do next. Besides, maybe Rosie was wrong.

The bus slid to a stop, and a Javanese woman and her kids jostled me on their way off the bus. I watched them cross the circular driveway of a local hotel. The hotel's wooden double doors bounced open, and Laura Taylor stepped out, looking striking as usual in a loose white skirt and a low-cut, lace top. She stopped and turned. A man followed her out, twirling her and placing a quick kiss on her lips. They skipped around the side of a taxi, both laughing, Laura's hand tucked firmly into the crook of Nick's arm.

The bus pulled away. I twisted, straining to watch them climb into a shiny SUV.

Nick and Rosie were both on the porch when I arrived back at Kevin's house, although Nick looked like he'd just settled in.

"Guess who called me while you were gone?" Rosie asked as

soon as I arrived at the top of the stairs.

"Who?" I asked automatically and Nick groaned.

"That psychopath, Arnaud. He threatened me again."

"Did you give him the bloody photo?" Nick asked.

"No. But I'm not giving it to him now. I'm keeping it to protect myself."

"Rosie, you are not keeping that damn photo. He'll leave you alone if you just give it back to him. You're acting like a silly little girl."

"I'm not. Mel—" Her voice caught and her eyes filled with tears. "Melvijn told me to keep it and I'm going to." Her voice rose. "You're so mean. I don't care what you say. You don't understand. You don't even believe—" She collapsed into loud sobs.

Nick dropped his head into his bunched fingers, yanking at his hair. Under his breath I could hear him counting and muttering. "Ten, nine, eight . . . Don't strangle her, bad form, and the last couple of hours were going so well, take a deep breath. She's got a few kangaroos loose in the top paddock. She can't help it. Six, five, four . . . That's good. Another deep breath."

Rosie continued sobbing in between dramatic heaves. I kneeled next to her, patting her head. And despite my own anger at Nick, I said, "You're okay, Rosie. Don't listen to Nick. He didn't mean it. He was just joking. You know how he is."

Nick raised his head, rolling his eyes. But it worked. Rosie was already wiping off her tears and sitting up. She watched Nick, still wary.

Nick sighed. "Fine, I didn't mean it. I'm sorry, Rosie."

Rosie blossomed, even with what could barely be termed an apology from Nick, much less a compliment. She leaned forward, wiping away her possibly fake tears and smiling. "Guess what?"

He leaned back, spreading his arms along the top of the

couch cushions. "Surprisingly, I'm going to let you tell me, Rosie. You've caught me in a rare generous mood." He smiled at me, but I looked away.

Rosie jumped up, pulling down her short skirt. "Remember the boyfriend I told you about? The married one? He arrived last night. I had an e-mail waiting from him. I was thinking maybe he could come back to Kasima. He wants to cleanse the cabins of spirits."

Nick buried his face in his hands again. "I don't—"

"Oh, Nick, please!"

"No."

"Please!"

"Fine, maybe when Alice leaves. But that's not for another week. And no cleansing of cabins!"

Rosie gave him a hug and ran inside the house, leaving me alone with Nick.

He and Laura had passed me as I climbed off the bus, not even stopping to offer me a ride in the falling rain. Although, to be honest, they probably hadn't seen me. But I knew why he was in such a good mood. Over Laura.

"Where'd you run off to?" he asked me.

I glared, barely able to bring myself to respond. "Just went in to buy a phone card and see if any Peace Corps volunteers are in town."

"Yeah? Anyone in particular?"

"No one was around," I said, rather than answering his question.

"We put you in a room with Rosie. Hope you don't mind." He pointed down the porch. "Last window on the end, although you have to access it through the living room and down the hallway. Hey Rosie, you down there? Stick out your head."

Rosie peeked out, waving from the end of the porch.

"Okay," I said, not sure what else to say to Nick, especially with listening ears.

"Speaking of phone cards, your friend Ramesh called Kevin trying to get hold of you earlier."

"Oh?" I said, trying to convey indifference. "What'd he say?"

"Besides the breathless moaning, disbelief, and horror over what happened to Melvijn?"

I tried a smile, but it may have come out as more of a grimace.

"Said he's coming by shortly to take us out for drinks. He wants to hear all the details."

"Did you invite Diane?"

"Yes," he answered, sensing my rising anger. "I told both Rosie and Diane, and Alice too. Do you not want us to come? Everybody's edgy. I thought it would be nice for us to get out. Diane—"

"No!" I said, a little too loud and lowered my voice. "I need time away from you all. If you want to go out, go on your own. You can't come with Ramesh."

"Where's this coming from? He invited all of us—"

"No!"

Nick shook his head, making me feel like a three-year-old throwing a tantrum. "Look, I'm sorry—"

I didn't listen to the rest of the sentence. Instead, I raced past him and into the house.

Rosie was lying on her bed in our shared room, her jaw hanging open.

"I guess you overheard. I don't mind if you come, Rosie, but I'm not sitting around all evening with Nick and Diane when I've spent the whole day trying to get away from them." I yanked off my dusty shorts and t-shirt and grabbed jeans and a black tank top from my bag, pulling them on.

"You're being too hard on Nick."

"I don't think so. I'm going outside to wait for Ramesh." I stomped down the hallway, crossed the now empty porch and sat on the front steps.

Ramesh took his time. Twilight settled in, and still I was wait-ing, tapping my foot impatiently, alone in the dark, wishing I'd tried harder to find a phone card. A door squeaked open above. The wooden planks creaked rhythmically as footsteps crept across the porch and down the stairs. A hand tapped me on the shoulder and I turned around, expecting Nick.

# Chapter 28

Instead it was Alice. "Ramesh called. He can't make it, but we're all going out anyway with Kevin. You coming?"

I stood up, noticing the rest of the group was just behind her on the porch. "Sure," I said, realizing I'd lost the fight. Besides, during my long wait in the dark, I'd decided not to let Nick or Diane get to me anymore.

Kevin parked across the street from the noisy, cheerful courtyard, and I took a detour to the restroom before joining the group at their white plastic table. I splashed my face and pulled out my handkerchief to wipe off the water while studying myself in the mirror.

What was I still doing in Suriname? What was I staying for? The rainforest? There were plenty of rainforests in the world. Nick? That was a waste of time. I needed to let him go. How many more people had to die before I realized I didn't belong here, that it was time to go home? Then I remembered I couldn't go home. Not until the police caught Melvijn's killer.

When I came out, Laura was there, the last person I wanted to see. She looked perfect, as usual, in a blue linen dress, her shiny black hair pulled up.

"I'm staying at the hotel, just across the street," she said while watching the door to the courtyard. "I'm going to have a drink with you all and then head back to my hotel room. Would you mind making an excuse to come with me? I need to talk to you in private. I've been trying to think of an excuse, but my mind doesn't seem to be working in this heat."

"Ah, I guess so," I said, assuming she wanted to talk about Nick. Well, best to get that over with too. Like ripping off a Band-Aid.

She went into the restroom and I crossed the courtyard, taking a seat between Kevin and Rosie at our plastic table under the twinkling white lights. It was turning into a beautiful night, the rising moon bathing the hotel across the street a milky blue, Kassav party music drifting down from the second floor of a nearby restaurant. It was the same courtyard bar where I'd first met Alice on what was supposed to have been my last night in Suriname. What probably *should* have been my last night in Suriname. If I'd gone home, none of this would have happened. Or at least I wouldn't have known anything about it—not about Nick or the murders.

I glanced at Alice. She was the same, laughing with Kevin, pounding her beer. Why had she pushed so hard for me to come to Kasima? Or was I remembering it wrong?

Nick called from across the table, "Em, are you—"

"Holy shit. It's T'om," Rosie said, interrupting Nick and grabbing my arm in distress.

"Who the hell is Tee Om?" Nick asked.

"T'om, my friend from the States. The married one. I told him—I . . . oh, no!"

A lanky man stopped to let a car pass and then continued across the busy street. Arnaud, the guide from Natuur Tours, otherwise known as Rosie's stalker, trailed behind him.

"How'd he know where you'd be?" I asked.

"I don't know," Rosie said, her shoulders hunched and her eyes downcast. "I told him to hang out and wait for me until tomorrow. What the hell is he doing with that psycho?"

"Hey, Rosie." T'om waved his arm and grinned. "Surprised? I missed you too much. I had to see you."

T'om approached our table near the street, Arnaud trailing a few feet behind. "I met this friend of yours in the smoothie shop you recommended. He offered to show me around tonight. I can't believe we found you—"

"You psychopath!" Rosie screamed at Arnaud, cutting off T'om and pushing back her chair. "Get away from me." She ran across the street, a car skidding to avoid hitting her as she raced into the hotel.

T'om, a forty-year-old man with a short beard and long, wild hair, stared at us in confusion.

Arnaud rubbed his angular face and said, "I want my photo."

"What photo?" T'om asked. "What's going on?"

"I've had enough of this shit," Nick said, standing up. "Arnaud, go away and take T'om—what the hell kind of name is that anyway?—with you. I'll get you your bloody photo, but not if I see your face again tonight. T'om, if you're lucky, Rosie will see you tomorrow. Not before. Now rack off, both of you."

Neither T'om nor Arnaud paid any attention to Nick. Kevin and Arnaud began arguing in Dutch, and T'om asked me if I was a Sagittarius, which, unfortunately, I was.

Laura used that moment to announce she was going back to her hotel room, and I offered to walk with her, to look for Rosie.

"Why don't we all go?" Nick said. "They have a bar inside."

I glanced at Laura, who shrugged. She wasn't being much help. We paid the bill and left T'om and Arnaud in the courtyard as quickly as possible, before Nick could strangle T'om, who was giving me an astrological reading about how perfectly matched I was with Arnaud, a Leo.

We crossed the busy street to the spacious hotel lobby, a parrot in a massive gilded cage shrieking a welcome. I left the group in the lively bar overlooking the pool, announcing I was off to search for Rosie. Instead I followed Laura up to her room, the number to which she'd managed to whisper to me before leaving us in the lobby.

She opened her door immediately, looking furtively along the hallway before grabbing my arm and pulling me inside.

"Want a glass of wine?" she asked.

"Sure, thanks," I said, although I was thinking I'd made a mistake, that I didn't really want to know details about her relationship with Nick.

She poured the wine at the small bar, handing it to me. "I heard you found Melvijn. That must've been horrible for you."

"Yeah." I watched her over the rim of the wine glass, taking a small sip, wondering where this was going. "You must be upset too. I know you were good friends."

"No, not really, although it seemed like he would've been an asset to the park."

"Uh-huh." I took another sip of wine. I suspected she was lying, given I'd seen them disappear together that night at the party, but her answer did seem understandable.

"I wanted to talk to you about something else," she said. "I saw Melvijn for a few minutes when he came over to Loiri Island last Wednesday. He asked me a lot of questions about Jack. He seemed to be hinting he knew who killed him. I didn't believe him, of course, which he took personally."

"What do you mean hinting?"

"I guess that isn't the right word. He claimed he knew what happened."

I leaned forward. "What'd he say?"

"That's the problem," she said, pacing the room. "He wouldn't tell me exactly. He said he couldn't yet. That he was working on an angle and was going to be making a lot of money soon. Like I said, I didn't believe him at the time. But now . . ." She stopped, watching me. "After what happened to Melvijn . . . I don't know."

"Why are you telling me this? Instead of the police?"

She ran a shaky hand through her hair. "Because Melvijn said he thought you knew who did it too, and I didn't want to go to the police with so little evidence."

I stared at her in shock, not answering.

"Do you know who killed Melvijn?" she asked.

"No! I don't know what he was talking about. He didn't mention anything like that to me. What exactly did he say?"

"I . . . I didn't really believe him at the time, so I didn't pay a lot of attention to details. I just thought he was showing off. He hinted it was one of the American women, but he wouldn't tell me which one."

"One of the monkey researchers? He used those words?"

"Yes, but I got the feeling he meant Rosie or Diane."

"Why?" I asked.

"I don't know. I guess I just never considered Alice."

"Didn't you ask for any details?"

"He wouldn't tell me. I told him he had to go to the police, and he said he was taking care of it in his own way. We fought about it . . . and the next day he was dead."

"How do you know he wasn't talking about Nick or me?"

"Because he mentioned you knew who did it too. He said it in a way—as if you were his backup, not like you did it."

"And Nick?"

She laughed. "Oh, I know it couldn't have been Nick. We go way back. He doesn't care about anything enough to kill. Certainly not Jack or Melvijn."

I frowned at my barely touched glass of wine. "How do you know Nick?"

"Through some mutual friends. We met in Costa Rica a couple of years ago when he was working on his dissertation. He's great. I'm excited—" She shook her head. "Never mind. So you don't know anything?"

"No," I said. "Honestly."

She grabbed my arm. "Are you sure?"

"I'm not really sure about anything at the moment."

She tapped her unpainted nails rapidly on the side of the table. "I guess that's all. If you say you don't know anything . . ."

"I don't," I said. "But maybe you should talk to Kevin."

"I'll think about that." Laura pushed me toward the door, now ready to be rid of me, regardless of my still full glass of wine.

"Wait a minute," I said. "I wanted to ask you about Nick—" But she had already shut the door in my face and turned the deadbolt.

I stood there for a minute, surprised at my abrupt dismissal. I considered knocking on her door again but decided against it. It was probably better to hear the truth from Nick anyway.

I was halfway to the elevator when the corridor went dark, leaving me helpless in the pitch black. A door opened behind me but no light appeared, although I could hear soft furtive footsteps creeping along the thin carpet.

# CHAPTER 29

I froze, listening to the footsteps. "Hello. Is anybody there?" I called, my heart pounding. The movement was near Laura's door and barely audible over the canned laughter from a muffled television in a room just behind me. Light drifted up from under a door on my left. A glowing exit sign was visible farther down. The sign went dark then reappeared. Someone had passed in front of it and was now tiptoeing along the wall.

I raced for the elevator in the opposite direction, running my hand along the wall to keep my bearing in the dark. The footsteps followed, closing in. The elevator's lit arrow was my beacon and I slammed against it, repeatedly pressing the down button, hoping the elevator was still there. A body barreled into me, shoving me against the elevator doors and grabbing for the purse wrapped across my chest. I held on to the straps and the doors crept apart, highlighting a hand pulling on the straps.

The hand let go and I tumbled inside. The light was blinding after the dark hallway, and I pushed at the elevator doors, trying to speed them closed. I held my breath, expecting hands to reach out of the dark to hold them open. I was still holding my breath when the doors slid shut and the elevator descended to the lobby.

I ran out of the elevator and straight for the bar, where I found Nick laughing with a group of drunken men. No one else from our group seemed to be around. I gasped out my story of an attack on the second floor to my gathering audience, all of them tall and muscular and shouting questions. All ten of them followed us out of the bar as we rounded up the desk clerk and crowded into the elevator. I was pressed tightly against Nick, the smell of sweat and alcohol intense in the small confined space.

"Who are these guys?" I whispered, nearly forgetting how upset I was with him.

"Soccer players, from Holland," he said. "They won a game earlier."

We squeezed out of the elevator only to find the hallway lights shining brightly, the terror wiped clean. Twelve pairs of male eyes turned to watch me in silence.

"The lights were out," I insisted. "I swear."

I turned to the desk clerk. "Where do you turn the hallway lights on and off?"

The clerk reluctantly showed me a small, unlocked room filled with towels and lotions at the end of the hallway near Laura's room, the same direction from which I'd first heard the footsteps. He closed and locked the door in front of us, gesturing at me while giving what sounded like a stern lecture in brisk Dutch before he turned and walked away, leaving me alone with Nick and the soccer players.

"He says the room should have been locked," one of the soccer players translated, "but he also says you're fine and he isn't going to call the police. He . . . ah . . ." He cleared his throat. "He thinks you made up the story."

"Jerk," I yelled in English down the hallway to the clerk waiting at the elevator. "You don't even have backup lights in case of an emergency."

The soccer players, apparently disappointed they couldn't thrash anyone, slapped Nick on the back, glanced at me in pity, and headed back to the bar.

"You believe me, don't you?" I asked Nick while we waited

for the next elevator.

"Of course," he said, his hands shoved deep in his pockets. He stepped into the elevator, not meeting my gaze.

I was feeling both vulnerable and angry about the attack, heaped on top of the trauma of finding Melvijn . . . it went on and on. But if Nick had put his arm around me then, or showed any kind of affection, I might have forgiven him about the girlfriend in Australia, or even Laura, admitted everything that was happening, and probably saved ourselves a lot of trouble.

But he didn't. Instead, he added, "You're not that kind of crazy, just a little reckless. Now Rosie . . . I could see her making up a story about being attacked. For attention."

The elevator doors slid open at the lobby and I turned to Nick, my emotions solidifying into a bitter determination to figure out what was behind the madness of the past two weeks. Even if I had to go it alone.

"Where is everybody else?" I asked.

"Who?"

"Rosie and Kevin. Diane. Everybody."

"Alice and Diane walked out to the dockside pier. I told them we'd come find them once I tracked you down. I haven't seen Rosie."

"You weren't working real hard at that, were you?"

"At what?" he asked.

"Finding me."

"I'm not your keeper. You left, supposedly to find Rosie. I figured you just needed some privacy after your blowup earlier. What was that about?"

"I . . ." I took a deep breath. "Look, I'm sorry about earlier. It was an accumulation of things, the whole situation with Melvijn . . . I know you told me it would be difficult, and I said it wouldn't be a problem, but I can't keep doing this. But I am sorry for acting like that."

Nick didn't respond immediately. The tension was unbearable, but I let the silence hang between us.

Finally, he said, "I understand things are kind of confusing right now. But why make any rash decisions? Why don't we just enjoy this for what it is? Take it a day at a time and see . . ."

"No. I'm sorry. I can't."

He grabbed my hand, his thumb rubbing the inside of my palm. "What's wrong, Em? What's this really about?"

I pulled my hand away. "Rosie told me you have a girlfriend back in Australia."

"Ah."

"Well?"

"Well, what?"

"Do you?"

He frowned and glanced at the screeching parrot. "Girlfriend. What does that word even mean?"

"Personally I think it's a fairly straightforward word."

"I guess the best answer I can give is no, I don't have a girlfriend back in Australia."

"Then why does Rosie think you do?"

"Because I told her I did. Frequently. Every time I spoke to her when she first arrived."

"You're telling me you lied?"

"Of course. You know Rosie. She desperately needs a man, and she picked me five seconds after she climbed off the plane. She wouldn't take no for an answer. I felt violated." He shivered dramatically and I had to hold back a smile.

"I thought she got together with Melvijn right away."

"She did. Shortly after the Arnaud mess. But I picked her up from the airport and spent three days in the city with her before we went out to Kasima. I made the mistake of taking her out for drinks and she followed me back to my room and didn't pick up on my hints. I finally told her I had a girlfriend so she'd leave me alone. I talked about my ex whenever Rosie was around, just to make sure she understood. Besides Alice's reaction, and my being your boss, she was the primary reason I wanted to keep quiet about you and me. I didn't think it would help relationships at camp, and I didn't want to hurt Rosie either. She's not a bad sort, just a little needy. And grabby."

It hadn't missed my attention he'd said he didn't have a girlfriend *in* Australia, which didn't preclude miscellaneous women scattered throughout the world.

"Then what about Laura?" I added. "I saw you with her earlier today."

He looked surprised. "Oh, yeah. Actually, I've been wanting—I mean, I just wasn't sure if—I mean, I wasn't sure how . . ." He paused in frustration. "Let's get out of here." He pulled me through the front lobby's double doors, stopping at the taxi stand just outside.

He waved for a taxi and turned back to me. "Sorry, I couldn't think in there with that poor parrot. I was afraid this would happen. That's why I tried to stop it, why I didn't want to get involved—"

"Excuse me?"

"Shit, I'm saying this all wrong. I'm sorry, I didn't mean for it to come out like that. I'm a little confused right now."

"I'll save you the trouble. I already—"

"Nick!" Rosie called, pushing through the lobby doors, Diane appearing just behind her. Rosie slipped her arm through Nick's. "Where have you been? We've been looking all over for you two."

"Damn," Nick muttered under his breath to me. "Ah, perhaps it's for the best. We'll speak about this later." He turned to Diane. "Did Alice and Kevin leave?"

"They left a half-hour ago," she answered.

"What have you two been up to?" I asked as I climbed into

the cab, glancing at their fingernails.

Rosie popped her gum, turning around from the front seat of the taxi. "We were wondering the same about you. You don't look so good."

"I'm fine. I just have a little headache."

"Emma had an incident," Nick said. "Someone tried to steal her purse."

"No way!" Rosie said. "Do you think it could have been Arnaud? I've been dodging him for the last hour, but he was still around. I talked to T'om. It wasn't his fault. He didn't know about Arnaud. He's going to stay away from him."

No one responded to Rosie. I leaned my head back against the cab seat. "What about you, Diane? What have you been up to?"

"Why would you suddenly care?" she asked, not answering my question. I gave up, closing my eyes. I felt Nick's hand reaching for mine in the dark of the cab. I let him take it. His finger formed an A and then a question mark on my hand, but I shook my head in the dark. I knew it wasn't Arnaud. The hand clutching my bag's strap had been white and female, the nails painted a light pink. A color Diane and Rosie were both wearing.

# CHAPTER 30

A pack of roaming dogs barked ferociously through the night. I tossed and turned, the crescendo yanking me awake each time I drifted into disturbing dreams about Sonia, Jack, and now Rosie, who was sometimes Diane. I didn't sleep until the neighbor's roosters joined in the chorus outside the window, signaling the coming morning light.

A firm whack to my stomach woke me. I forced open a heavy eye. Something was dragging wet sandpaper across my cheek. I forced open another eye. The massive white cat moved to my stomach, purring and kneading, restricting my breathing. I sat up, careful not to knock off Kiwi, and was immediately accosted again, this time by Rosie. She was already dressed, her shiny red hair bouncing in excitement.

"I've been thinking about what happened last night," she announced. "It must have been Arnaud. Nick's insisting I give him the photo back. I said I would think about it, but—"

"God, what time is it?" I set Kiwi carefully aside and rolled onto my stomach, finding my watch. "Rosie, it's too early to talk right now. I need coffee first."

"But Nick said—"

"Not now, Rosie. Please."

She lowered her voice to a whisper. "Did you decide it doesn't matter about Nick's girlfriend? You definitely shouldn't worry about that. You're the one with him now, right? What can she do? Best to enjoy yourself while you can."

"They've broken up."

"Is that what he told you?" She turned away in pity at my naiveté. I caught a slight, satisfied smile.

I rubbed my sleepy eyes, focusing on Rosie. "Were you and Diane together last night? Right before we all met up in the lobby I mean."

She fidgeted with her bra strap, slipping her bare feet to the floor. Her toes were painted the same pink shade as her fingernails. "No. I was talking to T'om. I didn't see Diane until right before we found you and Nick."

"Did Diane say where she'd been?"

Rosie shrugged. "No. Why do you care?"

"Just wondering what you all were up to."

Rosie peered at me intently, her face twisted oddly. "Okay . . . so what do you think? Should I keep the photo?"

"No," I said. "Give it back. I'm going to shower."

Alice, Kevin, and Diane were at the dining room table when I entered the kitchen twenty minutes later. Alice jumped up, giving me a quick hug. I glanced at her nails, but they were unpainted. "Sweetie, Nick told us what that deranged man did to you. I think we should go to the police."

"We've had enough of the police for a while," Kevin said as Nick strolled into the kitchen.

"I have to agree with Kevin," Nick added. "I've told Rosie she has to give back the photo today or she can't come back to Kasima. That should take care of it."

I watched them carefully. Like Rosie, they all seemed genuinely convinced it was Arnaud who'd attacked me. Yet one of them was lying.

Later that afternoon, the taxi driver dropped us on a broken, muddy sidewalk crowded with clapboard houses in a rundown neighborhood. It was my old stomping ground; I'd lived there for almost two years and I knew it well. The rainy season was in full swing, and the street was flooded ankle deep with filthy brown rainwater. We waded through the muck to reach the sidewalk. Singing drifted down from the jalousie windows of the small wooden Church of God. I didn't mention it as we climbed the worn steps in silence, but I'd been here before. Once.

We were late. The ceremony was close to starting when we slid into the last pew, my heart pounding. The church was small and held only about thirty people, a mix of Creole, Hindustani, and Javanese. Laura and Kevin were there, the only IWC representatives. They were sitting toward the front of the church and didn't turn around when we arrived. Ramesh was nearby, just behind Brian, who was surrounded by family. The casket was open, just like Sonia's. Involuntarily, I pictured Sonia's neck, red and bruised, although they'd attempted to cover it with make-up. I couldn't see Melvijn's neck from the back of the church, just the top of the open casket.

The heat was oppressive in the small space, with the jalousie windows shut and no fans or air conditioning. The family finally sat down. With luck, the service would be quick. I took a gulping breath as an older Creole man in a dark suit yanked the double doors shut, dislodging chips of yellow paint. I took another breath, the last of the fresh air, and the paint chips settled on the dusty wooden floor, joining the termite piles and exploring ants.

The minister was talking, but I couldn't concentrate. My heart raced. The air was stale and moldy, and I couldn't get enough into my lungs. I glanced at Alice on my right. She looked uncomfortable, shifting in her seat and pulling at the collar of her white t-shirt. I took another gulping breath. The pounding was overwhelming, echoing in my head. Sonia's husband had been right that day at the funeral. Her death *was* my fault. God, the heat was unbearable. Sweat was streaming down my back. It was too much. I couldn't breathe.

I stumbled up, shoved open the double doors, and threw myself down the worn steps, gasping for fresh air. At the bottom, I collided with a boy carrying a mesh wire cage packed with scarlet macaws. The cage fell to the muddy sidewalk and the macaws screeched in terror. The cage door broke open, the macaws tumbling out, a blur of shiny red feathers and beaks. The boy shrieked for me to help him catch the birds. Instead I collapsed on the worn steps, remembering . . .

*A beautiful full moon lit the quiet street. I didn't sense anything unusual when I passed her neighbor's overgrown yard. The Rottweiler growled from behind the cement wall, but I wasn't afraid, not even when I heard the kids crying from inside the house. I called "cluck, cluck" from her chain-link fence but Sonia didn't come to the door. The gate was open, and I found the stairs in the dark, growing nervous as I ran up the steps, wondering why more lights weren't on and why the kids were still crying. I knocked on the door, but nobody answered. I tried the handle. The front door crept open and John rushed to me, tears streaming down his cheeks.*

*"Sonia," I called again, my voice echoing across the empty living room.*

*"John, where's your mother?" I asked in Sranan.*

*He clung to my leg and I picked him up. The baby was on the couch, alone but unharmed. Where were the other kids?*

*"Sonia," I yelled. I crossed the empty living room, grabbing the baby off the couch and carrying both up the three steps to the bedrooms. I glanced into the bedroom on my left (my bedroom for three months during training) but turned to the right, toward Sonia's room. The hall was dark, but I could see a light from under her doorway. John struggled but I held him tight, nudging the door open with my foot and stepping into the nightmare.*

# CHAPTER 31

*Sonia was there, hanging from the ceiling fan, a rope around her neck. She twisted slowly in the air, her open eyes lifeless. A single light next to the bed lit the stool turned over on the floor below. John started to cry again, and I turned his face into my shoulder, although I knew it was too late. He was old enough to remember.*

Ramesh tapped me on the shoulder, startling me back to the present. "I thought you might be upset about the church," he said.

I stood up, dizzy, and wiped away my tears while we walked to his ancient white Toyota.

"You okay?" he asked.

"Not really," I said, wiping at more tears. "Her husband was right. It was my fault."

"It wasn't your fault, Emma."

"But I told her to leave him."

"He wouldn't let her drive or have friends. Or leave the house. She was miserable. You did what you thought was right."

"But it wasn't, was it?"

"She asked for advice and you gave it. She took her own life. How can you guess she do something like that? You said leave your husband, not kill yourself. Now it's your fault?"

"I know. I know," I said. "I try to tell myself that. But she didn't have anywhere to go, did she? Not with four kids. That was pretty arrogant and stupid advice on my part. And what about the children? They'll grow up without a mother. I feel like she thought it was my fault. That's why she let me be the one to find her."

"She had parents. Why not go to them? You can't blame yourself for that. You know what I recommend?"

"No."

"A ceremony. To release her spirit. She's still holding on to you."

Surprised, I didn't say anything for a long time, remembering Hortense had said pretty much the same thing. Finally I said, "You know I don't believe in any of that."

"Yes, you do."

I just shook my head, and Ramesh swung his arm around my shoulder. "Come on, you need a drink. I told Alice we wouldn't be back."

I climbed inside his car, nudging the door shut, afraid it might fall off if I pulled too hard. We zipped, to the extent a car with no shocks can zip, past the casinos and prostitutes and beautiful white colonial buildings. Ramesh kept his distance from the stray dogs, knowing the constant near misses made me edgy.

We stopped at a new bar in a refurbished colonial building along the river and found a table on the back deck with a view of a rundown freighter decaying in the river behind us. The patio was nearly empty, with only one other couple sitting outside in the heat; a sad mangy dog cowered under a table waiting for a scrap of food.

"It's so hard to believe Melvijn is dead," Ramesh said, slumping in his chair, his arms sprawled on the table. He was alternating between abject misery over the murder and breathless suspicion about who or what might have killed Melvijn, each theory becoming more preposterous than the last. His latest involved a roaming band of Amerindians with supernatural powers and a taste for vengeance against their Creole occupiers.

I let him talk on, relieved to be away from everyone, to have a small break with someone I knew couldn't have killed Jack or Melvijn.

A familiar booming voice roared across the bar, and I peered through the arched doorway, past the massive woodcarvings. It was Frank Van Landsberg with several well-dressed Surinamese couples. I jerked my eyes away, hoping he would stay inside the bar. But Ramesh was already gesturing for Frank to join us, which he did a few minutes later, bringing two Parbo beers. I should have told Ramesh the truth—that I wanted to be away from everyone and everything related to Kasima, if only for an hour or two. Now it was too late.

"We meet again," Frank said, collapsing in the chair. "It is good you came to the city, too much death in Kasima now. It is very bad, very bad what happened." He took a long swig of his red iced drink. "Not the same without Jack. You know, he was best man at my wedding. A great man. He understood Suriname. IWC will be finished now. They are mistaken if they think I will leave quietly." Frank called for the waiter, who was busy shooing away the dog, to bring him another Campari on the rocks.

I picked at my Parbo label. "You're leaving IWC?"

"Your precious Alice did not tell you?"

"No, what happened?"

"First Jack and now me. Those miserable monkeys. She will do anything for them." He swirled his ice, taking a sip of the melting water.

"What do the monkeys have to do with you leaving IWC?" I asked.

"Not the monkeys. Alice. She stays with Kevin? Yes? At his house?"

"Yeah, we're all staying there," I said.

Frank squinted at both of us and slammed his hand against

the table. "I'm not stupid. I know she tries to destroy my reputa-tion. But she will regret it soon. Kevin does not understand anything. Look at what happened to Melvijn. He knew nothing. He did nothing."

"What do you mean?" I asked. "What didn't Kevin do about Melvijn?"

"See. This is why I say the truth. You don't even know. What everyone in Suriname knows." He muttered under his breath in Dutch and shouted for the waiter to hurry with his drink.

Ramesh spoke sharply to Frank, and they argued back and forth in Dutch so fast I couldn't catch more than a word or two. Frank finally waved his hand, saying in English, "As anyone who is *important* knows, the police arrested Cedric Weidman for the murders of Melvijn Hardveld and Jack West this afternoon."

"What?" I gasped. "Why?" overlapping with Ramesh, who said, "I don' believe it."

"It is the truth. Melvijn was smuggling wildlife with Cedric out of Kasima. The police say they fought over money. Cedric killed him."

"I knew it!" I said. "I mean, how do they know? Cedric wasn't even there the day Melvijn was killed. He was on the island."

Frank shrugged, seeming unconcerned about details. "He had time in the morning or after he dropped off Alice."

"But how do they know for sure?" I asked.

Frank looked around, scanning the deck. He leaned in. "This is confidential. I know this only through my connections. The police found a note from Cedric asking to meet with Melvijn at the creek. It was in his backpack. They are very sure Cedric killed Melvijn."

I pulled away from Frank, wary. The waiter arrived with his drink, and I studied him gulping it down. It was Frank who'd carried Melvijn's pack back to camp. He could have planted the note then. Or before, if he was the person who murdered

Melvijn. If it had been premeditated. If Cedric had the ability to cross to the mainland and meet up with Melvijn, that meant Frank could have done it as well, in the afternoon, after his morning meeting with Kevin and Alice. And even if Melvijn *was* involved in the smuggling, it didn't exclude Frank from also being involved.

"How do the police know about the wildlife smuggling?" I asked.

"*I* suspected something was going on out there," Frank said, crunching his ice between his teeth. "I told Kevin not to hire Melvijn, but he wouldn't listen. I informed the police of my suspicions days ago. I am sorry it was too late to stop another death."

That, I knew, was probably a lie. Alice had said Kevin wanted Brian to have the job, that it was Frank who had offered it to Melvijn. But it was easy enough to check. I would ask Kevin.

"What time were they supposed to meet, according to the note?" I asked.

He appeared startled by the question and shook his head. "I do not know."

"I just can't believe Cedric would murder anyone," Ramesh said.

"And why Jack?" I asked, but neither of them answered.

"It is all settled now. This sad business." Frank slapped me on the back, standing up. "Best to leave the past in the past and move on. What do you say?"

"I don't believe it," I said, watching Frank rejoin his jovial group of Surinamese couples.

"You mean Cedric?" Ramesh asked. "He's not gon lie 'bout that."

"No. I believe him that Cedric has been arrested. I'm just not sure Cedric really killed Melvijn and Jack."

"Then who did?"

"Maybe Frank."

"Emma!"

"I don't trust him." Frank was now telling a story to his group, their laughter turning heads throughout the crowded inside bar.

"I know, you keep saying that. Why not?"

"Because Jack had just fired him a few hours before he died. There had to be a reason for the firing. If it wasn't the wildlife smuggling, what was it?"

"I don't know. But it doesn't mean he killed Jack. They were best friends."

"I don't believe that either. They didn't sound like best friends in the conversation I overheard."

Ramesh shrugged. "Poor Cedric. If Frank did it, he's not gonna be caught."

"I know," I said, remembering how disliked Maroons were in Paramaribo. "The police are probably happy to blame it on a Maroon. So much easier for everyone."

Ramesh's cell phone rang and he grabbed it, answering in a rapid mix of Sranan and Dutch. I studied him, remembering how he'd reacted to my bringing up the wildlife smuggling when he was visiting Kasima. I drank my beer, waiting for him to finish his call.

He finally clicked off the phone and I asked, "Did you know about Melvijn?"

"Know what?" he asked, setting his phone back on the table.

"That he was involved in wildlife smuggling."

"You believe that?"

"Kinda. What about you?"

Ramesh looked down, his face suffused with guilt. "I heard rumors. From Arnaud. Others. And Melvijn was spending money like he a king."

"Why didn't you say anything when I asked?"

"It was a rumor. There always rumors, some true, some not. I didn't want you thinking just 'cause he smuggling wildlife, he kill Jack."

"You know, I did see Melvijn and Cedric arguing that day you came out to Kasima with the missionary couple. Melvijn said Cedric owed him money."

"Then the police must be right," Ramesh said. "Cedric killed Melvijn. Forget about Frank. I'm hungry."

I hadn't eaten anything since breakfast, I realized. I'd been so obsessed thinking about Nick and Melvijn, I hadn't even thought about food. Ramesh called over the server and we ordered sandwiches. It became a complicated process since they didn't have a cook that night, and the bartender was going to make the food. I settled back in my chair while Ramesh discussed options with the waiter in Dutch, only partially understanding the conversation. I had tried to learn Dutch, which was the official language, but it hadn't been easy, not when English was so common in the city and Sranan so much easier to learn. Besides, Dutch was such an ugly language—at least that was the excuse I told myself.

The air was boiling hot, with barely a hint of breeze coming off the hazy river, and I already missed the cool night air at Kasima, the dazzling stars and soothing hum of insects and howler monkeys. It was a magical place, despite the deaths. I wondered how Hortense was handling Cedric's arrest, or whether she even knew yet. Hearing Cedric had been arrested had reduced my anger and self-pity. What if Melvijn had told Laura the truth? What if Cedric was innocent? I had to be sure of what happened or I'd never be able to forgive myself. Nick was right, I realized. I was a born meddler.

"Do you think Jack was really Cedric's father?" I asked once Ramesh had finished with the waiter. "Cedric didn't seem very upset after Jack's death. Do you really think he could have killed his own father?"

Ramesh shrugged. "I don't know. It's just another rumor, because of his looks. I thought you asked Hortense."

"I didn't know how to tastefully bring it up, and I got a little distracted after she told me Sonia's soul was somehow attached to me."

"I told you!" he shouted.

# CHAPTER 32

I woke late and stumbled into Kevin's kitchen, looking for coffee. All he had was instant, but I tried not to judge—a freeloading guest complaining was probably bad manners. It was Monday, and the house was quiet, empty. I helped myself to bread and Gouda cheese from the refrigerator and peered out the back window while I ate.

Nick was out there, swinging lazily on a hand-woven hammock stretched between two shady avocado trees, the whitewashed garden wall behind it suffocating under a tangle of hibiscus, bougainvillea, oleander, and angel trumpets. The cat was curled between his legs, and Rosie and Alice were nearby drinking coffee. I ignored my urge to join them, taking my less than perfect, but still lovely coffee to the front porch instead.

Nick eventually found me there and joined me on the couch, although he kept a wide distance between us. The morning air was hot and smoky, with a lingering trace of burning rubber, probably from backyard fires burning the week's trash on Sunday.

"Where'd you go to yesterday?" he asked. "I was worried about you, although Alice said you were with Ramesh."

"I was." I sat up, pushing away my empty coffee mug. "Did you all hear the news about Cedric?"

"Yeah, Kevin told us last night. Who'd you hear it from?"

"We ran into Frank. He says Cedric killed Melvijn. Jack too. Is that what you heard?"

"More or less," Nick said. "The part about Melvijn anyway. Pretty unbelievable. But I'm glad it's over."

"I hope so." I wasn't any more convinced the mess was over this morning than I had been the night before.

"Is Kevin around?" I asked.

He gave me a strange look. "I think so. You and Alice are supposed to drop us off at the IWC office in a few minutes. Then I think you and Alice are going grocery shopping. We're going back to Kasima tomorrow with some twitchers—excuse me, bird watchers. We've just been waiting for you."

"So soon?"

"You know Alice. The second she heard Cedric had been arrested she went searching for a ride back. Want to tell me what was wrong with you yesterday? Why'd you run out of the funeral?"

I stood up. "I . . . This isn't really the best time to talk about it."

"So you can tell Ramesh about it and not me? Is that it?"

"It's not like that," I said.

Nick lifted an eyebrow. "So what's it like then?"

"It's a long story about a friend who died. Ramesh already knows all the details. Maybe we can talk about it another time. I'm just not up to it at the moment."

"I see," he said, but I could tell he didn't.

"Listen. I need to find Kevin. We'll talk later." I went to Kevin's bedroom, worrying I was about to make a huge mistake in trusting him. I knocked on his door anyway. He opened it immediately, looking surprised to find me standing outside.

"I . . . I wanted to talk to you about something," I said. "In private. Before we go back to Kasima. Do you think we could meet later? Somewhere in town?"

He touched my shoulder, concerned. "You're okay, right?"

"Yeah, yeah. I just wanted to—" I stopped when Nick appeared in the hallway, glancing at Kevin's hand on my shoulder.

"Ah, sorry to interrupt," Nick said, frowning. He turned, then stopped to glance back at us before heading back into his room. He'd come down the hallway on purpose, of that I was sure.

Kevin dropped his hand and looked at his watch. "I've got meetings all day. This transition has been overwhelming. How about dinner tonight? Bali. Six o'clock."

"That works. I'll meet you there."

"I can pick you—"

"No, I'll meet you there. I've got some things to take care of this afternoon if we're really going back to Kasima tomorrow."

The car ride across town with Alice, Kevin, and Nick was tense. I sat in the back with Alice, who tried hard to strike up a conversation with Nick and Kevin, but both seemed pre-occupied with their own thoughts, and she wasn't able to get more than a grunt out of either of them. We dropped Kevin and Nick at the IWC office—a beautiful whitewashed colonial building with swirling balustrade balconies and detailed green woodwork set against a sun-dappled street lined with grizzled mahoganies. Definitely not a bad place to work. Between their office and Kevin's luxurious house, I was beginning to think I needed to get myself a job in conservation overseas.

We both climbed out too, switching to the front seats, with Alice taking over driving. She pulled out with a shriek of gravel and a cascade of honking horns when she cut off several cars in the traffic.

"Sweetie, is there something you want to tell me?" she asked, waving her hand in dismissal of the still blaring horns.

I glanced at her in surprise. "What do you mean?"

"About Nick! I just heard the news. I'm so happy for the both of you. You're perfect for each other."

"Ah . . . I'm not sure what you're talking about, Alice."

She waved her hand. "You don't have to keep it from me. Nick is so silly. I don't know why he thought he had to hide it. I mean, it's true some relationships have caused problems in the past, but you two aren't like that. You're adults. Even if things don't work out, I know you'll both act appropriately and behave yourselves. Unlike some people I could mention."

"Who told you?"

"No one has to tell me, munchkin. I can figure things out for myself. Why do you think I invited you out to Kasima, anyway?"

I frowned. "What do you mean?"

"For Nick, of course. I knew he was getting restless and talking to Kevin about other jobs. I couldn't lose him so soon, he's too important. And cheap. When I met you that night with Ramesh, I was sure you'd work well together."

I shook my head, completely befuddled. "Seriously? You invited me out to Kasima to set me up with Nick?"

"Sure, sweetie. You were the complete opposite of both Rosie and Diane, who he didn't seemed interested in, so I thought, what can it hurt?"

"Alice . . . I don't even know what's going on with Nick. I certainly—"

"Don't worry, he'll figure out soon enough what's important. Men take a while, but I can tell he's smitten."

My face flushed. This was worse than talking to my mom about relationships. "Thanks, Alice. I guess."

We finished with the shopping by early afternoon and returned downtown to pick up Nick, who'd been looking at boat engines and purchasing more supplies from the central market. We were loading his supplies into Kevin's SUV when we heard yelling in English. We turned in unison, watching in horror as Arnaud came barreling toward us along the busy sidewalk, Rosie's boyfriend T'om racing after him, pushing people out of the way and shouting, "Stop him. He stole my photo! He stole my photo!"

Arnaud slowed when he saw us, and T'om took the op-
portunity to leap through the air in a rolling tackle. They landed
on the sidewalk, grabbing at each other's clothes and shouting
in English and Sranan. Arnaud held a small piece of paper in
his right hand, which he waved over his head. T'om scrambled
on top of him, reaching desperately for what appeared to be a
photo.

Rosie came running up behind them out of breath, but she
stayed at the edge of the gathering crowd, her USC hat hiding
her eyes. I glanced at the hat, remembering something Alice
had mentioned about Jack. T'om was now straddling Arnaud,
still grabbing for the photo, but Arnaud was waving it out of his
reach while yelling in Sranan. A police officer finally arrived and
pulled them apart.

"He stole my photo," T'om said, standing up and shaking the
dirt and trash off his clothes, his hair bushy and jutting in all
directions.

The policeman looked at Arnaud, who was heaving deep
breaths and still holding the torn, crumpled photo in his hand.
He handed the photo to the policeman. I peered over the officer's shoulder, glimpsing Arnaud posing on one of the beds on
Loiri Island, his hand propping up his chin. I looked downward
and gasped, jerking away.

"Fucking hell," Nick muttered.

The policeman looked back at T'om. He held up the photo
and the crowd leaned in for a better look. "This is your photo?"
he said in heavily accented English.

T'om remained defiant. "Yes. He stole it."

Arnaud smiled and began talking rapidly in Dutch.

Nick skirted the edge of the crowd, grabbed Rosie's arm, and
pulled her away, leaving T'om to argue with the police officer.

"What the hell's going on, Rosie?" Nick demanded, yanking

Rosie toward the SUV.

"I was trying to give the photo back. We, I mean, I, just wanted to make a copy first. We didn't know Arnaud was following us. He came into the store and grabbed the photo before we could copy it and, like, T'om had to chase him."

"*Had* to chase him?" Nick took a deep breath and yanked on the top of his hair. "I hate to ask this, but *why* were you copying it?"

"T'om didn't think I should give it back completely, just in case Arnaud kept threatening me."

"She needed it for her protection," T'om said, appearing next to Rosie.

"Mate, I hope you haven't made any plans to come to Kasima," Nick said, facing T'om. "Because you're not welcome anymore."

T'om didn't seem particularly upset. "I need to go out to Kasima and help Rosie cleanse the cabins. Arnaud told me Melvijn put a spell on her. That's probably why everyone keeps dying. There's some bad—"

"Rack off."

"What?" T'om said.

"Get out of my face," Nick said slowly and deliberately this time. He pulled Rosie toward Alice, who was waiting at the SUV, keeping her distance from the scene.

I turned back to Arnaud, who had just finished with the policeman, his photo still clutched firmly in his hand. "What really happened with the photo?" I asked him in Sranan. "Quickly."

"I don't understand you," he said.

"Between you and Rosie," I added. "How did she get your photo?"

"I gave it to her."

"Did she ask for it, or did you just give it to her?"

215

"She asked me for it," Arnaud said. "She said she wanted to remember me when I was away. But she lied. She let Melvijn have it. He used it to make magic so he would make all the money and I would go broke."

"How do you know that's why she wanted it?"

"Why else would she not give it back? He was a bad man. He convinced her to do bad things."

"Like what?" I asked. "What bad things?"

"I lose a lot of money because I can't take tourists to Kasima. It's Melvijn's fault. He wanted to start his own tour company to Kasima. He made Rosie lie for him. I never threatened her. Melvijn told her to say those things so I couldn't get to Kasima anymore."

He pointed to Alice, who was watching us from the SUV and frowning. "She knows me. I help her. I brought the rum for her. For the party. She will tell you I say the truth."

"Why don't you tell *me* the truth? Were you with Rosie when she attacked me last night? At the hotel?"

"No! Did Rosie say I attacked you? She lies." He turned and disappeared into the crowd of anonymous shoppers.

I returned slowly to the vehicle, not looking directly at Rosie. It couldn't be her. I didn't want to believe it. I preferred Diane. But something was bothering me, and I had to check.

"What did Arnaud want?" Alice asked.

"Nothing," I said. "I'll meet you all back at Kevin's house later on tonight. I have some errands I need to finish."

I crossed the palm-shaded street, entering a small Chinese corner store. The owners followed me through the dusty aisles, convinced I was pocketing their canned sardines, until I finally handed over my money for a coke and phone card. I entered the code into my cell phone and called Ramesh first, confirming everyone thought Melvijn had been using Rosie to punish Arnaud, whom he was fighting with. It didn't prove anything though, other than there were two sides to any story.

I went to the Internet café next, waving at the American Mormon boys on the sidewalk trying to convert the passing teenagers, their shirts somehow managing to stay bright white and pressed in the Suriname sun and rain. That alone seemed a miracle. Unfortunately, they weren't the same boys who were on my flight out to Kasima. As the only sober people the night of the party, they might have been useful witnesses.

I paid for two hours and settled myself in a corner far away from the windows. I didn't do any e-mail. Instead, I searched the Internet. The site I wanted took me almost an entire hour to find, mostly due to the slothful pace of the Internet connection, but I confirmed my worst suspicions about what had happened to Melvijn and Jack. I was now pretty sure who'd attacked me the night before. I just wasn't sure how to prove it.

# CHAPTER 33

Dinner with Kevin wasn't developing quite the way I'd planned. I wanted to talk about Jack and Melvijn, but he wanted to talk about relationships. The sinking feeling I might be on a date was confirmed when he ordered the Indonesian *rijsttafel*, which involves an elaborate number of dishes over several hours.

"They have an excellent caipirinha," he added, ordering us each one. "I may need several. Today was hellish."

"What happened?" I asked.

At least work was a safer topic than relationships. As usual, I blamed Nick. If he hadn't insisted on being secretive, this would never have happened. Under different circumstances I might even have been interested in Kevin, but life was way too complicated at the moment. And even if things were not working out with Nick I was still half in love with him. Maybe more than half.

"Frank is challenging our right to fire him," Kevin said. "It's difficult enough to let anyone go here, much less someone with Frank's connections."

"Why was he fired? Did it have anything to do with the wildlife smuggling?"

He looked surprised. "How'd you know about that?"

"An educated guess."

"I probably shouldn't tell you this, but yes. Jack found out Frank knew about the smuggling but had let it continue because one of his government connections was involved. Jack was furious."

"Do you think you would have gotten management of Kasima without Frank?"

"Maybe, maybe not. We've brought in a lot of money . . . But now with this battle with Frank, it could get ugly."

"Could IWC lose control of Kasima? I saw Frank a couple of days ago and he seemed to be threatening that."

He rubbed his forehead. "I know. It's possible."

"I don't understand what was going on out there," I said. "How could they fill planes full of animals and no one notice?"

"Who says people didn't notice? But why should they say anything? They got paid some cash to keep quiet about the mysterious planes, some more to trap animals. Other than the monkey researchers, there weren't any outsiders at Kasima regularly enough to know what was going on. And it was impossible for anyone to arrive at the island quickly or unannounced."

"Has Cedric admitted to anything?"

"Not much," Kevin said. "But I don't think anyone believes Cedric and Melvijn were really in charge. Illegal trade in endangered species is a multi-billion dollar industry. Drug cartels diversified back in the eighties, moving into wildlife and human trafficking because of the lower risks and huge profits. And the legal trade in exotic species is even bigger. The wildlife was illegally trapped in Kasima, but much of it could legitimately be exported."

"Why did you offer Melvijn the park manager job if you knew what he was doing?"

"We didn't know about Melvijn. Besides, Alice recommended him."

"Alice?"

"Yeah, I think she was trying to get him out of her hair. She begged and I said I'd give him a try as a favor. We'd heard rumors about the wildlife trapping at Kasima, but not Frank's involvement until just recently. Jack and I met with a DEA agent and an official from the Surinamese police the morning we came out to Kasima for the party. They were suspicious of Kasima but didn't know who was involved. They weren't so much concerned about the wildlife smuggling as the connection to some drug runners."

"What will happen to Cedric?"

"He'll go to trial. Cedric claims he worked for Melvijn and doesn't know anything else. He says Melvijn approached him shortly after joining Alice's team with the proposition he look the other way and allow certain planes to land regularly on the airstrip. He says he wasn't involved beyond that. He's denying he killed Melvijn or Jack."

"Someone told me Jack might have been Cedric's father. Could that be true?"

Kevin shook his head wearily. "No, of course not. I mean I've heard that rumor, but it isn't true. Jack wasn't perfect in terms of his relationships with women, but if Cedric was his, he'd have been living in the U.S. attending the best schools money could buy. I think Jack just favored Cedric because he was fond of Hortense and had known them both for years."

I took a long sip of my caipirinha. It was sweet and strong and gave me the courage to continue. "So the police don't really have any real evidence about the deaths, do they? They're just guessing?" I paused, letting that sink in. "What if Cedric didn't kill Melvijn? Or Jack? What if it was one of us? You were suspicious that first day we came in to the city, weren't you?"

The waiter arrived with our first round of Indonesian side dishes and Kevin waited until the waiter left to respond. I stared at the small plates of shrimp cakes, fried *loempias,* and noodles, not feeling the slightest hunger.

"This is quite a conversation we're having," Kevin finally said.

"Yeah, but then it's been quite a month I've been having."

He covered my hand. "I know. I'm so sorry. But the truth is, I don't know who killed Jack or Melvijn. I don't want to believe it was Cedric, but who else could it be?"

I played with my glass, turning it in my hand. "Do you know Laura very well?"

"Ah, sure. We've worked together for about five years or more. She's fairly straightforward. Dedicated to her job. Maybe not the best taste in men . . ."

I laughed bitterly at that, thinking of Nick. "I had a strange conversation with her after the funeral yesterday. She said Melvijn told her one of the monkey researchers killed Jack. She says he was vague, but hinted it was either Rosie or Diane."

"Laura told you this?"

"Yeah."

"This might sound rude, but why you? I mean why not tell the police? Or me?"

"Believe me, I asked her the same thing. She seemed to think I had the same information. I think she didn't quite believe Melvijn and was looking for confirmation from me before mentioning it to anyone else. I thought Melvijn was maybe lying to her, although he did make some strange hints to me too. But then someone tried to attack me in the hallway after I left her room."

"Arnaud, right?"

"No, it couldn't have been Arnaud. At least not alone. Whoever it was wanted my purse, and I saw her hands when the elevator door opened. There were white, feminine. The nails were painted a pale pink. The same color both Rosie and Diane happen to be wearing."

"But why would Rosie or Diane attack you? Or kill Jack and

Melvijn, for that matter?"

"I . . . I'm not completely sure yet, but I think . . . I think one of them had a relationship with Jack. Maybe it ended badly. I don't know. What if she killed Jack and Melvijn saw her do it, but instead of telling the police, he blackmailed her? I'm worried that this isn't really finished, that . . ."

I didn't want to mention Rosie specifically, although I was sure it was her, as much as I'd wanted it to be Diane. I'd found her connection to Jack. Alice had mentioned Jack left to work at the University of Spoiled Children, which I'd confirmed after an Internet search was the University of Southern California. He'd taught there on and off for the past ten years, even after creating IWC. And Rosie had studied there. Probably under Jack. From what little I knew of both of them, it seemed likely they had a relationship. Although I had no proof. Yet.

Kevin pushed away his plate of food. "I'm not really hungry anymore. Are you?"

"No."

He waved for the waiter. "I think I should talk to Alice tonight."

"Why? What can she do?"

"You're probably wrong about this. I'm sure it's nothing, but I did hear a rumor about Jack. I doubt it's even true, but Alice usually knows what's going on at Kasima. If she thinks it's safe for you to return to camp, then I don't think you have anything to worry about."

We found Nick on the porch reading his book, a tall lamp casting a warm glow over him. He glanced up, raising an eyebrow in surprise at finding us arriving together.

"Interesting combination," he said, his voice ice cold. "What have you two been up to?"

"Dinner at Bali," Kevin said. "Nice Javanese place. You should check it out." He touched my shoulder, steering me onto the porch.

Nick jerked forward then stopped. He settled back on the couch, unclenching his fists and picked up his beer, tipping it toward us in a cheer. "Maybe someday."

Kevin glanced at me and back to Nick, frowning. His hand dropped away.

"It's been a long day," I said. "I'm going to bed."

"Yeah, I'll bet you're exhausted," Nick said. "Double juggling can do that to a girl."

"Unlike men who can keep three or four balls going at once and never miss a beat."

"One's always been complicated enough for me. Case in point."

"Ah . . ." Kevin said, taking a step away. "I . . . ah, I'm going to go see if Alice is still awake."

"She's in the kitchen," Nick said, "with Rosie and Diane."

Kevin turned his back on Nick. "If I don't see you before you leave, just in case, radio if you need me. Or try the satellite phone. You have my number, right?"

I nodded.

"I'll talk to Alice, but I'm sure the police are right." He squeezed my hand and walked away.

"That was touching," Nick said.

"I'm going to bed."

"Emma," he called, but I didn't turn around.

He caught me in the dark hallway, pushing me against the wall next to Diane's closed door. He plunged his hands into my hair, pulling it from the loose ponytail, his body trapping me against the wall. His hands slid downward, molding me against him, his lips and tongue hot and urgent. And then he was gone.

# CHAPTER 34

We all woke before dawn and met on the edge of the bustling central market to claim our seats. Then we waited for several hours until the packed DAF truck, an old, U-Haul truck with gaping holes for windows, pulled away from Saramaccastraat, the assorted metal components screeching like ring wraiths as we passed over the city's rain-gutted potholes.

We were in the back of the truck next to shrieking parrots, their cages balanced precariously on top of boxes of dead fish. The blocks of ice protecting the fish were already melting, creating small rivers through the dusty grime-covered floor. At least the fish smell was minimal, or possibly disguised by the fumes of gasoline drifting off the bouncing gallon drums.

Nick didn't say anything when I chose a seat next to Rosie. In fact, he hadn't said anything all morning, which made his jealous kiss all the more confusing. Did he really think it was okay for him to be with multiple women, but was jealous just because I had dinner with Kevin? I shoved away the thought. I didn't have time to figure out Nick at the moment; I needed to focus on Rosie.

"What's T'om going to do?" I asked her when she was finished hanging out the window blowing him kisses.

"He plans to hang out and wait for the next tour to Kasima after Alice leaves next week."

"What's T'om's wife think of his visit to Suriname?" I asked.

"Oh, they're polyamorous, so she's okay with him coming here."

"What's that mean?"

"They're allowed to have multiple relationships."

"Uh-huh," I said. "Sounds . . . ah . . . like an interesting guy."

"More like a nutcase," Nick said, leaning across the aisle to rest his arm on the back of my worn bus seat. "You seem to have a special talent for attracting them, Rosie."

Rosie stuck out her tongue, and Nick fell back against his own seat when the truck picked up speed. I tried to focus on Rosie's face, but the truck was now bouncing and shaking like a carnival ride gone off the rails, and I had to stare ahead just to keep my breakfast down.

"Yyyyou kkknow, it just hit me that Jack West used to work at the University of Southern California," I stuttered, propping my arms under my breasts, wishing I'd worn a better bra. "Did you ever have a class with him?"

"No. I'd heard about him of course, but he hasn't taught there in several years."

"Really? His name's still on the website."

"I think he was still affiliated, but he didn't teach classes."

I shifted in my seat, pushing a curling piece of metal back into the gaping stuffing. "So you'd never met him until the party?"

"Nope. Hhhow about you?"

"Nooo. Never."

"Diane and Nick knew him though," Rosie added. "Diane said they'd both met him at conferences."

"Really?" I glanced at Nick, disappointed my theory was falling apart, although Rosie could be lying. Nick was slouched in his seat across the aisle, Brian on his other side. His eyes were closed, but I knew he couldn't possibly be asleep, not with the bouncing and intermittent shrieks of metal that pierced at the cellular level. Which he proved by opening one eye and letting it cruise lazily over my body before sliding it shut.

We didn't make it far: stopping a few blocks down the street at a *winkel* for assorted drinks and noodle dishes, then again to load a boat engine, and finally a long stop on the outskirts of town for gas. As soon as the engine shuddered and died, the men perched on the drums of gasoline crawled over our heads to scramble out the windows, tossing their cigarettes to the truck floor. Diane raced out the front door, another gaping hole, followed by Alice. I jumped up to stamp out the chucked cigarettes burning out next to the gasoline and followed Diane and Alice off the bus.

"I'm not getting back on that thing," Diane was telling Alice when I hopped to the dusty ground, followed by Brian. "I'll wait in town for a tour group or pay for a plane myself. I can't even breathe." She made a dramatic show of coughing while lighting her cigarette.

"You'll survive," Alice said, heading for the small store.

I followed Alice, asking, "Did Kevin speak to you this morning?"

She headed for the drinks section, piling cold cokes and orange sodas in my arms before answering. "You mean his concerns about Jack's relationship with Diane?"

I nearly dropped the glass bottles. "I . . . ah . . . I didn't . . . What do you mean, Jack's relationship with Diane?"

Alice frowned. "Oh? You didn't know? Don't tell Diane I told you then. That won't go over well. I warned you Jack was a misogynist brute didn't I? Poor Diane. Jack's been traumatizing her for the past year. He used her, then tossed her aside once he got what he wanted. I warned her. But you don't have to worry, sweetie. Diane didn't—Shh! Here comes Brian."

Brian, who had spent most of the morning chatting with

friends on Saramaccastraat, joined us, taking half the sodas from my arms. He was friendly, but underneath I sensed a new formality around me, as if he was keeping his distance. I couldn't tell if it was because of Melvijn's death or something else. I didn't have a chance to ask Alice anything more about Diane before we climbed back on the DAF truck, finally leaving town behind and moving onto the dusty Afobaka road.

So Diane hadn't been with Melvijn. Thinking back, it made more sense. The afternoon I saw Melvijn coming out of Diane's room, I hadn't seen Diane. At least not until later, when I saw her walking across the yard with her towel on her head, aiming for her cabin. And she took long showers. Rosie must have been imagining the relationship. And Diane must have been crying about Jack that night at the party. But then, what had Melvijn been doing in her room? Had he stolen something from her and she thought I'd taken it? It might explain why she kept calling me a thief.

Diane had probably followed Jack to Tigrikati, fought with him, and pushed him in the river. And Melvijn must have seen it on his way back from walking Laura to the lodge and had been blackmailing Diane. He'd even hinted as much to Laura. And Diane obviously had money, with her designer bags and clothes.

Eventually, gas and cigarette fumes intermingled with red dust lulled me unconscious. I missed the turn past the aluminum smelter and didn't surface until we were passing through the village of Brownsweg, created when the Suriname River was dammed. For some reason, the trees were left standing as the water rose, creating a lake either creepy and surreal or spectacularly beautiful, depending on your vantage point.

Several hours later, all of us caked in a layer of fine red bauxite dust, we arrived at the upper Suriname River. I stumbled off the bus, completely shell-shocked, and collapsed next to a shack selling sodas, canned goods, and lukewarm beer. And waited. We continued waiting for three frustrating hours, a light rain causing us to take shelter under a leaky mango tree. Some point during the hot, sleepy afternoon, the DAF truck left, winding its way along the lonely road until it disappeared into jungle.

By the time the American birders arrived, it had been a very long day and we climbed gratefully into the dugout canoes. I sat next to Rosie with Diane in front of us, the tourists' luggage piled behind us. Brian was in the back with the Maroon boat captain, whom he seemed to know, and Nick and Alice were entertaining the tourists in the other boats as part of our payment for the free ride. I slumped back, watching a light mist steam off the dark brown river while Rosie snored on my shoulder.

Diane was awake now, sipping from her canteen with the bottomless spring of coffee. She glanced back at us, frowning.

"So how long are you going home for?" I asked her, our first direct conversation since the night on the island.

She narrowed her eyes. "A month."

Although I should have been prepared, the anger oozing from her every pore was startling. I took a deep breath and kept going anyway. "It . . . It'll be a nice break for you I guess. I know you were close to Melvijn and Cedric."

"No, I wasn't. I'm tired of your stupid games. I want my—"

Rosie jerked awake. "You're lying. I know you were screwing Melvijn. Why don't you just admit it?"

Several tense seconds passed before Diane said, "Why would I have sex with Melvijn? I'm sorry about what happened to him, but I didn't even like him. Unlike you, I have that as my starting point."

"Whatever," Rosie said. "I know you're lying, whether you admit it or not. And I'm no worse than Emma. She left the party with Jack and came back with Nick. At least I stick to one man a night."

Diane's canteen splattered across the wooden planks, the tepid coffee splashing my toes. Rosie jerked back so abruptly, the boat wobbled. I leaned over to wipe off my feet, catching my breath. Was that why she'd killed him? Was I somehow the catalyst? Because of Rosie's teasing that I'd run off with Jack? I shook myself. No. She couldn't have just pushed him. His neck was sliced open, probably by a machete. Just like Melvijn's. Which meant his murder was planned.

But where had she hidden the machete? She didn't have it when I saw her by the bench. And it wouldn't have fit in the small Gucci overnight bag she'd brought from camp. If she'd killed Melvijn, did that mean she'd also left the note framing Cedric? Or had the note been real and just bad timing for Cedric? I could almost, just barely, understand a passionate murder—in the heat of the moment. But what kind of person planned a murder and then let an innocent person take the blame?

# CHAPTER 35

The next morning arrived too quickly. Rain drizzled against the metal roof of the cabin, and I woke thinking about Nick rather than Diane. But I couldn't let myself get distracted. I pushed aside the thoughts, along with my sheet, and crawled out of bed to dress in the dark. We'd jumped right back into the normal schedule, which meant I had the morning off. It would probably be my only chance to search Melvijn's boxes before Brian took them back to the city.

Melvijn's clothes were still scattered around his room, but his supplies were piled in a plastic storage box, and I started there. I found a manila envelope with letters from a variety of women, including several former researchers. I became engrossed in the letters until rustling outside the window jerked me back to the present. My heart pounding wildly, I crept to the window only to find a giant tegu lizard waddling through the dead leaves.

I turned back to the box, reluctantly setting aside the letters. My job was to find whatever Melvijn might have stolen from Diane, not dig ghoulishly through possessions that were none of my business. I finished Melvijn's room without finding anything useful and climbed up the thin wooden ladder leaning against the cabin wall, popping my head into the dark, confined space of the attic. Melvijn had been doing something up here the morning he was killed. My only hope was that he'd been hiding something that would lead conclusively to Diane. Shining my flashlight over the trash bags and discarded rubber boots, I noticed several boxes of mildewing data against a back wall.

I pulled myself onto the dusty wooden floor. A bat fluttered past my head in the dark, and I ducked down to creep across the attic in a half-crouch, the floorboards squeaking in protest with each gentle step. I stopped at the first box and lifted off the lid. I flipped through the paperwork, but didn't find anything and moved on to the next box. A flash of bright white paper caught my eye, and I pulled it out. It was an envelope addressed to Diane, and next to it were several more, all from Jack. Next to them was a mini-cassette tape.

Below me, the front door bounced shut, echoing across the silent cabin. I froze in my half-squatting position, holding the letters and cassette, listening carefully to the footsteps. There was movement in the room below, Melvijn's room. It felt like an eternity passed while I waited, my legs growing numb. I glanced down at my watch, barely breathing. I heard more noise, possibly the scraping of Melvijn's storage box across the cement floor. I couldn't take the suspense. I had to know who was in the room.

I slipped the letters and cassette in my pants pocket and lowered myself to the attic floor, crawling across the wooden planks to peer through the hole. Melvijn's door swung open and a tall dark head passed under the opening in the attic floor. It was Brian, still in his field clothes. The cabin door slammed against its frame, and I scrambled down the ladder.

Brian was under the overhang assembling his fishing pole. I hid in the shadow of my room, watching, and then followed him halfway down the trail. I waited until he climbed in the canoe and paddled downstream, the water calm and glassy as he drifted around a curve in the river.

Alone again, I opened the letters and read through them. One was a breakup letter, short and not so sweet. Another ordered Diane to stop all communication or Jack would have her kicked out of the park. So I was right. Sort of. It *was* Diane. Melvijn must have stolen them right after Diane killed Jack. It was enough to convince *me*, but it wasn't proof. There had to be something more. I pulled out the cassette. I'd have to find the player and listen to it.

I searched the main room of both cabins next, but couldn't find a cassette player. I looked into Alice's room too, thinking she might have it. I'd just opened one of her boxes when a movement startled me and I glanced out the window, catching my breath. Brian was watching me through Alice's wide open window. In panic, I slammed her box shut and rushed from the room. I stumbled out of the cabin toward Brian, tripping on the doorstep and falling into the dirt.

The mini-cassette tumbled out. I grabbed it before standing up, shoving it back into my pocket and shaking off my dusty pants. "I had a craving for a cigarette," I said. "I thought I'd borrow one from Diane, but I wasn't sure which was her room. I don't smoke much anymore, but, you know, every once in a while I absolutely must have one." I giggled. "I didn't think Diane would mind. She's always offering them." *Stop rambling,* I told myself. "I thought you were in the field . . ."

"Alice gave me the day off to pack Melvijn's bags. And fish." He held up a serrated knife. It glinted in the sun.

I took a step back then stopped myself. I didn't have to be scared of everyone anymore. Just Diane. I knew what had happened. At least most of it. Brian lowered the knife and turned to climb down the side path to the beach.

"Wait, Brian! I need to radio the city, to send a message to Kevin. I have to go to the field now, but can you radio me if anyone comes from the island? It's really important."

He frowned. "I'm not sure anyone will stop by today, but if they do I'll let them know you want to go back."

"Thanks," I said and went to change into my field clothes. I was replacing Alice, who was taking the afternoon off.

Several hours later I was following a subgroup as it traveled further away from the main troop toward a tributary of the Suriname River, and I was a little worried that the river smelled like rotting eggs. I had a bad feeling it might be pingos and radioed for suggestions. I'd been keeping my radio on all afternoon, hoping Brian would call and it was now nearly dead. It wasn't check-in time, and only Alice answered from back at the cabin. I told her about the river and smell but she didn't seem worried.

"Sounds like any pingos are still pretty far away, sweetie. You should probably start heading toward camp though. If you see anything strange, climb a tree. I'll let the rest of the group know where you are and what's going on."

"My radio's about to die," I added, but it was already too late. The red light was gone, the battery dead. I shoved it in my backpack and turned southward on the path. A few minutes later I heard a "whoo" and "whooed" back, hoping it was Nick coming to save me from the pingos. Instead Diane sauntered up the path, her machete out and hacking at the overgrown bush on the rarely used trail.

"I think I smell pingos," I called out, pulling out my machete just in case she tried anything. "I told Alice I was just going back to camp." I tried slipping by her on the tight path but she clawed off my backpack when I passed and ran several feet down the trail.

"Where are they, you bitch?" she yelled, tossing my supplies onto the ground.

"Where are what?" I asked. "Give me back my pack, Diane."

"You know what I'm talking about!" She kept searching the bag, tossing my water bottle at my feet. "I want them back! Now!"

I backed down the path, still holding my machete in front of me, knowing she was getting close to finding the letters. "Diane, why don't you calm down? It's too late. I've already called Kevin. The police know all about your relationship with Jack now. I know Melvijn was blackmailing you. That he took your letters. Did he tell you it was me? You're not going to get away with killing anyone else. If you try to hurt me, they'll know you did it."

"I didn't kill anyone!" she screamed. "I don't know what you're talking about. No one had to tell me. I knew it was you who took the letters. You're just a fat, jealous pig."

"Nice, Diane. Classy. You can call me anything you want, but you're still not going to get away with this. I know you attacked me at the hotel. I saw your hands and your pink fingernails." I kept backing down the trail away from her. She was stronger than she looked—she'd been able to hack open both Jack and Melvin's necks.

"I was only taking back what was mine. These are none of your business. You stole them just to hurt me, to make fun of me with Nick." She pulled open the outside flap, tossing several fecal sample bottles and the mini-cassette tape onto the path.

"I didn't take the letters, Diane. Melvijn did. The day after you killed Jack."

"I didn't kill Jack!" she screamed again. "You're a liar!" She dug into an inside pocket, emerging triumphantly with the letters. "I knew it! I'm going to the police to report you."

"That's a good idea, Diane. Let's walk calmly back to camp, and we can both go to the police together. You can report me."

She turned and ran down the path, taking the letters, but leaving my backpack's contents scattered along the trail.

I knelt in the leaves, setting down my machete to pick up the scattered pieces. I was surprised Diane had run off so quickly without trying to kill me. Maybe she thought no one would believe me, which was probably true. A hiking boot crunched the small cassette to fragments just in front of me. I jerked back, feeling something odd. A push. I toppled sideways, although nothing was next to me, just as the machete swung at my neck.

# CHAPTER 36

The blade whispered past my neck. Still not understanding what was happening, I scrambled out of the bushes, trying to stand up, but stumbled in confusion and fell again. She swung immediately, hitting my calf and cutting into my boot.

"What the hell—" I stopped, my senses finally focusing on Alice's wild grin as she lifted her machete.

"Alice, no!" I yelled, scrambling to my feet again. She swung, hitting the back of my thigh. Intense pain spread up my body. I dove for my machete on the path, jerking it up and catching her in the face. It was a horrifying moment when my machete ripped open her cheek and warm blood splashed across my face, blurring my vision, dripping into my mouth. She lunged again and I ran, crashing through palms and thick shrubs toward the river.

I came out of the trees on a rocky shore, searching desperately for somewhere to hide. The massive boulder about ten feet out in the river seemed my best bet and I waded toward it, planning to hide on the backside. Movement in the rushing water reminded me piranhas are fond of blood, and I changed my plan. In a rush of adrenaline, I pulled myself on top. I tried to stand, but I was too dizzy and collapsed in a heap.

Alice appeared at the edge of the trees and raced toward my rock. I took a deep breath and coughed. The stench was overwhelming.

She came to the edge of the water, her face still dripping blood. She wiped at the gash, smearing it into her spiky bangs.

"Emma, sweetie, why don't you make this easier on both of us and come down? You can't possibly escape."

"Why, Alice? I don't understand." I pushed myself up, out of reach of her machete.

"I'm sorry, Emma. I don't want to kill you. I like you. Like a daughter. But you couldn't mind your own business."

"I don't know what you're talking about, Alice."

"Melvijn told me you're the one who gave him that cassette."

I frowned. "You mean the blank cassette you dropped?" I asked. "Why would you care?" And then I knew. "Oh, of course. Snoring. You sneaked out the window, didn't you? And left a recording of your snoring looping in the bedroom."

She laughed harshly. "Don't lie. You must have been in on it with Melvijn. I would never have suspected it of you. I feel betrayed."

"I wasn't, Alice. I didn't know."

"Don't claim ignorance now. You were caught sneaking around my room this morning. And Brian told me he saw you with a mini-cassette. I wondered where Melvijn had put that. I'm not going to let you mess things up. Not when I'm about to sign my agreement with IWC. They're such idiots. They still haven't figured out what this place is."

"What do you mean? What is it?"

"It's a prehistoric indigenous site, maybe even a city. The hill our camp is located on is teaming with archaeological artifacts. It's going to be huge! I can't believe no one else has noticed. I'm convinced Jack knew. But I have to get my contract signed before IWC finds out and tries to steal this spot from me."

She really was crazy, but maybe if I kept her talking, I could figure a way out of being murdered. "So Melvijn saw you kill Jack and was blackmailing you? That's why you killed him?"

"He didn't see it. He only figured it out after he listened to the cassette you gave him. He actually saw Diane and Jack fighting and thought she'd killed him. As you probably know, he wanted ten thousand dollars in cash when I returned to Kasima or he was going to the police."

"But why did you blame Melvijn's death on poor Cedric?"

"Because Melvijn and Cedric had the nerve to capture Julia's baby. For the pet trade. Melvijn was stupid to think he could mess with me. Just like you. I wondered if you were up to something after I saw you talking to Arnaud, but I wasn't sure. Until today."

"What does Arnaud have to do with any of this?"

Alice sighed and wiped at her bloody face. "Maybe you aren't as smart as I thought. I paid Arnaud to bring in the rum for the party. To make sure everyone was extra drunk. IWC was only providing a few beers. Cheapskates."

"You won't get away with another murder," I said, swaying and starting to feel dizzy from the gash in my leg, which was soaked in blood. I moved my feet apart to keep myself upright. It was a mistake. Alice jumped, swinging at my foot. I scooted back just in time and swung my arm. Our machetes clanged, and a series of pig-like squeals responded from the river.

Alice swung again, hitting rock. "Oh, people drown all the time, and everyone knows how you like to take a swim."

She tackled the rock, swinging the machete across the top. Startled, I jumped and lost my balance, falling backwards into the river and losing my machete. I landed with a splash and let myself sink to the bottom. Alice charged around the edge of the rock, wading through the water toward me. I stayed on the bottom, holding my breath and swimming into the current. She caught my foot, but I kicked her hard in the stomach, a specialty from my water polo years, and she let go with a squeal I could hear even underwater. The river swarmed with bristly boulders that morphed into massive pig-like creatures. They knocked against me, their hooves scraping my back where I clung to the river bottom, pulling myself deeper.

My lungs were about to explode, but I stayed on the bottom, swimming forward, letting the hooves pass overhead, now barely visible in the murky water above. I finally came up for air in the middle of the river, gasping in horror at the scene on land.

Ugly boar-like creatures were marching out of the river—hundreds of them, some scrambling onto shore, others circling my former rock in the shallow water, clawing and grunting, their tusks clicking in creepy unison. They probably smelled my blood still sliding down the side of the rock and dripping into the water.

Alice was backing up on the beach, trying to avoid detection, but the biggest male must have smelled her, because he turned and charged. Fifty or sixty pingos followed, and Alice shrieked in terror and ran into the dark jungle. Several stragglers stayed behind near shoreline, circling and clawing at the rock. I pressed my hand around my leg wound to stop the flow of blood, and let the current pull me downstream.

I kept myself awake long enough to land on a boulder in the middle of the river and crawl to safety in a little dip in the rock, away from the piranhas. At least Alice wouldn't be able to see me from the shore, and I could finally rest. I slipped off a sock and tied it above my leg wound, but the blood flow was already slowing. I lay on my side, watching the river slide peacefully past; the skies opened and rain poured down. My eyelids slid shut. I felt calm and safe because I knew Sonia was there, protecting me.

"Why did you do it, Sonia?" I whispered and slipped into unconsciousness.

I woke to the sound of a foghorn blowing in the distance somewhere upstream. I blinked at my watch, tears, or possibly rainwater, blurring my vision. It was four-thirty, and the rain had stopped. Where was I? Was Sonia here? I sat up and tried yelling, softly at first, still feeling weak, but remembering the pingos. No, the pingos went ashore. Chasing Alice. How far had I floated downstream? I couldn't remember. I fell silent, worried my yelling might bring Alice rather than help.

I began to feel stronger and pushed myself up, scouting the river and jungle. The vultures were already circling above. Blood and rainwater had soaked through my clothes and I was cold. I needed to get to shore and back to camp before dark came. I searched the edge of the jungle, looking for a rocky outcropping or a sandy shore. I didn't want to land on roots. Too many chances for snakes. But I also didn't want to drift any farther from camp. I spied a patch of white and slid into the current, swimming toward the sandbank.

It wasn't easy, pushing through the swampy undergrowth, but I had to stay close to the river; it was my only hope for finding my way back to camp. The sun was almost gone by the time I stumbled across the river trail. I crept along its edge, watching for signs of movement, still worried Alice might be waiting near camp. There were voices on the beach, and I recognized Nick's distinctive accent. I tiptoed closer, trying not to step on branches or make any noise. I was better at that now. I peered through the shadows, seeing first Brian, then Nick. There was no sign of Alice. Brian whipped around, looking in my direction.

Nick was talking and pointing up river. Brian grabbed his arm and pointed at me through the trees. I nearly fled.

"Emma?" Brian called. "Is that you?"

I stumbled onto the beach and Nick rushed forward, pulling me into a painful grip. He kissed my hair and face, murmuring, "Thank God, thank God."

"I thought you didn't believe in God," I said, pulling away.

He laughed, kissing me again. "We found Alice. We didn't know what happened to you. We've been searching for hours. I kept thinking of Melvijn—"

He let go, noticing my leg for the first time. It was dripping blood again. "Did the *pingos* get you too?"

I grabbed hold of his sleeve, my words tumbling out, "Where's Alice? She tried . . . she tried to kill me. And Sonia was there. Sonia saved me. She pushed me away from the machete and then, and then, the pingos. Where are the pingos? There were hundreds. Everywhere. Where are the pingos, Nick?"

"Everything's okay," he said. He squeezed my hand and pulled me toward Brian. "Do you think you can make it up to the cabin on your own, Em? There's something we need to take care of."

"No, no, Nick," I said, grabbing at his sleeve again. "You don't understand. Alice killed Jack and Melvijn. Where is she?"

He patted my arm. "It's going to be all right, Em."

"You believe me, right?"

He glanced at Brian, frowning. "Of course we do. But the pingos are gone, and Alice is hurt. Badly. We're not even sure she's going to live. Rosie's with her, but we need to carry her back."

"Give me your machete."

"I may need it, Em. There are more up at the cabin."

"Are you sure Alice isn't up there?"

"Em, everything's okay. Just wait for us at the cabin. Diane will help you. She's right at the top."

I trudged up the hill, feeling numb and let down, sure Nick hadn't believed me about Alice.

Diane was in the front yard, cursing at the satellite phone. "The stupid phone just went out." She slapped the phone, barely glancing at me. I didn't even bother trying to explain the situation to her.

I showered and tried to bandage my leg wound as best I could, thinking about Sonia and Alice. Did Sonia really push me away from Alice's machete? How was that possible? I lay down on the kitchen table bench and closed my eyes. I felt weak, probably from all the blood I'd lost.

A motor roared in the distance. Sometime later Nick came inside.

"A plane's on the way. Can you manage packing a bag? We're going into the city. They've already taken Alice over to the island. Brian's with her, but they'll be back to pick us up in about fifteen minutes."

Nick sat next to me at the kitchen table. "Were you together when it happened? I found your backpack on the path."

"When what happened?" I tried sitting up, but little white lights were spinning around my head.

"When the pingos attacked."

"No." I propped my heavy head up on the table. "The pingos didn't attack me, not until later. They didn't hurt me. It was Alice! She slashed open my leg with a machete. She killed Jack and Melvijn too. She thought I knew, but I didn't. The pingos charged her. I didn't know—"

Nick stared at me in shock.

"I knew you didn't believe me," I said, turning away.

"I believe you," Rosie said, walking into the kitchen. "Alice is nuts. I've always known that."

# CHAPTER 37

Two long days later, I finally had a chance to talk to Nick. I'd visited Sonia's family that morning on the way to the police station and said goodbye to the kids. I tried talking to Sonia's husband about why she'd killed herself, especially on that particular night when I would find her, but he still blamed me. It was awkward and sad and I didn't stay long. I'd finally found peace with the fact that I'll never know for sure why Sonia wanted me to find her, but I don't feel guilty or responsible for her death anymore. I think in saving my life, she'd finally let me go. Even without a Winti ceremony. Plus, she'd help me come to terms with who I really was.

I'd spent most of those two days, hour after mind-numbing hour, speaking with various police and embassy officials. The police were still searching for Alice, who'd escaped from the island once she'd learned I'd been found alive. She'd been hurt by my machete and the pingos, but apparently not as badly as everyone had thought. She might not have escaped if they'd listened to me, but I kept that thought to myself. I hadn't seen much of Nick, even though we were both staying at Kevin's house. I knew I'd never see him again once I left, and I was sad about that. But I understood it was time to move on to something new.

We finally met up on Kevin's balcony, the evening air thick and humid, as usual.

"Is there any news about Alice?" I asked him. He looked

exhausted, having flown back to Kasima earlier in the day with both Kevin and Brian, who had both stayed behind.

"She's vanished," Nick said. "We think she must have gone back to the cabin at some point though. There were a lot of supplies missing: medicine, food. The police think she's heading south. Into Brazil. But I think she may go toward French Guiana. She did her dissertation research there. She knows the land and may still have friends."

"Do you think Hortense helped her escape?" I asked.

"No," Nick said. "Not after Alice blamed Melvijn's death on Cedric."

"What's going to happen with Kasima now?"

"Brian is the new park manager, and it seems like Frank is backing down. The police finally released Cedric yesterday. He flew out with us."

"So, how long are you staying in Suriname?" I asked.

"I figure it'll only be another week or two. I'm going to help Kevin with a couple of projects and then . . . then onto other things."

"I'm happy for Brian. It's been a bad couple of weeks for him, losing both Melvijn and Alice. He's known Alice a long time."

"He feels horrible that he told Alice about seeing you in her room and the cassette. He thinks it's his fault she tried to kill you."

"I know. He's apologized a half-dozen times over the last few days. But it wasn't his fault. He didn't know what she was. God, I hope things are a little calmer out there for him. He deserves a break."

Nick reached along the couch, grabbing my hand. "So what are you going to do back in the States?"

"I . . . I don't know . . . probably fall into depression for a while. That's what most Peace Corps volunteers do their first few months back home."

He laughed softly. "That's an honest answer."

"Truthfully, I have absolutely no idea. I don't even want to think about it. I'm going to miss Suriname."

"Do you remember I mentioned a documentary project that might or might not find financing?"

"Vaguely."

"Yeah. It's a film on leatherback turtles. But it's really more focused on my old mentor. It's an IWC project, and they've finally pulled together the funding. They want to hire me. I'd like to think I got the job strictly because of my world-renowned expertise on sea turtles and friendship with their 'conservation hero,' but it's slightly possible Laura pulled some strings. We start shooting in three months. I was wondering . . . maybe you'd like to join me in Costa Rica? I'm sure we can use you somehow. You do have a film degree."

"Why would Laura pull strings for you?"

"Because I'm a charming bastard." Nick grinned.

I pulled my hand away. Dogs barked in the distance, and I watched one of the table candles burn down and flicker out, not saying anything.

"What's the matter, Em? You seem mad."

"I'm not mad. I just don't understand why you would want me to join you in Costa Rica when you seem to have something going on with Laura."

He sputtered, "With Laura?"

"You know what I'm talking about. You admitted it at the hotel."

"At the hotel? What are you talking about? When?"

"The night Diane attacked me in the hallway."

"Em, you misunderstood. I was trying to tell you about the film."

"Don't lie. I saw you kiss her."

He stared at me, puzzled, for several seconds before he burst out laughing. "Oh, yeah, I guess I did. I was excited. She'd just told me the funding came through, and I couldn't believe my good luck. It didn't mean anything."

"Then why have you been avoiding me the past couple of days?"

Nick sat back against the couch, not meeting my eyes. "I . . . I've been trying to talk to you."

I studied him and he looked down, sheepish.

"You're right. I didn't try very hard. I needed some time to think. To decide what to do . . . about you, about my feelings. This, you, it all happened so fast. I didn't expect it or really want it, until I didn't have a choice."

"And now you want me to drop everything and follow you when you barely know what your feelings are from one minute to the next?"

"No, I want you to do what you want. What feels right for you." Nick fidgeted, trying to look unconcerned about my answer.

"How do I know I can trust you? That you're not going to change your mind a week after I've arrived in Costa Rica?"

"Em, there are no guarantees in life. We're not getting married. I'm just asking if you want to keep going. See where this leads. I want to be with you. I'm in love with you."

I closed my eyes. It wasn't the most concrete declaration, but it was something. I opened them again, staring into his. "I'm in love with you too." He wrapped his fingers in my hair, leaning in, but I held up my hand to stop him, afraid if I let him kiss me I'd never finish what I needed to say. "If I come, this relationship has to change. You might have to actually acknowledge that we're in a relationship. You sure you want that?"

"Yes," he said, playing with my hair, his fingers leaving a tingling trail along the back of my neck.

I wiped a discreet tear from my eye. "Just so we're clear, no more kissing other women on the lips unless they're related or over sixty-five."

He let his hand slip down to my back, rubbing softly. "Cross my heart. But I should warn you, it's going to be long hours and maybe no pay."

"Sounds familiar. Women always get screwed on pay."

"I was thinking I could sell you as an intern."

"Intern? How about production assistant? If they're not going to pay me, they can at least give me a halfway decent title."

"I suppose that can be arranged." His roaming hand moved to mine, his thumb circling my palm, his eyes half-closed and watching my mouth.

I licked my lips, trying to keep myself from sinking. "There's something I need to tell you, something I haven't been completely honest about. And since my mom's arriving tomorrow . . ."

He frowned. "What do you mean?"

I squirmed on the couch, knowing he was going to think I was crazy. And frankly, I could understand his point of view as I regularly thought the same thing. "When Alice swung her machete at me, she would have killed me, except for one small detail."

"Yeah?"

I took a deep breath, preparing for the inevitable tears. "Sonia, my friend Sonia. She was my Peace Corps host mother, so I lived with her and her family when I first came to Suriname. She killed herself three months ago. To be more precise, she hanged herself. We were supposed to have dinner that night and make my favorite cheese cookies, maybe watch a movie. Her husband was working. I found her."

He squeezed my hand. "Em, I'm so—"

I wiped away a tear. "Wait, I'm not finished. I have to tell you this before I lose my nerve. The thing is, I've been having nightmares ever since it happened. I know that is probably normal, but these nightmares were different. They were real, more like a haunting, and Hortense . . . Hortense knew. She told me Sonia was with me. You know, attached somehow. Her spirit, or ghost, or soul. Whatever you want to call it. I know this is going to sound crazy—"

"*Going* to sound crazy?" Nick asked.

"Nick!"

"Sorry, continue."

"The thing is, Sonia saved me. She pushed me out of the way of Alice's machete before I even knew what was happening. She was there. I felt her."

"Ah . . . okay . . . You know, Em, there's a perfectly good explanation for what's been happening to you, any competent psychologist would—"

"Believe me, I know all the rational explanations. I've been repeating them to myself for the past couple of weeks. Most of my life, actually. But the problem is, I can't keep explaining it away anymore. Not now it's happened to me. This sort of thing isn't completely unknown in my family. Not in the female contingent anyway. My grandmother was a renowned water witch and psychic in Missouri. My great-grandmother, too. I mentioned my mom's a doctor, and that's true, but I didn't mention she's kind of into the *alternative* side of the medical field, quite famous actually. But I've never wanted to believe. I've tried to *not* believe. But now . . . I *know* Sonia was there."

Nick took a long, deep breath. "And what exactly is a water witch?" he asked.

"They can find underground wells, water, using a forked tree branch. It was very useful in the countryside years ago."

"Seriously? That's kind of a random skill."

I bit my lip. "So you're okay with this new side to me?"

"I believe you think it's real, especially given your family. I figure it'll be my job to prove it's a load of bullshit."

"Got it," I said. "I know where you stand on the issue, but just be nice to my mom when she asks for your birth time. Okay? You do know it right?"

"Why the hell will she ask me for my birth time?"

"For our compatibility chart. You know, to see if we can be together. Astrologically speaking."

"Listen, Em, I know a fair amount about crazy mums. My own's full-on Greek after all, and I've not run halfway 'round the world for nothing. But *you* don't actually believe in that do you?"

I shrugged. "I don't know. Consider me an agnostic. I just thought you should be forewarned." And then I kissed him.

# AUTHOR QUESTION
# AND ANSWER

*How did you end up in Suriname?*

I joined Peace Corps and received a dream assignment as the education and communications officer with WWF Guianas (known as World Wildlife Fund in the U.S.). I didn't know anything about Suriname, other than it was a small country on the Northeast coast of South America, squeezed between English speaking Guyana and French speaking French Guiana. Together the three countries are often referred to as the Guianas.

Lucky for me, Suriname is an amazing country, especially if you love unique cultures, wildlife, and wild places. And scorching heat. The population is still small, less than 500,000 people, and gathered around the capital, Paramaribo, near the coast. Culturally, Suriname is Caribbean, with a population that includes Amerindians, Creoles and Maroons, Europeans, Hindustani (East Indians), Javanese (from Indonesia), Chinese, and most recently Brazilians.

The interior rainforests and savannah, part of the greater Amazon region, are relatively pristine and cover 80% of the country. The coast still has large tracts of mangrove forests and hosts some of the most important beaches for nesting leatherback turtles in the world. You haven't truly lived until you've seen a massive, panting leatherback lay her eggs on a rain soaked beach at midnight—the setting for the second book in the series.

*What inspired you to write* Monkey Love and Murder?

I'd wanted to write a mystery for years but was never quite sure how to begin. When I finished Peace Corps, I joined a capuchin monkey research project and lived in a remote cabin with a few other researchers for six months. Between the isolation, malaria prophylaxis inspired dreams, and stories of epic feuds between researchers, it seemed an ideal setting for a mystery.

*Is Kasima National Park a real place?*

Kasima is inspired by a real place in the Central Suriname Nature Reserve called Raleighvallen (Raleigh Falls), which is where I spent those six months researching monkeys. Since the book is a mystery, I obviously had to have a murder and lots of people up to no good. I didn't want to suggest that any of the wonderful people I worked with at Raleighvallen were associated with my characters in *Monkey Love and Murder,* so I made up my own park in another area of the country, but used some of the characteristics of Raleighvallen.

*What is your experience working with monkeys?*

I have an environmental science master's, but I'm not a primatologist. I joined the monkey research project "just for fun" as my nephew likes to say. A lot of the work was routine, but there were definitely aspects that needed specialized skills, and I had a steep learning curve.

The project I worked on was researching capuchin monkeys, and to a lesser extent squirrel monkeys, but we regularly encountered howler and spider monkeys, as well as plenty of other wildlife. I fell in love with the elegant spider monkeys, called *kwata* in Suriname, but I never spent enough time watching them—because they'd throw branches at me and dash away—so I had my fictional researchers follow a spider monkey troop.

*What kinds of monkeys live in Suriname?*

Scientists believe primates migrated from Africa to South America sometime around 30 million years ago, probably by island hopping and/or drifting on rafts of vegetation. There are eight New World monkey species in Suriname. These are: red-handed tamarins (*Saguinus midas*), squirrel monkeys (*Saimiri sciureus*), brown capuchins (*Cebus apella*), wedge-capped capuchins (*Cebus olivaceus*), bearded saki (*Chiropotes satanas*), white-faced saki (*Pithecia pithecia*), black spider monkeys (*Ateles paniscus*), and red howler monkeys (*Alouatta seniculus*). Suriname is unique in that none of its monkey species are currently at high risk of extinction. However, they do face threats from loss of habitat, overhunting, and the pet and wildlife trade.

*Who are the Maroons?*

In Suriname, Maroons are descendants of West Africans who fled the colonial Dutch slave plantations and formed villages along the interior rainforest rivers. In the 1760s, after years of guerilla war, Maroons signed peace treaties with the Dutch granting them territory and independence. To this day, the six main Maroon groups in Suriname have retained a distinct identity based on West African languages, culture, and religion adapted to the Surinamese rainforest.

Following Suriname's independence from the Netherlands in

1975, the government was overthrown in a military coup in 1980 and then fought a lingering civil war with the Maroons that seriously impacted the infrastructure and social fabric of the interior of Suriname. Traditionally, the Maroon economy was based on female subsistence farming and male hunting and fishing. Today, many women sell goods in the Paramaribo market, while men are laborers in and around Paramaribo, or work in bauxite mining or small-scale gold mining.

*Is Winti a real religion?*

Yes. Winti is an Afro-Surinamese religion that combines the religious beliefs of the slaves brought to Suriname from West Africa with the environment and cultures of Suriname. The foundation of Winti is the belief in a creator god, lower level gods or spirits called Winti (which means wind), and ancestor worship. Spirit possession and supernatural phenomena— magic—are also part of the religion.

You can visit my website at www.edithmcclintock.com to learn more about Suriname, New World monkeys, and their conservation and research.

# ABOUT THE AUTHOR

When not writing mysteries, **Edith McClintock** works in the conservation and development field and blogs about her travel adventures. She was born in a school bus in the woods of Tennessee on the largest commune to come out of the sixties, and moved to downtown Miami in the early eighties, during the days of the Mariel Boatlift and Cocaine Cowboys.

Although a lifelong reading addict, she didn't start writing fiction until after Peace Corps, when she joined a monkey research project deep in the Amazon. Trapped in a jungle cabin for six months, there was little to do but imagine creative ways to kill off her fellow researchers. All of whom, she would like to note, were too nice to make it into her first novel, despite their begging.